Jack Batten, after a brief and unhappy career as a lawyer, has been a very happy Toronto freelance writer for many years. He has written thirty-five books, including four crime novels featuring Crang, the unorthodox criminal lawyer who has a bad habit of stumbling on murders that need his personal attention. Batten reviewed jazz for the *Globe and Mail* for several years, reviewed movies on CBC Radio for twenty-five-years, and now reviews crime novels for the *Toronto Star*. Not surprisingly, jazz, movies, and crime turn up frequently in Crang's life.

Books of Merit

CRANG PLAYS THE ACE

CRANG PLAYS

A Crang Mystery

THE ACE

Jack Batten

THOMAS ALLEN PUBLISHERS
TORONTO

Library and Archives Canada Cataloguing in Publication

Batten, Jack, 1932–
    Crang plays the Ace : a mystery / by Jack Batten.

First published: Toronto : Macmillan of Canada, 1987.
ISBN 978-0-88762-746-0

I. Title.

PS8553.A833C73   2011   C813'.54   C2010-908131-5

Cover design: Sputnik Design
Cover image: Hans Neleman/Getty Images

Published by Thomas Allen Publishers,
a division of Thomas Allen & Son Limited,
390 Steelcase Road East,
Markham, Ontario L3R 1G2 Canada

www.thomasallen.ca

ONTARIO ARTS COUNCIL
CONSEIL DES ARTS DE L'ONTARIO

Canada Council
for the Arts

The publisher gratefully acknowledges the support of
The Ontario Arts Council for its publishing program.

We acknowledge the support of the Canada Council for the Arts, which
last year invested $20.1 million in writing and publishing throughout Canada.

We acknowledge the Government of Ontario through the
Ontario Media Development Corporation's Ontario Book Initiative.

We acknowledge the financial support of the Government of Canada
through the Canada Book Fund for our publishing activities.

11 12 13 14 15   5 4 3 2 1

Text printed on 100% PCW recycled stock
Printed and bound in Canada

For my crime-fiction friends
Julian, Sandy, Chris,
and especially Marjorie

CRANG PLAYS THE ACE

1

MATTHEW WANSBOROUGH was saying he was sorry to be where he was. He was in my office.

"I'm embarrassed to have to come here, Mr. Crang," he said. "That's unfair to you. I apologize."

"Save the apology," I said.

Wansborough let out a small smile.

"You may not need it," I said.

The smile widened a fraction.

"Second thought," I said, "hold the apology in reserve. I know you at second hand, and far as I'm aware, you don't know me at any hand."

Wansborough made a clearing noise in his throat. He was in his mid-fifties and had grey hair like Gary Grant's and wore a deep blue custom-tailored three-piece summer suit. Six hundred dollars, I'd say, Holt Renfrew. Wansborough had phoned that morning for an appointment. I knew his name from Zena Cherry's column in the *Globe and Mail*. Zena writes with affection about the fun times of people around Toronto with old money. She mentions Matthew Wansborough about once a month. Zena says he likes to ride to hounds.

Wansborough said, "I've come because my people said you were the counsel who might assist me."

"That's a good start. Who are your people?"

"McIntosh, Brown & Crabtree. They look after my legal affairs."

"I'll just bet they do."

McIntosh, Brown & Crabtree is number one or two among the big law factories in the bank towers along King Street. It has 150 lawyers and another 275 people in support personnel, which is what big law factories along King Street call paralegals, title searchers, articling students, computer operators, and other lesser legal folk.

I said, "Tom Catalano in the litigation department down there give you my name?"

"He spoke well of you," Wansborough said.

"Hey, hold him to it."

"Mr. Catalano didn't say what sort of people you ordinarily represent, Mr. Crang."

"Mostly guilty people," I said. "Break and enter, drug charges, sometimes a bank holdup, the kind with guns. Paper offences are a minispecialty of mine. You know, fraud."

Wansborough was sitting on the client's side of my desk. He had his left leg correctly crossed over his right. He was showing a bit of blue silk sock and a lot of sturdy black Dacks oxford. He recrossed his legs, right over left, lifting his pant leg by the crease with thumb and forefinger. He didn't say anything.

"My people are usually guilty," I said. "But sometimes they're not guilty of what the police charge them with. It's a matter of degree. The police say manslaughter, the evidence says a variation of assault. Or maybe there's bad identification of my client. Or maybe the police knocked him around and he talked more than he intended. These things come out when I get a chance at cross-examination in court."

"You make it sound matter of fact," Wansborough said.

I said, "It's what I'm good at, asking questions in court. Outside court too. I'm nosy."

Wansborough pursed his lips. Maybe he didn't approve of my clients or my office or, heaven forbid, my clothes. I had on jeans, a light blue broadcloth shirt, and a pair of Rockport Walkers with spongy soles. It was my uniform on days I wasn't scheduled for court. On days I had a case on, I looked downright spiffy, gown hanging from my shoulders without an undue wrinkle, vest free of mustard stains, tabs and dickey snow-white from the laundry. The model of a criminal lawyer. My office had a wooden desk, a swivel chair on the business side of the desk, three chairs like the one Wansborough was sitting in on the other side, a green metal filing cabinet, and bookshelves that held bound volumes of *Canadian Criminal Cases* going back to 1912. It wasn't listed on a tour of notable offices of Toronto. Or maybe Wansborough's lips were always pursed.

"Have we got to the part where you're embarrassed?" I said.

Wansborough plunked both Dacks on the floor. Decision time.

"It comes to this, Mr. Crang," he said. "I am showing more profit than I ought to be doing."

"Some people that happens to, Mr. Wansborough, and nobody calls it trouble."

"I manage the family's business interests," he said. "They're extensive, and I have maintained us at a steady profit even in the economy's downturn. I invest in companies whose management is familiar to me. I know the people and the corporate performances."

"That ought to get you a profile in *Canadian Business*," I said.

"I hold seven directorships," Wansborough continued. "In six other instances, with smaller companies, I have a controlling interest."

I swivelled a few degrees to the left in my swivel chair and looked down into the street. A kid was walking by. From my angle, the top of the kid's head looked like a Walt Disney skunk. Pinkish-white stripe down the middle, jet black on the sides. My angle was straight down from the second floor over a unisex clothing store called Trapezoid. The office I practised out of was on Queen West near Spadina. When I moved in a dozen years ago, it was working-class commercial and heavy on Middle European shopkeepers. A few years back, in some unfathomable shift of Toronto custom, the street went New Wave. It was farewell to the Czech ma-and-pa hardware store and the goulash restaurant. Now it was science-fiction bookstores and diners that charged three dollars for *café au lait*. I didn't mind the change. It could have been worse. It could have been a Burger King and porno shoppes.

Wansborough paused in his business catalogue.

"Mr. Crang," he said, "mightn't it assist us in the long run if you take notes?"

"That what you're used to at McIntosh, Brown?"

"A junior attends the meetings and records pertinent details, yes."

"One, Mr. Wansborough, I have no junior in residence, currently or ever. And, two, you ever see *The Thirty-Nine Steps*? Old Hitchcock movie?"

"I recall reading the novel at school. Didn't Lord Tweedsmuir write it?"

"I'm Mr. Memory."

"Pardon?"

"The guy in the movie who remembers everything or, if you prefer, in the book. Mr. Memory. That's me. Mind like a steel trap. Nothing escapes. Trust me."

"I see," Wansborough said.

"He was John Buchan when he wrote the book," I said. "Lord Tweedsmuir was."

Wansborough cleared his throat again.

"The information I've given you," he said, "is in the nature of background. I want you to understand that my investment in a company called Ace Disposal Services is a departure from my customary practice."

I said, "Ace Disposal doesn't sound like it ranks up there with the blue-chippers."

"I'm aware of that, Mr. Crang."

Wansborough's voice had a snap to it. For all his prissiness, he didn't strike me as anybody's pushover. When he rode to hounds, I'd put my money on him as first rider to the fox every time. He had a squared-off face and jutting eyebrows and he was as tall as I, five eleven or so, and heavier, over two hundred pounds. I'm built along the lines of yon Cassius. Lean and hungry.

"What about the aberration, Mr. Wansborough?" I said. "Why Ace Disposal? And what is an Ace Disposal?"

"The investment was to show support for my cousin," Wansborough said. "I advanced $300,000 four years ago last February. My cousin wished to buy into a company as a working partner and chose Ace Disposal for the purpose. The investment made the family a minority shareholder and obtained my cousin a vice-presidency. Ace's business, as far as that is concerned, is in transporting waste from construction sites to municipal dumps. Its assets consist of a great many large trucks and a maintenance area here in the city. In the first two years after my investment, the company showed negligible profits, as I rather expected would be the case. Beginning in the second quarter last year, however, it has yielded what I consider a disproportionately high profit. That puzzles me."

"Let's go back to your cousin," I said. "What's he have to say about the new bonanza?"

"She, Mr. Crang," Wansborough said. "My cousin is Alice Brackley. On my mother's side. She attributes the change to improved management. My cousin, I tell you this in confidence, has been the difficult member of the family. Intelligent enough for a woman but terribly stubborn. I believe she went into Ace Disposal to show she was as competent in business as any of the men in our family. Especially into such a business as Ace Disposal."

I said, "Headstrong."

Wansborough liked that. He said, "One doesn't hear such an adjective these days."

"One doesn't."

Wansborough said, "The change for the better in the company coincided with a new group purchasing a majority interest. A man named Grimaldi has been president for the past twenty months."

"Fine old Monacan name."

"That would be another branch of the family," Wansborough said. The snap was back in his voice.

"Mr. Grimaldi has an expansive charm," he said. "I concede that. And his operational manner is aggressive. He keeps the trucks on the road six days a week, that sort of thing. Charles is Mr. Grimaldi's first name, and certainly my cousin praises his person and his methods. But he is in my view evasive when I inquire into the company's recent success. So is Alice. I have never read the company books."

I swivelled around to face Wansborough and put on my summing-up look.

"What we have here," I said, "is an outfit doing better business than you think it should and an executive officer who isn't to your taste."

Wansborough's head made a brusque nod.

I said, "And you're retaining me to ease your mind about both."

Another nod. I was a whiz at synthesizing information. I said, "At the worst, you want to know if there's hanky-panky."

Wansborough said, "Mr. Catalano said you have had previous experience in the sort of inquiry we're discussing."

"Tom's talking fraud," I said. "One of McIntosh, Brown's corporate clients, big printing firm, it developed a leak in its treasury. The company was coming up a few hundred thousand short and nobody could find the hole. Catalano hired me to poke around on the quiet. Turned out the two women at the top of the accounting department, long-time employees, much beloved by all, were running a sweet racket. They invented employees on paper. Gave them names, social security numbers, bank accounts. Put them on the tax roll, handed out T-4s, filed their income tax returns in the spring. And every week they issued pay cheques to the employees' bank accounts. Except the employees were paper people and the two old darlings ended up with the cash."

Wansborough's lips did their pursing number.

I said, "In accounting parlance, that's called a dead-horse fraud."

Wansborough's face looked tight.

"Don't take it as a precedent," I said. "Your problem doesn't sound in the same league."

I couldn't tell whether I'd reassured Wansborough. He left the office and I watched him from my window. He was walking east on Queen behind a girl with a haircut I'd last seen on William Bendix in *Wake Island.*

2

STREETS WHERE BIG FINANCIERS take care of their financing are narrow. Wall Street, Threadneedle Street, Bay Street. After Wansborough left, I rode a Queen streetcar over to Bay, got on a trolley bus headed south, and sat in the traffic. Bay is two lanes wide each way and lined with buildings where stockbrokers and money men make deals. Delivery trucks park in no-stopping zones. Cabs pick up fares. It takes ten minutes to travel a block. I watched a spruce old party in a white seersucker suit and a panama hat totter down the front steps of the National Club. Bet he'd had a swell day—a couple of gimlets at lunch, a few games of hearts with his cronies, some reminiscing over the good old days in killer financing, and now it was home, James, for a nap. The bus broke free of the scrimmage at Front Street and made time under the tunnel by Union Station and through the scramble of east-west expressways near the Lakeshore. I got out at Queen's Quay and walked a block east to the Toronto Star building.

It doesn't look like a newspaper building. It looks like insurance salesmen or government clerks lurk within. But whatever architect did the cookie-cutter job on the design, he couldn't mess with the smell. It was there when I pushed through the revolving door, the smell of newsprint. It's a smell of promise, maybe only the promise of news but that's good enough. I like it when newsprint rubs off on my hands. I remember when the old *Toronto Telegram* was printed in pink editions.

The type still rubbed off black. Do young people get the same kicks these days? Do videos have a homey smell? Do ghetto blasters rub off on their hands?

I took the elevator to the fifth, the editorial floor, and walked around a couple of corners to the library. I asked a clerk who'd done favours for me in the past for the news clippings on Ace Disposal Services. She punched into the wall of big mechanical drawers where all *Star* stories are filed in brown envelopes in tidy alphabetical order. Nope, she said, nothing under Ace Disposal. I asked her to try disposal services. Drew another blank. Waste? Zip. Garbage? Bingo city.

It wasn't much. I sat at a table in the library and read a two-part series from six months earlier about organized crime and the garbage business. The lead paragraph in part one announced mighty revelations to follow, but what the series delivered was a few thousand words of generalities. It leaned on those two familiar dancing partners, unnamed sources and police spokesmen. Unnamed sources disclosed that crime syndicates, looking to launder their profits from drugs, loan-sharking, strippers, and the like, were dropping money into the private garbage industry. Police spokesmen hinted at signs of gang infiltration of said industry. No specifics, no numbers. Ace Disposal made the series twice, both times as "the largest company in the garbage field in Toronto." Period.

The byline on the stories read Ray Griffin, and I went looking for him in the city room. A copy girl steered me to the section of the floor where feature writers hang their hats, the ones with "press" in the brims. Griffin, the copy girl said, was the sharp dresser. She giggled when she said it.

Griffin had his feet up on a desk just like an old-timey reporter, except there was a computer terminal beside the desk and he was young, in his late twenties. He had unwashed black hair, a droopy bandito moustache, and a large residue of acne scars on his face. He was wearing an emerald-green short-sleeved shirt, plaid Bermuda shorts, and sandals with a lot of strapping. I would have giggled too.

I introduced myself.

I said, "The garbage series seemed a little short on what you journalists call hard news."

"The lawyers took the guts out of it," Griffin said. He talked fast. "They've been nervous ever since the Mafia guy in Quebec won his libel case against a Montreal paper. But I'll go back to it. Another year or so, it'll make a hell of a story."

"Some lawyers are like that," I said.

"Aw shit, I had the stuff," Griffin said, rushing his words. "I knew which guys belonged to which families, where their money came from originally, and where they went to scrub it up."

"Grimaldi?" I said. "That one of your names? Charles Grimaldi?"

"I got all kinds of Grimaldis," Griffin said.

He leaned over and opened a lower drawer of his desk without taking his sandals off the top. Nice feat of balance. He came up with two red file folders, put one on the desk and opened the other. It had a thick stack of pages of computer printouts held together perfectly squared with a large paper clip and six or seven stenographers' notebooks. He chose one notebook and turned through the pages. He was very methodical. The handwriting in the notebook was as rounded and legible as a private-school girl's.

"The Grimaldis," Griffin said. "I'll tell you all the dirt on the Grimaldis."

I said, "It's okay by me if you hold it down to Charles."

"I got to go at this from the beginning." He stopped turning the pages of the notebook in his lap, looked up, and started talking at full throttle.

"The old man, Pietro Grimaldi, that's Charles' father, he's numero uno up in Guelph and has been since the end of the Second War. He came to Canada from Calabria and opened a grocery store. That's what he still is today, a grocer in Guelph, Ontario. He's also what you'd call the godfather up there. I'd call him godfather everywhere except in the newspaper or the lawyers'd go bananas. It sounds ridiculous anyway, godfather of Guelph. The whole area's got maybe two hundred thousand people, but everything that's organized crime around that part of the province, old Pietro's in charge. The drugs, the girls, the counterfeiting, all that, and he's never served a day in jail. He's never been in a courtroom. Very sharp old guy."

I kept waiting for Griffin to look at his notebook. He didn't.

"The funny thing about these people, they don't think of any of that stuff, drugs and prostitution and everything, as crime. It's business." Griffin's pace had hit lickety-split. "But they know that all the rest of us think of it as criminal. That may be simple-minded to you and me, but it's crucial if you want to understand the psychology of a guy like old Grimaldi."

"I'm with you," I said, just to give him a chance to take in some oxygen.

Griffin said, "Pietro was one of the first guys in the big crime scene to figure that all the money he's making, he shouldn't just turn it over into more drugs, more hookers, more whatever. He should put it into businesses that the rest of us citizens consider legitimate."

"Which brings us to garbage," I said.

"Not yet it doesn't," Griffin said.

"Right," I said. "You have to go in order."

"Pietro wasn't going to run these straight businesses himself," Griffin said. "He's still a grocer. You should see him waiting on the customers. You'd take him for your kindly old Uncle Pete, and all the time, in the back room, he's masterminding this whole network of bad guys. Anyway, he's sticking at home, so he sends his three boys out into the world to look after the up-and-up operations."

I said, "Garbage."

"Wait," Griffin said. The notebook was still open in his lap, unconsulted. "Pietro's got three sons. The oldest, Pete Junior, he gets a string of laundries in Hamilton. Number two boy, John, he's in car-washes through the southwest part of the province, London, Woodstock, down there. And Charles, the youngest, for him Pietro buys Ace Disposal, which is the largest garbage company in the city."

"I read that somewhere," I said. "You ever meet Charles?"

"Dark, good-looking guy in his early thirties," Griffin said, not easing up on the speed. "He took me to lunch at Fenton's when I was doing the story and talked a lot of bullshit about the challenge of garbage. He must've spent seventy bucks on the food and wine."

"The old slyboots," I said, "trying to purchase your favour that way."

"Charles is the one in the family who's different," Griffin said. "He's the only son with a record, two assault convictions when he was a kid. On the second, he was ten months in reformatory. That was thirteen years ago. Charles was nineteen. He hit a guy with the lever from a tire jack. Fractured his skull."

Griffin closed the notebook on his lap.

I said, "You're probably just as good without all the help from that thing."

"Huh?"

I thanked Griffin for his time.

"Don't forget," he said, "I told you I'm still interested in the story."

I said, "When I break this case wide open, you'll get it first."

He said, "Nobody talks like that any more."

There was a Diamond Cab at the taxi stand in front of the building and I took it home.

3

MY HOUSE is in Goldwin Smith's old neighbourhood. I moved in about eighty years after he moved on. Goldwin Smith was a wise old duck who wrote on political and social affairs around town in the late nineteenth century. He didn't make much money out of his writing, but he married a rich woman. That was another thing Goldwin and I had in common. My rich woman was named Pamela. She was beautiful and talked through her nose. Her family had a lot more money than Matthew Wansborough and the money was a couple of hundred years older. Pamela married me when I was a law student in part because she thought I was quaint. My father thought Pamela was quaint. I come from a long line of working-class toilers and my father was a photo-engraver. Banged at pieces of metal for all his employed life. He died ten years ago, around the time Pamela stopped thinking I was quaint and we divorced. Goldwin Smith stayed married.

At the northwest corner of Beverley Street and Sullivan, there's the Chinese Baptist Church, then a row of square red-brick houses. Mine's up at the north end. It faces across Beverley to the park that used to be Goldwin Smith's front lawn. His house was called the Grange and still is. It has a stone porch and stone pillars almost as tall as my house. The Art Gallery of Ontario uses the Grange for offices. I divided my house into two apartments, mine upstairs and one downstairs where a gay couple and their Irish setter have been in residence for six years. Alex is a civil servant, Ian sells real estate, and the dog slobbers on everyone he gets close to, friend or foe.

I got the Wyborowa out of the freezer compartment of the refrigerator and poured some over three ice cubes in an old-fashioned glass. Whether Matthew Wansborough knew it or not, he had the mob for a partner. He wouldn't want his pals who put on the funny red jackets and ride the horses with him on weekends to find out about that. On the other hand, he wanted the answer to the question he started out with: How come Ace Disposal was suddenly making money? Did Charles Grimaldi have a touch with garbage? Was the Grimaldi family using Ace as a front for other purposes? Lucrative purposes? Illegal purposes?

I put a Bill Evans album on the stereo, *You Must Believe in Spring*, and went out to the kitchen. I spread a thin layer of Paul Newman spaghetti sauce on two large pieces of whole-wheat pita bread. Fine slices of mushroom, green pepper, cooking onion, zucchini, mozzarella cheese, and asparagus went on next. I organized them in jolly little patterns and covered them with flakes of parmesan. Boutique pizza, a woman friend of mine calls the recipe. It's one of two in my repertoire. Chili is the other. Makes for a cramped diet and sends me out of the house for dinner most nights. I put the two pizzas in the oven at three hundred degrees. They needed twenty minutes. Bill Evans had reached the final bars of "We Will Meet Again," the last track on side one.

I turned the record over, poured another vodka, and phoned my answering service. A Mrs. Turkin had returned my call. Mrs. Turkin was the mother of an eighteen-year-old kid I acted for. The kid's girlfriend had got in the front seat of a taxi late one night and told the driver to let her off in the underground garage of a downtown apartment building. When the cab driver and the girl were concluding the transaction in the garage, which the driver may or may not have interpreted as a prelude to some quick and nasty sex, my kid jumped in the back seat of the cab. He made threatening noises at the driver while the girlfriend lifted the poor sap's wallet. The cabbie said he got a good look at my kid as he and the girl were hot-footing it out of the garage, and a couple of weeks later he spotted my kid in front of Sam the Record Man's on the Yonge Street Strip. The police reasoned that my kid's girlfriend had set up the robbery, a variation on the old badger game. My kid said something to the cops when he was arrested. To wit: "The driver deserved it. He was just looking to get laid." Clever. I jock-eyed around with the crown attorney on the case for a month and we made a deal. She reduced the charge from robbery to assault with intent and I pleaded my kid guilty. Not bad considering my kid had a record, nothing violent before the waltz in the garage but a record. He'd been in jail for the month and was coming up for sentencing.

I phoned Mrs. Turkin. At her end, the television was on in the background. More like the foreground.

"We been worried sick about James, Mr. Crang," she said. She had to talk up over *Family Feud*.

I said, "He may go to jail, Mrs. Turkin."

"What we done for that boy, there wasn't nothing more we could," she said. Even talking up, her voice was whiny.

"How long he goes to jail," I said, "may depend on you and your husband."

"He got the marks in school," she said. "We never made him quit or nothing."

I said, "The judge is going to sentence James on Monday morning, Mrs. Turkin. I'd like you or your husband to be in court."

"What?" The whine was gone.

"Judges are usually impressed favourably, Mrs. Turkin, when the parents of a boy James' age take the trouble to appear for sentencing."

She had put her hand over the receiver and was shouting at someone else. The shouting lasted ten seconds.

"We can't get off work, neither of us," Mrs. Turkin said to me.

I said, "It could make a difference of months in the sentence, Mrs. Turkin."

"Me and my husband got jobs to think of and that's more than James can say."

She hung up.

The pizzas were beginning to bubble in the oven and Bill Evans was halfway through "Sometime Ago."

I made another phone call and got Tom Catalano's wife at home. She said Tom was still at the office. Her tone was in the small gap between patience and resignation. I dialled the night line at McIntosh, Brown & Crabtree, and someone said he'd dig Catalano out of the library.

"This wouldn't be a prodigal son call?" Catalano said when he knew it was me.

Years earlier, I'd worked my eighteen months as an articling student at McIntosh, Brown. Catalano kept wanting me back.

"I don't get it, Crang, whatever it is that makes you stick it out in the criminal courts," he said on the phone. "It's grubby stuff and fundamentally boring. Come down here and I'll guarantee you a Supreme Court civil trial first time out of the box."

"I'd flunk the dress code you got down there," I said.

"I'll hand you the kind of cases they write up in the *Dominion Law Reports*," Catalano said. "That ever happen with the clients you got smelling up your waiting room?"

"Haven't got a waiting room," I said. "Anyway, one point in favour of my clients, so far none of them have been serious enough to consort with the guys who wear black suits and leave their associates in the trunks of cars out at the airport."

"Meaning?"

I told Catalano about Matthew Wansborough and Ace Disposal and the Grimaldis, father and sons. He was silent for about three beats and asked if I had told Wansborough my news. I said no and asked him if Wansborough was likely to get himself involved in something shifty and keep it from his lawyers. Catalano said, was the Pope Jewish? He said a newspaper reporter's unprinted allegations weren't much to go on. I said Ray Griffin impressed me as sound on his research. Catalano said he'd hold off on reporting to Wansborough, and in the meantime, I should find out what I could about the Grimaldis and Ace and do it about as soon as yesterday.

"Listen," Catalano said when we were through with Wansborough's troubles, "one of our juniors came to work this morning in corduroy pants and a tweed jacket. We let him walk around that way all day."

I said, "Tell me when he shows up in a windbreaker from his bowling league."

I called my answering service again and told them I wouldn't be in the office next day. I phoned my secretary and told her the same thing. Part-time secretary. In a practice like mine, paperwork is minimal, mostly a matter of reports to the Legal Aid Society on cases they send me, a few letters, subpoenas. Mrs. Reid is a proper lady in her early sixties who will forever be Mrs. Reid to me and I will be Mr. Crang to her. She comes in two or three days a week to type things and file other things. On days when she doesn't come in and I'm not around, the office is unmanned. And unwomanned.

I ate the pizzas at the table in the kitchen, and afterwards I poured another vodka and watched television. Barbara Frum on *The Journal* was carrying on a four-way interview with an economist in Halifax, the Minister of Finance in the Toronto studio, a union man in Hamilton, and a former provincial premier in Regina. The subject was interest rates. After a while, the camera-switching made me forget whether I was being enlightened.

I flicked off the set and turned out the lights. Across the street, three gentlemen who looked in need of fresh barbering were sitting at one of the tables under a light in the park passing around a bottle in a brown paper bag. Maybe they weren't winos. Maybe they were free and questing spirits come to commune with the shade of Goldwin Smith. I went to the bedroom at the back of the apartment and slept straight through for eight hours.

4

I **WAS DRINKING** my second cup of coffee, and when it got to be eight-twenty, I turned on the radio in the kitchen. The radio was set at the CBC station. The morning show was in its third hour and time had come for Annie B. Cooke to do her movie reviews. I never miss Annie B. Cooke.

The show's host introduced her, and after he and she had engaged in fifteen seconds of what passed for witty badinage at eight-twenty in the morning, Annie B. Cooke waded into a movie about Tarzan. I gathered it was a movie that its makers intended to be taken seriously. Ms. Cooke wasn't having any of that.

"The movie reveals how Tarzan was raised in semi-dark Africa by a bunch of guys dressed in costumes left over from *Planet of the Apes*," she said in a voice that was a match for Debra Winger's, "how Tarzan grew up and shopped at a jungle emporium for a loincloth by Giorgio Armani, and how he was taken to London, where he freaked out when he discovered his former jungle colleagues locked in cages at the zoo. The movie is pompous and makes you yearn for the good old days of Johnny Weissmuller."

The host chuckled, and Annie B. Cooke praised a French movie with Lino Ventura, trashed a directing job by Paul Mazursky, and recommended a comedy that Carl Reiner had written the script for. The host thanked her and it was over to the weatherman to size up the prospects for more July heat wave.

I turned down the radio and poured a third coffee. When five minutes had gone by on the clock on the stove, I picked up the phone and dialled a number I knew by heart.

"You have a nimble way with a phrase," I said when Annie answered at the other end.

"Aren't you the loyal listener," she said. She sounded out of breath. It takes her five minutes to walk rapidly out of the CBC Cabbagetown studio where the morning show comes from, half a block north and two blocks east to her flat on the third floor of a renovated house. Renovated is the only way houses come in Cabbagetown these days. Annie always walks rapidly after her morning reviews, something about the adrenalin pump of working live radio.

"Listening to you," I said, "it beats going to the dud movies."

"Hang in there, Crang," Annie said. "Next month, the Roxy's running an Anita Ekberg retrospective."

"Just my speed."

"We'll go to the seven-o'clock screenings. My treat."

"Does this mean we're steadies?"

"Pinned. It's a progression: dating, pinned, steady, engaged, married, cheating, an entry on the court calendar."

"Let's plan on vamping somewhere between pinned and steady for a decade or two."

"You're not otherwise entangled tonight, is that the reason for this early-morning chat? You're not labouring on behalf of people who probably should stay in jail anyway?"

"It's Thursday," I said, "date night all over the world."

"Seems to me you once described Saturday as date night all over the world."

"Next I may say Friday," I said. "It's a shifting kaleidoscope out there."

"Okay, I've got a screening of the new Richard Gere at four," Annie said. She spoke in her down-to-brass-tacks tone. "You can come by at seven. This is for dinner, I take it. I wonder how many times Gere's going to drop his pants in this one. Seven o'clock and I'll brace you with one of those vodka martinis before we go out. Or whatever it is you do with one of those vodka martinis."

"Drink it."

I went into the bathroom for a shave and a shower. My bathroom is decorated with a framed poster Annie gave me for my last birthday. It's from a 1940s movie called *The Mask of Dimitrios*. It shows Peter Lorre, Sydney Greenstreet, and Zachary Scott trying for a snarl in their expressions. My kind of guys.

I fell for Annie B. Cooke's voice before I met the rest of her. It kept turning up on the radio in the morning. One day the program Annie does the movie reviews for had me on in a four-minute guest spot. I was in the news with a weird defence I'd worked out for a teenage hooker who'd retained me. The defence got her off. Other criminal lawyers picked up on it and the CBC morning show wanted me to explain the defence on the air. I agreed. The program's host was hyped-up and energetic and got in more jokes than I did until the four minutes were over and someone was tapping me on the shoulder. It was Annie. She was next up on the show and wanted the microphone I was sitting in front of. I hung around and asked Annie out to dinner. She accepted. That was a year and a half ago.

We get along pretty well together. Annie isn't keen on my clients, but that isn't a problem. More a point of vigorous debate. Everything else is jake. I like her line of patter, she likes mine. We're attracted to one another in the physical department. We may even be in love. But we aren't saying. We don't discuss marriage or moving in together. Gun-shy. Or maybe that's partner-shy. I've had a marriage that didn't pan out. She had a live-in guy for a couple of years and I gather it ended messily. For Annie and me, it's comfortable the way it is, keeping our own places, stepping out on plenty of dates, maintaining mutual faithfulness. We're still getting to know one another. I trust it'll be a lengthy process.

5

IT DOESN'T LOOK LIKE A CAR that anyone who has a regular job would drive. It'd make a grand third car in a rich stockbroker's family, something for the kids to wheel over to the country club. It's a Volkswagen convertible, small, white, and sporty.

I drove it out from behind the house. I went over to Spadina and headed south. I wanted to get out to the west suburbs and I had a choice, Lakeshore Road or the Gardiner Expressway. No sense putting the Volks up against the speed merchants on the Gardiner. I turned off Spadina on to the Lakeshore.

I'd always wanted a convertible. Indeed, lusted for one. The Volks wasn't what I'd had in mind but it came as a gift. I was defending a client who'd served time for robbing banks. He was on trial for another holdup. My client was black. At the preliminary hearing, the bank teller who'd emptied his till when someone pointed a gun at him described the robber as a look-alike for Sammy Davis Jr. My guy was tall and light-skinned. He looked more like Lena Horne than Sammy Davis Jr.

At the trial, I read the teller's testimony to the jury. I showed them a dozen photographs of Sammy Davis, including the one of old Sam embracing Richard Nixon at the 1972 Republican Convention in Miami. I asked the jury if that man resembled my client. They took fifteen minutes to acquit.

My guy paid his fee. He said he was so grateful he had a present for me. A convertible. I was thinking something flashy and American. My guy was thinking miniature and German.

The traffic was light on the Lakeshore and I dawdled along. On my left, the sun glinted off the water. Lake Ontario was almost motionless in the still of the morning. I passed the Argonaut Rowing Club. Three strapping lads in blue singlets and shorts were easing their shells into the water. Farther along, a dozen ladies were taking a tennis clinic on the courts at the Boulevard Club. The soft thunk of racquets meeting balls drifted on the air. Another few hundred yards down the road, kids splashed in the Sunnyside pool. Ah, the wide, wide world of sports.

Up ahead, the Palace Pier signalled the end of the public stretch of lakefront. The Palace Pier is a tall, bleak condominium on a small piece of land that juts into the lake, and it isn't the real Palace Pier. The genuine article was a dance hall of the same name that stood for years on the site. I heard Duke Ellington's band there near the end. They were getting long in the tooth, Hodges, Carney, Lawrence Brown, and the rest, but when they played, they still made your stomach lift.

I followed the ramp off the Lakeshore on to the Queen Elizabeth Way. The lake disappeared behind rows of squat factories and warehouses. I stuck on the Queen E to Kipling Avenue and turned north. According to the street guide I keep in the glove compartment, Ace Disposal's address put it on one of the back streets west of Kipling and south of Dundas. It was an area that catered to man and his car. I drove past a Speedy Muffler outlet, a coin car wash, a Rad Man, and half a dozen body shops.

I turned left off Dundas, and in a couple of blocks, on the other side of an unpainted garage where you could have your transmission overhauled, the premises of Ace Disposal announced themselves in a large square sign that hung about twelve feet in the air on a steel pole. The sign had red lettering on a yellow background. Beyond the pole was a chain-link fence. It enclosed four or five acres of asphalted property. The fence stood as tall as the pole with the sign and had a thick trimming of barbed wire at the top. I didn't bother checking for a welcome mat.

I pulled beyond Ace's land, made a U-turn, and parked on the other side of the street in front of a bar and restaurant that advertised exotic dancers from noon to midnight. Just the ticket to pass the hours while your car is getting a lube job up the street.

There were two gates in Ace's fence. Both were closed. One gate was for people and the other for trucks. The people gate led on to a cement path that crossed a patch of brown grass to a long rectangular one-storey building. The building was glum and red-brick and had air-conditioning units sticking out of every second window. No doubt typists, bookkeepers, and various office workers laboured on the other side of the air conditioners. If I wanted to chat up Charles Grimaldi or Wansborough's cousin, Alice Brackley the headstrong, that was where I figured to find them. But I didn't want to chat up Charles or Alice. Not yet. I didn't have the right questions. I was on a reconnoitring mission. Reconnoitring was a word that made me feel efficient.

In the middle of the property, a bigger grey-brick building had a small office area at one end. The rest of it opened up in large bays for servicing trucks. There were eight bays, and four of them were in business. Six or seven men in mechanics' overalls swarmed around the trucks. The asphalted surface that surrounded the buildings had painted-in spaces for at least two hundred trucks, but only ten spaces were occupied. The rest of the trucks must have been out on the job. Whatever precisely that was. Maybe reconnoitring would enlighten me.

The trucks in the parking spaces were uniform in appearance, big and blunt, a dusty red colour, and looked like they'd been put together from a giant set of kids' Lego blocks. The largest piece of Lego sat on the back. It was a bin, a good ten feet deep and probably that much across. If I read correctly the series of bars and chains that led from it to the cab of the truck, the bin could be hoisted on and off the truck when you pushed and pulled the right buttons and levers in the cab. As toys go, it was probably a lot of fun.

I sat in the Volks for fifteen minutes. A man came out of the office end of the grey-brick building and walked toward one of the parked trucks. From the distance, all I could make out of the man were jeans riding low on a bulging stomach, a black T-shirt, and a face covered in a thick, dark beard. He swung into the cab of the truck with a nonchalance that said he'd done it more than once before. He started the engine and steered the truck slowly toward the larger of the two gates. A man in a security guard's outfit stepped from a small hut near the gate, pulled it open, and waved the truck through. The driver turned left and the truck rumbled up the street toward Dundas. It had me for company.

I followed the truck on a route that took us back to the centre of the city. We came off the Lakeshore at York Street and headed north toward Queen.

The Ace truck slowed down a block and a half short of Queen, just south of Osgoode Hall, the elegant nineteenth-century building that houses Ontario's Supreme Court. It turned into the opening in a construction site that was surrounded by smart orange hoardings. There were glass and chrome skyscrapers on either side of the construction site. If I knew my downtown Toronto developers, there'd soon be a third of the same. Three identical skyscrapers in a row. The guy who'd designed Osgoode Hall wouldn't have understood.

The orange hoardings had a dozen glassed-in viewing spots for interested citizens to catch the action. I parked in a tow-away zone and took up position at one of the viewing spots. The excavation dropped fifty or sixty feet. At the bottom, workmen were laying foundations for the new building. My truck had braked its way down a steep incline to the base of the excavation. My truck. Already I was feeling proprietorial.

My truck wheeled in a semicircle and stopped. The driver opened his door and leaned over the side of the truck, half in and half out of the cab. As he leaned, he operated a couple of levers with his right hand. In response, the empty bin on the back of the truck lifted up and out and down. Gradually it settled on the bumpy ground of the excavation.

I patted myself on the head. Metaphorically speaking. The truck operated in just the way I'd thought back at Ace's yard.

The driver closed himself back in the cab and jockeyed the truck several yards north in the excavation. He backed up to another bin that was sitting on the ground. The second bin overflowed with irregularly shaped chunks of cement, broken two-by-fours, and other construction debris.

The driver worked with the levers in the cab. An arrangement of forklifts reached out from the back of the truck and hoisted the full bin into the spot that had been vacated by the empty bin. Rube Goldberg couldn't have diagrammed it better.

The driver gave a ho-hum wave to a group of workers in yellow hard hats and steered up the incline out of the site. I crossed the street and started the Volks. The truck driver picked his way through the streets east and south away from downtown. I remained in surreptitious pursuit.

Following a large truck through slow traffic in clear daylight. Did that qualify as surreptitious pursuit? Close enough for a beginner.

The driver got the truck on to Leslie Street and aimed south at the lake. He drove as far as he could go. That brought him to a sign that read "Metropolitan Toronto Dump Site. No Admittance."

The driver ignored the instruction.

I didn't.

I pulled off to the right and parked on the shoulder of the road. I watched the truck through the side window of the Volks.

The truck passed through an opening in the wire fence around the dump. It stopped fifty feet inside at a building that was about the size of a booth on a parking lot. On either side of the small building were large metal platforms.

I gave the metal platforms a solid five seconds of scrutiny. Right, got it, the metal platforms were weigh scales. Time for another metaphorical pat on the head.

The truck drove on to the weigh scale at the west side of the small building. At an open window with a counter on it, a man in a short-sleeved, open-neck white shirt consulted a little gadget in front of him. He jotted something on a sheet of paper that looked like it had three or four carbons attached to it. The little gadget figured to be the weigh-scale indicator. The man in the white shirt had weighed my truck. He gave a nod of his head at the driver. The truck pulled away and disappeared out of my sight into the mass of mounds and hillocks that made up the dump.

I waited.

More trucks arrived at the dump. Some were dusty red and had Ace's name on the side. Some came from other disposal companies. The trucks stopped on the weigh scale at the west side of the building.

Other trucks, some Ace and some not, came out of the dump. They stopped on the weigh scale on the east side of the building.

The man in the white shirt took care of both sides. He consulted the weigh-scale indicator on the west side and a similar indicator on the east side. For each truck, he wrote down something on a different sheet of paper with carbons, giving the bottom copy to the driver. He moved purposefully back and forth between the two windows in his little kingdom. He didn't appear rushed. None of the drivers honked a horn at him. A professional at work.

My truck came out of the dump in twenty minutes. It had a jolly bounce that told me its bin had been emptied of the construction debris. The truck pulled on to the east scale. The guy inside the booth jotted his notations, tore off the bottom copy, and handed it to the Ace driver.

Presumably—no, certainly—the sheet was the same paper that the man in the white shirt had used for his notations when my truck arrived at the dump and weighed in on the west side.

Old white-shirt gave a nod of the head to the driver. The truck moved off the scale.

I turned my head from the side window and looked straight ahead. The Volks was parked under a tree, and the front window was in shadows. My face reflected back at me in the semi-darkness. The expression on it was studied. When I look studied, I also look like I should be wearing a tall hat in a conical shape. I let the studiedness slide off my face.

My truck had weighed in with a full load.

It weighed out empty.

The man in the small building had recorded the two weights.

Subtract the second weight from the first and you had the weight of the load.

That figure was the basis on which Ace paid Metropolitan Toronto for the privilege of dumping waste on Metro land.

Ace passed on the charge to its customers. Customers like the guys who were putting up the skyscraper on York Street. Ace charged the customers the amount of the charge it paid Metro plus something for its own services in hauling the stuff to the dump.

All very legitimate and businesslike.

I checked my reflection in the window. Nobody in there wearing a conical hat on his head.

Hot dog, I'd mastered the basics of the disposal business.

6

I FOLLOWED THE TRUCK around for the rest of the day. Maybe more surveillance would firm up my analysis of the Ace operation. Maybe I'd discover something dodgy about the disposal business. Maybe I'd pick up a light tan with the top down on the Volks. Maybe the George Hamilton look would come back in style.

The truck made two more runs. Each took us to a different construction site and back to the dump. Empty the bin, take the paper from the man in the booth, move on.

After the third trip, it was two o'clock. The driver parked his truck a few blocks up Leslie from the dump in front of a place called Jerry's Tavern. The driver went in. Jerry must have been a cheery soul. His tavern was painted canary yellow and had more than its complement of neon. It was also ancient enough to offer two entrances. The custom dated back to genteel days when Ontario law required ladies to arrive in drinking establishments through a door exclusive to their sex.

I went into a variety store across the street from Jerry's. A small Korean lady was selling a fistful of lottery tickets to a large black man. When they finished, I bought a quart carton of two-per-cent milk and a package of butter tarts. A sugar hit to carry me through an afternoon of surveillance. I sat in the Volks, sipped the milk, and tried to pin down the flavour of the butter tarts. Band-Aids. The tarts tasted like Band-Aids.

An hour after the driver entered Jerry's, he exited. He stood on the sidewalk and belched. I noted two fresh pieces of information. His T-shirt wasn't all black. It had Duran Duran printed on the front in faded white lettering. At his right hip, hooked on a belt loop, he wore a ring of many keys. It looked heavy. If I carried a load like that on my belt loop, my pants would fall around my ankles.

The driver climbed into his cab and drove north on Leslie. I did likewise.

Duran Duran. Was that the name of the guy or of the band? You didn't run into such conundrums in my kind of music. Stan Getz was the guy. The Stan Getz Quartet was the name of the band.

The truck drove straight across the city to a residential street in the Annex district near Bathurst and Bloor. A triplex was going up on a lot between two Victorian houses. The driver dumped the empty bin from the truck on the front lawn and scooped up another binful of construction trash. All as before.

What wasn't usual was that a short, heavy man in green pants counted off several bills from a fat roll in his pocket and handed them to the driver. It was the first time all day I'd seen money change hands.

The truck went north on Bathurst Street. Bathurst is long and narrow, and as you get farther north, apartment buildings line the street. Out of polite earshot, some Torontonians call it the Gaza Strip. It's a middle-class Jewish neighbourhood peopled by families who have moved up the immigrant corridor of Bathurst Street from the earlier ghettos downtown.

North of Steeles Avenue, about the time I began to ponder the question of our destination, the high-rises peter out. Rural Ontario breathes a few defiant last gasps, maple trees, oaks, and elms. Housing developments would take care of them in another half-generation. The truck caught the orange light at Highway 7. I pressed the accelerator and hung on its tail.

Past Royal Downs Golf Club, the truck turned left on to a dirt road. The driver hadn't signalled for the turn. My tires squealed when I followed him in. I didn't follow him far. He stopped twenty yards down the dirt road. By the time I braked, the driver was jumping down from his cab.

He waddled in my direction. His hands were hitching up his pants and he was speaking to me.

"Hey, you, shit-face," he said.

It wasn't going to be an invitation for drinks at the Park Plaza.

The dirt road was too narrow to turn the Volks around, and accelerating backwards on to Bathurst seemed more chancy than a confrontation with fatso. I got out of the car and watched the driver come the rest of the way toward me. The waddle had been upgraded to a swagger.

"All day I look in the rearview, I see you, turd," the driver said. He was near enough that I could smell Jerry's beer.

"Tenacious son of a gun, aren't I," I said.

"You and that fag car."

"Steady," I said, "let's leave the vehicle out of it."

Up close, with all the gut and beard and black T-shirt, the driver had a tendency to loom. He weighed about two-fifty, but he looked as fit as Oliver Hardy. That might help my cause if it came to fisticuffs. I didn't want it to come to fisticuffs. One of us would get hurt. Probably me.

"You got a smart mouth, asshole," the driver said.

His punch began below his belt line, somewhere behind the ring of keys. He might as well have winged it in by way of Pearson International Airport, I had so much time to move my head and left shoulder inside the swing of the punch. His forearm landed on the back of my neck. It made a loud, slapping noise and rocked me forward. The slap was worse than the rock.

He'd already launched another arcing shot with his left fist. Didn't this guy watch the Saturday-afternoon fights on ABC-TV? Didn't he know rainbows like he was throwing were what Marvelous Marvin Hagler had for lunch? I kept my arms high, and his punches thudded onto my elbows and shoulders. The punches didn't have much steam, but they kept me swaying back and forth on my feet. Professional boxers call it rolling with the punches. I called it making the best of a bad situation.

Every time the driver swung his arms, his black T-shirt pulled up over his belt and showed a strip of hairy gut. I opted for a display of offence. I dropped my right shoulder and aimed a fist at his bare belly button. It seemed an efficient punch, straight, hard, and not more than a foot. It made no impression on his stomach. Either I was power-deficient or the gut was all muscle.

While my right hand was down and going about its useless manoeuvre, he landed one of his roundhouses. It hit hard on my ear. The inside of my head turned red. I staggered a couple of feet to my left and bumped up against the Volks. It didn't have as much give as bouncing off the ropes in a ring.

I squared around and faced my worthy opponent. He had a small, mean grin on his face, and his right hand was cocked over his shoulder. He was measuring me.

The redness had gone from behind my eyes. I shot out two fast left jabs. It was a reflex move inspired by fear and desperation. Both jabs landed on the driver's nose. He looked surprised. I felt surprised. He hadn't thrown his right hand.

I was the first to recover from our mutual amazement and hit the driver with two more left jabs. His head popped back. I hit him with a right to the beard. It was like punching a porcupine. He made an oomph noise and sat down in the dirt road. The man with the gut of iron had a glass jaw.

My right ear was ringing. I touched it and it felt hot. The driver climbed up from the dirt. He crouched over and rushed at me. His arms were reaching out in front of his body. If he got the arms around me, his weight would give him a large edge. I was faster on my feet than he was. But he had the bulk.

I got up on the balls of my feet and danced out of the path of the first rush. He turned and rushed again. I danced to the side. It couldn't last much longer, him charging, me making like Manolete. Fatigue was catching up to my legs.

On his third rush, I planted my feet and timed a right-hand upper cut. Now or never. The punch caught him under the jaw at the point where his beard stopped and his throat was exposed. He straightened out of his crouch. I hit his cheek with a left hook. He fell over backwards. He raised his head. I kicked it. Too bad it wasn't winter. I might have had my Grebs on.

I turned and opened the door of the Volks. The guy in the black T-shirt was pushing himself up with his arms. I got behind the steering wheel and started the engine. The guy fell over on his side. I drove out the dirt road and turned south on Bathurst toward the city.

My right ear hurt like hell.

7

WHEN I GOT THERE, the door to Annie's apartment was open and she was in it. She reached her hands up to my shoulders, stood on tiptoe, and touched my lips with hers. She made me feel like we were a couple of kids. Skipping across the meadow. Picking up lots of forget-me-nots.

Annie is in her mid-thirties. She is five feet tall and has fine bones and not enough muscle on them to nudge her much past one hundred pounds. Her hair is the colour of Mr. Poe's raven, and she wears it short and flat and pulled back behind her ears. Her cheekbones are high and her chin has a slight forward thrust. The combination gives her a feisty look about which she displays no self-consciousness.

She had on beige trousers with legs that narrowed and tightened until they stopped six inches above her ankles. They went with low-heeled white leather shoes and a white silk shirt that had billowy sleeves and was unbuttoned to the space between her breasts. The first time I met Annie, I said she looked Parisian. She said other men before me had told her the same thing. I said I'd see them at dawn with pistols. She said she grew up in a village northwest of Toronto called Palgrave. So much for the male powers of observation.

Annie had a Kir going. She went into the kitchen and made me a vodka martini on the rocks according to my favourite mix. Hold the vermouth, hold the olive, hold the twist.

I'd been home, showered, changed, and applied ice to my right ear. It still hurt. It was red and stuck out a little. It didn't go with the spiffy ensemble I'd chosen.

"I'll try two guesses," Annie said. I was watching her from the doorway into the kitchen. She had her back to me, getting out the ice and pouring the vodka. "The hot new fashion along your part of trendy Queen West is dyeing one ear vermilion. Or, my second guess, somebody's lodged a tomato in your right ear and the damned thing won't come out."

"Wrong vegetable," I said. "In the boxing world, we call this incipient cauliflower."

"You aren't in the boxing world," Annie said. She turned in the kitchen and handed me the drink. Our fingers touched on the side of the glass. "If I remember the tidbits of autobiography you've laid on me, you haven't been in it for twenty years."

"Technically I've never been in it," I said. We stayed talking in the kitchen. Cozy. "I boxed at university. That's as much like the real thing as Neil Diamond is like Dick Haymes."

"To me," Annie said, "fighting is fighting whether you do it at an institution of higher learning or at Maple Leaf Gardens."

"True."

"So how did you get the mean-looking ear?"

"I'll tell you over dinner. You'll love it."

"Dinner probably, the story I doubt it."

We ate at Costa Basque on the part of Avenue Road where the nice old houses have been converted into restaurants, stores that sell expensive *objets*, and offices for lawyers who handle lucrative divorce actions. Costa Basque is laid out on a series of balconies, each overlooking a central courtyard. We sat on the top balcony. It's more intimate up there, away from the guitarist on the ground floor and the conversation of the folks at the bar who ask him to play "Yellow Bird." Second-most-popular request in the place. First is "Raindrops Keep Fallin' on My Head." Good old Basque tunes.

The waiter handed us menus. He was young and trim and fey. I asked for a bottle of white Rioja. The waiter scampered after it. I studied the menu.

"About the ear," Annie said.

"Hey, first things first," I said from behind the menu. "Man's gotta think about his nourishment."

Annie said, "You're going to order the pâté followed by paella."

I looked up.

"I think you just called me predictable."

"You operate in patterns," Annie said. "You go at something long enough until you reason out the course of action you think is going to work best. From there on in, you never deviate. This restaurant, for one teeny example, we've come here, what, four times. The last three, you've had the pâté followed by paella."

"Maybe not predictable," I said. "Maybe pigheaded."

"I'm not being critical, old darling."

"Criticism is your game."

"Reviewer," Annie said. "Movie reviewer."

The waiter covered the bottom of my glass with wine. I tasted it and pronounced it splendid. The waiter beamed at me.

We ordered. Annie said she'd have green salad and grouper. I said I'd have pâté and paella. I gave the words a John Gielgud twist. Even, measured, lofty. It got a small snicker out of Annie.

"At the risk of doing an imitation of a broken record," she said, "the ear."

I started with the fight on the dirt road and worked back to Wansborough's visit to my office.

"Your first respectable client in living memory," Annie said when I was finished, "and you get yourself punched."

"Irony makes the world go round, as somebody must have said."

"Dorothy Parker?"

"Not sage enough for Lillian Hellman."

"Right. Too frivolous."

"Author unknown," I said.

The waiter arrived with the salad and pâté. The pâté was made with ham and chicken livers and had a grainy texture that was dandy. For a few moments we chewed and made approving noises.

Annie said, "Skipping right along to topic B on the agenda, let's consider your strange clients."

"You and Tom Catalano."

"Case in point," Annie said. "Your friend Tom has everything a good lawyer's brain can earn him, security and respectability and all those other qualities that our society legitimately salutes, and I don't think he feels he's compromising his standards by acting for people who actually wear ties."

A drop of tarragon dressing hung stubbornly to the side of Annie's mouth. I didn't blame it, but I reached over and dabbed it away with my napkin.

I said, "Shall I tell you about my insatiable appetite for the free-lance life? The urge to go it alone? Be my own man? The Jack London of the legal world?"

"Try for something more profound."

"How about this: I like short stories."

"That's profound? That isn't even relevant."

I put down my fork and picked up the last piece of pâté on the plate with my fingers.

I said, "The police arrest a guy. We go to court. People testify. The Crown has its version of what happened. I have mine. Themes take shape. Strands unravel. We get conflict, and in the end we get resolution. Someone makes a decision, the judge, the jury. Beginning, middle, conclusion. Sometimes a surprise conclusion."

"I'll grant you this, Crang, you give it the structure of a short story."

"Criminal cases are like that in court," I said. "John Cheever couldn't have written them better."

"More like O. Henry."

"Whoever. I'm hooked on the narrative every time I go to court. Can Tom Catalano say as much, him with his security and respectability? He expends that brain of his on civil actions that have one consistent theme, who owes how much to whom."

The waiter cleared away the empty plates. He put the grouper in front of Annie and the paella in front of me. He wished us bon appétit.

"There's something else," I said.

"Isn't there always."

"A relationship develops between me and my clients," I said. "Lousy word, relationship. Stop me before I say interface. Still, there's something that connects me and them. Guy in jail, at that moment he has only one positive element in his life, his lawyer. Family doesn't count in jail, if he has any, friends don't count, not other cons. He's cut off from what we might laughably call his normal environment except for me, his counsel. That circumstance, like it or not, means that my connection with him develops along upbeat lines. I like it."

"You're beginning to sound more social worker than criminal counsel," Annie said.

I shrugged. I was having a swell time with the paella. First a piece of veal, then a couple of mussels, an oyster, a tiny chunk of chicken, some rice, sniff the fumes, inhale the saffron. I felt like rubbing my tummy and saying goody goody.

"The trouble with it all," Annie said, "the way you feel about those people in jail, is that it's bound to distance you from the rest of the world."

"The straight world you're talking about," I said.

"There must be a better adjective."

"The straight world gets a trifle bent," I said. "Cops tell fibs. Crown attorneys push witnesses around. Judges reveal cruel streaks. Small points but true."

"Is there a larger point?" Annie asked.

The Rioja was all gone. I made motions at the waiter.

I said to Annie, "Maybe not larger but pertinent to what we're talking about. These people, my beloved clients, aren't entirely rational. If they were, I'd probably find them dull. They pull these crazy stunts. Get themselves behind life's eight ball."

"Everybody has a run of lousy luck now and then," Annie said. "The difference is, your people go looking for the eight balls."

"What makes them into bandits?" I said. "I'm fascinated to know if there's an answer."

"Maybe you'll never find out."

"The quest of a lifetime."

The waiter poured more wine from the new bottle into our glasses. He poured with his right hand and held the left behind his back at the correct slope.

"Tom Catalano's still a nice guy," I said.

"You'll do too," Annie said.

I gave her an aw-shucks smile.

"Do I sound cranky about you sometimes?" Annie said.

She didn't wait for me to answer. I would have fibbed anyway.

"It's the rewards," Annie said. "Or the status. I want the return for you that you ought to have earned. Okay, I'm talking from a perspective I might not be entitled to. I'll never make a big buck reviewing movies. Never expected to. But you, a lawyer, all those years at school, you . . . ah hell, Crang."

"You aren't going to say I could be a somebody," I said.

"Not that clichéd," Annie said. "I was almost about to ask you to be more serious, but that's not right either."

"Serious tends to be dull. Natural equation."

"Tedious you're not."

"This line of conversation has stalemated."

"Leave it at this," Annie said. "I hope your Mr. Wansborough is a harbinger of clients to come."

I couldn't locate another mussel in my paella. Out of oysters, too. I went on a search for chicken.

"On the subject of careers," I said, "how was Richard Gere's bare ass this afternoon?"

"Bare ass!" Annie said. There was an exclamation point in her voice. "We're talking full frontal nudity here. The man's basing stardom on his genitalia. What's worse, private parts aside, his acting's so bloody mannered, the Meryl Streep of his sex."

Annie had a thought or two about performing mannerisms. All actors include them in their equipment, she said; the good ones make them disappear. Annie's thought or two expanded to a thesis. She said she admired Robert De Niro's technique. She said it was close to seamless. Annie was intense as she talked, and at the same time she was having fun with her subject. She said the older English actors had technique that vanished before one's very eyes. Annie thought it was amazing.

She talked, I played audience, enjoying it, and after the wine was gone, we had Spanish coffees, and Annie began to wind down.

"Gere had a line in the movie today you could handle," she said to me.

"Set the scene."

"It's one of those 1940s nightclubs you only see in movies," Annie said. "Never existed otherwise. Women in slinky gowns, everybody smoking like mad, an orchestra with violins, waiters in tuxedos, and Gere's coming on to the gorgeous lady with the sultry look. Get the picture? The orchestra's playing a tango and Gere says—"

"—your place or mine?"

"Your reading lacks a certain *je ne sais quoi* but the wording's on the money."

We finished our Spanish coffees. I paid the bill and tipped the waiter, who looked pleased as punch. And Annie and I resolved the Richard Gere dilemma. We went to her place, and some of the time we slept.

8

FOR BREAKFAST, Annie made us an omelette with bits of tomato mixed in and we sat at the table in the bow window of her apartment. I ate my half of the omelette and most of hers and drank two cups of coffee. I did the eating and drinking in silence except for the odd slurp. A book had Annie's undivided attention. It was about an Italian movie director named Alberti and it was written in Italian.

"Damn," Annie said to her book, "I didn't know he wrote the script for that."

She had an interview with Signor Alberti in the afternoon. He was passing through town on a promotion tour for his new movie.

Annie said, "The entertainment editor at the *Sun* says he'll pay me for a thousand words on Alberti if I deliver first thing tomorrow for Sunday's paper."

"They take freelance stuff?"

"Their regular movie guy's out in California on a press junket and the editor said there was nobody else at the paper who knows as much about movies as I do."

"How complimentary."

"He did say European movies."

I went home and changed into jeans and a cotton sports shirt, something comfy for more surveillance duty. I drove over to the Metro dump at the foot of Leslie Street and parked under the tree outside the entrance. Thursday, I'd started at Ace Disposal. Friday, I was beginning at the dump. Sometimes my talent for improvisation frightened me.

I watched trucks pass in and out of the dump, on and off the weigh scales, for an hour.

"Hey," I said. Out loud. It was an exclamation of discovery.

I leaned across the front seat and fiddled among the odds and ends in the glove compartment. The street guide, a flask of brandy for swooning spells, a deck of playing cards with bicycle wheels on the back. Gloves, too, the kind with no fingers. They remain unworn. I'm saving them until I get my first Mercedes and can rightfully adopt the pretentious look in handwear. I got out a spiral-bound steno notebook and a ballpoint pen that wrote in black. I unstrapped my wristwatch and set it on my lap. I watched and I timed and I made notes.

Trucks arrived at the weigh scale on the average of about one every couple of minutes. Sometimes there was a lineup of three or four trucks. Sometimes five minutes went by without a truck in sight. They came out of the dump at the same rate. About half the trucks were from Ace Disposal, the rest from a variety of other companies. So far, so clear.

What prompted the "hey" was the amount of time it took the man inside the weigh-scale office to deal with the Ace trucks. It was the same man from the day before, the old pro in the short-sleeved white shirt. Maybe a different shirt. He consulted his weighing gadget, jotted numbers on his sheets of paper, handed out the carbon copies to the drivers as they left. Identical routine with each truck in and out. The fishy part was that the routine may have been identical with every truck, but according to my watch and calculations, it took him twenty to thirty seconds longer to deal with an Ace truck than with a truck from another disposal outfit. That was twenty or thirty seconds longer going in and the same coming out.

I started up the Volks and drove back on Leslie until I came to a phone booth. I looked up the number of the *Star*'s editorial department and let it ring seven times before somebody came on the line and told me Ray Griffin didn't get in till noon. That was an hour away. I said I'd call later.

Back at the dump, a variation in routine greeted me. A Cadillac was parked in back of the weigh-scale building. It was very large and very pink, on the order of the gaudy sort that Mary Kay cosmetics salespersons cruise around in. Maybe old white-shirt in the weigh office had run out of lip gloss. A young man wearing a straw hat at a rakish angle sat behind the wheel of the pink Caddie. He'd left the motor running. A couple of minutes later, another man came out the back door of the weigh building. He had black hair, a deep tan, and a nose that was champion size, and he was wearing a light blue summer suit with dark blue stitching around the pockets. He was carrying a thin black briefcase. He got into the front passenger seat of the Cadillac, and before he'd closed the door, the driver was reversing out of the yard and gunning up Leslie. In a cloud of dust.

I stuck it out for another hour. I timed and noted and got the same answers. Ace trucks took about twenty-five, thirty seconds longer to service. Whatever it meant, it was, as they say in the accounting business, a confirmed trend. I drove back to the phone booth, and when I got Ray Griffin on the line, I had a question for him.

"You got somebody tame in the disposal business?"

"Are you on to something?"

"I asked first."

There was a pause on the other end.

"What'd you mean tame?" Griffin asked.

"Somebody inside the industry who didn't mind feeding you material he probably shouldn't have. Somebody who spoke off the record."

"Oh sure, a source, you mean."

"I guess I do."

"I got plenty of stuff from a guy who used to drive for a disposal company."

"Ace?"

"Another one. Ace's drivers are heavies."

"I noticed."

"You're getting into this in a big way, it sounds like."

Griffin's voice had turned confidential. He was a reporter who sniffed a scoop. Except he wouldn't say scoop. Or sniffed.

I said, "I'd like to talk to your driver. That possible?"

"Easy," Griffin said. "He works right here now. Drives a *Star* delivery truck. I can have him for you around four-thirty. He's on the early shift and he'll just be coming off."

We arranged to meet at a restaurant near the Star building called the Press Grill.

"We don't call it that, us reporters," Griffin said. "We call it La Salle de Crayons."

"You sophisticated devils." I hung up.

9

THE PRESS GRILL was windowless and as fragrant as the prisons of Turkey. It smelled of fried onions, stale beer, and cigarette smoke trapped since the days when Holy Joe Atkinson ran the *Star*. Holy Joe died in 1956. Somebody had tried to update the room's decor in a style that ran to California manqué. The ferns drooped and were turning brown at their tips, the posters of 1970s rock groups had wrinkled in their frames, and the three waitresses were too matronly for the tight yellow dresses that passed as uniforms. The place wouldn't see a revival of the Algonquin Round Table.

Ray Griffin and a small, bouncy man with the sleeves of his blue work shirt rolled up tight over his biceps were sitting under a blow-up of Jim Morrison. They had a pitcher of beer in front of them.

"Crang," Griffin said, "like you to shake with Ernie Andrychuk."

Ernie had his first name spelled out in tidy script over the left breast of his blue shirt. He gave my hand a ferocious squeeze. Griffin had on a flaming-red tennis jersey with a green duck where René Lacoste puts his alligator.

Ernie Andrychuk said, "Mr. Crang, I already told Ray here everything I know about Ace when he done them articles of his."

"You want some of this beer, Crang?" Griffin asked.

Before I could say vodka, Griffin was signalling one of the visions in yellow.

"I appreciate your time, Ernie," I said.

"Well, I dunno," Ernie said. He had a puckish face and eyes as blue as the sky over Eire. Andrychuk? Maybe the skies over the Ukraine.

I said, "I've got some specifics you might be able to help me with, Ernie."

"Long's somebody else's paying for the beer," Ernie said with an elfin grin. The Barry Fitzgerald of the Steppes.

The waitress put a stein in front of me, the heavy kind that give lesser men than I a hernia.

I said, "Is there a Metro dump on Bathurst Street, pretty far up, north of Highway 7?"

"There's twelve dumps around the city," Ernie said. "None of them's on Bathurst north or south or any other part."

"Why would an Ace driver pick up a load at a small building site and take it up there?"

"That's easy," Ernie said. He looked as satisfied as a kid who knows the answer to the first question on the ancient-history test. "Probably one of them gypsy dumps," Ernie said. "The driver's doing a run on his own. Takes a payoff from the builder and dumps the load for him and nobody's the wiser at Ace."

"A little freelance finagle?"

"There ain't much in it for anybody. 'Cept maybe the builder. He don't have to go through Ace. He pays the driver maybe fifty bucks and the driver gives half to the guy who owns the land where he dumps the stuff."

"The dump's illegal?"

"All kinds of people do it that got the land out in the sticks and nothing on it."

I sipped my beer. It tasted soapy. To me, all beer tastes soapy. I drink it only on occasions of crisis or diplomacy. In the Press Grill, I drank it out of tact. Blend in with my companions. Be one of the guys.

"You're on to something, Crang?" Griffin said.

"Not what I want to be on to," I said. "But it's yours for the taking."

I wasn't looking for scams that lost money for Ace. I wanted the kind that might be turning Ace a profit.

"Let's take the usual drill a driver goes through," I said to Ernie Andrychuk. "He weighs a load in at the dump, drops the load, and weighs out empty. The weigh-master or whatever you call the guy in the building at the scales gives him a sheet of paper and he goes on his way."

"That sheet of paper, it's called your waybill."

"Got it."

"Weigh-master keeps the original and a copy and the driver gets the other copy."

I asked, "What does the driver do with the waybills he's accumulated at the end of the day?"

"Place where I worked, Donnelly Disposal, it was kind of small compared to Ace, nine or ten trucks is all, we handed them in to the dispatcher back at the yard."

"And from there, Donnelly billed the customers, that right?"

"Sure, the customer pays a flat rate, fifty bucks a pickup or whatever, plus more for the weight of the load which is what your waybill tells ya."

Ernie drained off the rest of the beer from his stein. The pitcher was empty and we paused while Griffin rounded up the waitress for a refill.

"Think about this one, Ernie," I said. "Why would it take the weigh-master over at the Leslie dump a half-minute longer to process an Ace truck than a truck from another company?"

Ernie's face lost its merriness. It scrunched into a puzzled expression. His busy little mind must have been telling him he was going to flunk ancient history after all.

"Don't sweat it, Ernie," I said. "Try another one. You know anybody in the business who rides around in a pink Caddie? Dark guy with a big nose?"

"Solly the Snozz."

Ernie came close to shouting the answer. Saved by the last question. Passed the test. Good grades to take home to Mum and Dad.

"That what you call him?" I asked.

"Well, me, I don't, not to his face anyways. He's Sol Nash. Works at Ace, I dunno as what, but I used to see him all over the place. He's got a driver who's a boxer, a pro I mean, when he's not suspended for hittin' the referee or something."

"Why would Nash drop in on the weigh-master at Leslie Street?"

"He goes regular to all the dumps. Who knows why? I never heard of office guys from other companies doin' that. But everything's different about Ace."

"Such as?"

"Bigger, that's for sure. They got two hundred trucks at least. I bet more, even. And the drivers they hire for them trucks, nobody messes with those guys unless you wanta get your arm broke or something. They're bikers, those guys, Hells Angels or whatever you call them."

Ernie poured more beer from the pitcher into his stein.

"How am I doin', Mr. Crang?" he asked.

"Peachy, Ernie," I said. "You earned a B-plus."

"Sorry about Ace's trucks takin' longer on the scales. Can't figure that one."

"You think it's important, Crang?" Griffin asked.

"Everything's important," I said, "if you don't know the answers."

"You're keeping me posted, promise?"

"I'd do anything for another visit to you scribes in your natural habitat."

Griffin turned in his seat and looked around the room. It was filling up with men and women who gave off waves of energy and panic. Reporters fuelling up for a deadline or coming down from meeting a deadline. Either way, they wanted their drinks in a hurry, and the three waitresses bustled back and forth between the tables and the bar. The decor still struck me as ersatz San Francisco. Griffin caught my reaction.

"One of the dames in Features, hell of a writer, she has another name for in here," he said. "She calls it Château Despair."

I put a ten and a five on the table to cover the pitchers of beer and promised Griffin he'd get the late-breaking news on Ace and Grimaldi. He winced.

Outside the restaurant, the sun had left its invisible message on the pavement. The heat off the asphalt in the parking lot seeped through the soles of my Rockports and gave my feet a soft, oozy feel. The sun was sliding behind the Harbour Castle Hilton across the street.

I drove up University Avenue, turned left before I reached the block where all the hospitals start, and switched through the side streets until I reached my place. The air in the living room was hot and stale. I didn't have air conditioning in the house. Air conditioning makes my body think it's gone to its final resting place in a Holiday Inn. I opened the windows in the kitchen and the living room, and in a few minutes a gentle cross-wind ruffled the staleness. I poured a Wyborowa on some ice cubes and sat in the chair that looks over the park across the street. A couple of guys with their shirts off were playing chess at one of the tables.

Little things. I propped my feet on the windowsill and took a swallow of vodka. Everything I had so far was little. Ace hired bikers to drive its trucks. The man on the Leslie Street scale needed a half-minute of extra attention to weigh in the Ace trucks and another half-minute on the way out. One of Ace's big shots made regular calls on weigh offices around the city. Three things and none of them significant in itself, but maybe there was a pattern. One of the shirtless chess players across the street stood up from his seat and paced back and forth behind his side of the board. Big move coming up. Another little thing was the bearded driver's run up Bathurst Street. But that didn't fit the pattern, if one existed. The pacing player in the park resumed his seat and moved one of his pieces. His opponent stared at the board. Everything except the freelance fiddle at the Bathurst dump spoke, albeit faintly, of something possibly shifty on Ace's part. The man across the street stopped staring. He swiped his right hand at the board and knocked the pieces to the grass. Sore loser. I'd concentrate on my three small items that were consistent with Ace's potential wrongdoing and see whether they led somewhere. The winning chess player was picking the pieces out of the grass. His friend remained in a funk. I went back to the kitchen for more ice and vodka and took my drink into the bathroom for a shower.

Ten minutes under the spray didn't do much for my ratiocinative powers but it worked up a swell appetite. I put on a clean collarless white shirt and the same jeans and Rockports I'd been wearing and strolled down Beverley Street to Queen. It was almost nine o'clock and Queen was humming. Every second female wore a Madonna get-up. The guys were harder to fit to type, everything from virile Bruce Springsteens in basic black T-shirts to candidates for the Hitler Youth in clumpy boots and leather gear. Commerce was brisk at the outdoor cafés and the boutiques that dealt in clothes my mother and father used to wear. A kid in a long white apron cooked and sold chapatis from a hibachi on a wagon parked at the curb. Two girls in their early twenties were projecting slides on the brick wall of a building beyond a parking lot. The night hadn't grown dark enough to give the pictures complete definition, but an ornately printed sign beside the projector invited one and all to purchase the paintings shown in the slides, all originals and nothing over two hundred dollars. The painting style was Dali-esque. So was the salesmanship.

I waved at the woman behind the cash register in Trapezoid, the clothing store under my office, and glanced at the windows above. Lights out, all safe and snug. The woman waved back. She was a dead ringer for Diahann Carroll and about the same age. If Annie B. Cooke didn't have a lock on my affections, I might have invited the Trapezoid woman around to look at my collection of old *Jazz Reviews*.

I kept walking until I reached the Rivoli a few doors past my office. The Riv, as we smart insiders call it, serves the best food on the block. It's a long, narrow room with taupe walls, a high hammered-tin ceiling painted burgundy, black tables and chairs, and fixtures done in a nutty variation on art deco. A booth was empty near the back and I squeezed in. Sitting room at the Riv is as tight as an economy seat on Air Canada, but the menu makes up for all sins. Even the sin of the music. The space cadet who selects the tapes for the Riv's sound system takes glee in playing musical mind games, Frank Sinatra's "Strangers in the Night" followed by John Cage ruminations. Set them up, knock them down. Or maybe I was the only customer who noticed. Maybe the undiscovered artists and out-of-gig rock musicians who frequented the place always dined to the sound of squeak and squawk. My waitress had Theda Bara eye makeup and three studs in her left ear. I ordered Thai red beef curry and a half-litre of the house white. The waitress gave me a winning smile and thanked me. She tacked on a "sir" at the end. If the Queen Street crowd in their far-out clothes and accessories were supposed to be the rebels of the generation, they'd struck out. They were too sunny and polite to think about overthrowing the establishment.

The curry was light and mild and made pleasing sensations on my tongue. Artie Shaw played "Frenesi" on the sound system. I tapped my toe but lost the beat when the tape segued to something punk rock. Or was it new wave? Was there a difference? Had I just defined middle age? I drank an espresso and sauntered back the way I'd come on Queen. Trapezoid had closed down for the night, but the building wasn't dark. The lights were on in my office.

The door that opens on to the stairs leading up to the office is on the front left of the building. I turned the knob. It opened. That wasn't right either. I couldn't hear any sounds from above, no footsteps, nothing furtive. I took it slow on the way up, putting my feet down on the outer corners of the stairs. Less chance of squeaking the boards. I picked up that piece of wisdom from Nancy Drew. I poked my head around the corner at the top of the stairs. The door to my office was open, but all was still and quiet. The hell with it. I stepped down the hall in forthright fashion and turned into the office. It was empty. So were my bookshelves, green metal filing cabinet, and desk drawers. Someone had dumped their contents in heaps on the floor.

I made a wide berth around the heaps and sat in the chair behind my desk. I contemplated the mess, and the longer I contemplated it, the more random it appeared. Whatever the aftermath of a burglary looked like, my office wasn't it. Files and books had been thrown on the floor for the sake of the throwing. The files couldn't have been examined paper by paper. The contents of most files remained intact inside the folders. I seemed to be looking at a piece of run-of-the-mill vandalism.

By whom? Not kids. There was nothing in the way of valuable loot to draw them into my office in the first place unless they coveted the framed Henri Matisse poster on the wall. They didn't. It was still on the wall. Besides, whoever had done the trashing job had been professional about gaining access. There were no broken windows or busted doors. Somebody had jimmied the lock on the door downstairs. It wouldn't be difficult, probably a matter of inserting a credit card at the proper angle, but it spoke of a practised hand.

I turned the lights off and walked home. Office cleanup could wait. Was this another little thing to add to my list of Ace transgressions? If so, it was a whole lot closer to home. My home. To take my mind off the little things, I got in bed with a new collection of Whitney Balliett's essays on jazz from the *New Yorker*. It didn't work. I went to sleep and dreamed that Charlie Parker broke into my bedroom. He raised his alto saxophone to his mouth, and when he blew, he sounded like a graduate of the Guy Lombardo reed section.

10

I **HAD A COURT** at the Downtown Tennis Club for ten o'clock Saturday morning. My opponent was an intense, dark-haired stockbroker in his mid-thirties. He and I schedule a few sets every week, and they're always close. He says tennis is what keeps him sane during the angst of the market's bulls and bears. I lifted weights for a year and jogged four times a week for another year, but gave up both. I couldn't stand the solitude. When I take my exercise, I want to bang against my fellow man. I beat the stockbroker 6-3 in the first set and was running away from him 4-0 in the second when our court time ran out.

"You were pumped up today," he said in the locker room.

"Must have been something motivating me," I said.

I called Annie B. Cooke from the phone in the tennis club's lobby.

"How's the definitive profile of Signor Alberti?" I asked.

"At a thousand words, nothing's definitive." Annie's voice sounded weary.

"Seminal?"

"How about superficial?"

"You that discouraged?"

"It's my old problem. I over-researched. Alberti gave me all the time in the world and I asked him approximately one hundred and forty-six questions for which he had approximately one hundred and forty-six articulate answers."

"That's more exact than approximate."

"The thing is, I can't make up my mind what to leave out."

"When's your deadline?"

"Twelve-thirty."

"I'll buy you lunch at one."

"Deal."

I went shopping. Two bottles of Côtes-du-Rhône at the rare-wines store on Queen's Quay, then up to Daniel et Daniel on Carlton Street around the corner from Annie's apartment. It's a classy patisserie-cum-French-style-deli, and I bought a bunch of salads—zucchini, pasta, shrimp, and hearts of artichoke. I got a couple of poached chicken breasts and two fat chocolate eclairs. I hit Annie's front door at five minutes past one. She answered my knock in a light blue dress, white sandals, and a wide-brimmed white hat like the one Anita O'Day wore in *Jazz on a Summer's Day*.

"Picnic time," I said.

"Take a seat," she said and walked to the back of her apartment where the bedroom is.

I leafed through a copy of *Cahiers du Cinéma* looking at the photographs. I lingered over one of Isabelle Adjani. She had on high heels.

"Ah," Annie said from over my shoulder, "the defence counsel searches for a weakness in the case."

"What do you suppose Isabelle was planning to wear with these shoes?" I said.

Annie had changed to wheat-coloured trousers and a navy blue tank top. She'd ditched the wide-brimmed hat and was carrying a wicker picnic basket.

"Knives, forks, paper plates, salt, pepper, napkins, plastic glasses, and a corkscrew," she said. "I gather you've got what goes with the equipment."

"Daniel et Daniel's best spread."

"Then I was right to pack the linen napkins."

We angled through Cabbagetown's back streets and came out at the Bayview expressway. The day was without wind or clouds, the sky was a bright blue, and it felt good not to be one of the hundreds of thousands of Torontonians who hit the highways on summer weekends for what radio traffic reporters call cottage country. We drove north on Bayview and east on Eglinton Avenue to Serena Gundy Park across the road from the Inn on the Park. The parking lot was crowded. I carried the bottles of wine and Annie looked after the picnic basket. She said it took a woman's fine sense of balance to keep the contents firm and steady. We walked south from the parking lot alongside a river that I remembered swimming in on Boy Scout camp-outs. I said so to Annie.

"I don't know which is more unbelievable," she said. "Swimming in that brown water or you joining the Boy Scouts."

"Everything was green and fresh back then," I said.

"The water or you?"

The path passed through a small woods and emerged on to a huge expanse of gently rolling hills. Families gathered around the picnic tables that dotted the landscape, and in between, little kids kicked around soccer balls and their parents tossed Frisbees. We turned to the left and soon put the athletic action behind us. There was another small wooded section on the edge of the park down the steep hill from the Ontario Science Centre. Not many picnickers bothered to hike that far. Annie and I arranged our goodies under a maple tree and I opened the first bottle of wine. While we gave it a proper savouring, I told Annie the story of my latest poking into Ace's operations and of the break-in at my office.

I said, "I think the two are linked or my name isn't Sam Spade."

"It isn't," Annie said, "and what did the police say when you reported the break-in?"

Before I could answer, she said, "Oh, forgetful me, you're the independent fellow who goes it alone when crime strikes."

"I think it might be someone telling me to back off," I said. "I haven't exactly made myself invisible to Ace. The truck driver I popped could have taken my licence number or the guy on the Leslie weigh scale might have done the same and passed it on."

"If the break-in was intended to discourage you," Annie said, "then the breakers-in have made the miscalculation of their lives."

Two squirrels scrambled through the branches of the maple tree over our picnic. Their blue-black fur was mangy, but they bounced around like the Flying Wallendsas.

"I have a client," I said to Annie. "I owe it to him not to bring the cops in until I know where he figures in the picture. That makes a difference."

"Give me a break."

"It doesn't make a difference?"

"I'm objecting strictly as a matter of form, okay?" Annie reached out her empty plastic glass and I made like the sommelier. She went on, "I know, O light of my life, you're determined to stick your face into whatever nastiness this Ace Disposal thing may represent until someone takes a poke at it. Correction, second poke. We can't leave out your scuffle with the bearded gentleman. Duty to the client and all those other noble sentiments, I appreciate their truth in the legal profession. But honestly, Crang, maybe you're using them as a cover. You just like playing the gallant snoop, which is okay except I think you've got Sir Galahad and Inspector Clouseau so mixed up you might do yourself real harm."

An emotion of the awkward sort covered the picnic. The sound of traffic on Eglinton drifted in from the far distance and the chatter of the two squirrels filled the middle distance.

I said, "I liked the part where you said, 'O light of my life.'"

"Who, me?" Annie said in a mock-innocent voice. She drew her left hand across her breast and cocked her head like a silent-movie heroine.

I leaned toward her. She met me halfway. We closed our eyes and kissed. It was a chaste kiss, nothing touching except lips, but it lingered long enough for something to go ping in the region of my solar plexus.

Annie opened her eyes.

"Nice," she said.

"Want to do something unspeakable?" I said. "Or shall we just make love?"

"Given your propensities, the food would spoil before we were sated. Do I mean that or satiated?"

"Spoil the food?" I said. "I could never face the Daniels again."

"Nor I."

We ate and drank and giggled, and after a couple of hours, we drove to the Carlton Cineplex and had cappuccino and watched a new French movie. Philippe Noiret played a police inspector who looked like he was bearing the weight of most of the universe's secrets.

"I think I'll find a mirror and practise my worldly expression," I said to Annie when we came out.

"You want to be Philippe Noiret when you grow up."

"You guess all my ambitions."

Alex and Ian, my downstairs tenants, had invited us for dinner. They wrapped a whole salmon in silver foil and put it on their stand-up barbecue that comes with more attachments than the Kennedy Space Center would know what to do with. While we waited for the salmon to cook, we sat on the patio and drank margaritas and took turns shooing away the tenants' slobbering Irish setter. His name is Genêt. Ian told funny stories about his early life as a devotee of leather and motorcycles and a club where the jukebox played Village People hits. By midnight we were full of salmon and asparagus and white wine and Alex was doing his impressions of Prince Charles chatting up Joan Collins. Annie succumbed to another fit of giggles, and after I steered her upstairs, we left a trail of clothes in a path that led to my bed. Annie lost her giggles and we made love until both of us were sated. Or satiated.

I tiptoed out at ten o'clock next morning to buy some croissants hot from the ovens of a bakery on Queen. I picked up a *Sunday Sun* on the way back. Annie turned to the entertainment section, and while I squeezed the orange juice and plugged in the coffee, she read her article on Alberti.

"Oh gawd," Annie said, "nobody's going to mistake me for Pauline Kael."

I said, "I'll take the original Annie B. Cooke any morning."

"Just don't read this thing while I'm watching."

I didn't. Annie took her juice and coffee and croissants into the living room. I sat in the kitchen and read. When I finished, I picked up my cup of coffee and crowded into the living room chair beside Annie.

"Fresh information for your everyday interested reader like me," I said, "and the writing flows."

Annie was quiet for a couple of seconds.

"You're not just bucking up my spirits?" she asked.

"Would I lie about things like that?"

Another pause.

"Probably not," Annie said.

I drove her home at five o'clock and spent the rest of the afternoon and early evening shifting the heaps of files and books on my office floor back to their proper homes. I didn't want Mrs. Reid, my part-time secretary, to deal with the mess. Never ask the help to do a job you wouldn't do yourself. It was one of my mottoes. I tried to think if I had other mottoes. By eleven o'clock when I fell asleep in bed with the Whitney Balliett collection, I hadn't come up with any.

11

TEN HOURS LATER, I walked out the front door wearing my lightweight grey suit. It was James Turkin's sentencing day, the kid who'd done the number on the cab driver in the underground garage. The sentencing would be held in one of the courtrooms in Old City Hall, and I didn't need to wear my counsel's gown for the occasion. As Toronto buildings go, Old City Hall is dowdy and lovable. It's made of red sandstone and sits in its old maid's pride on Queen Street at Bay. It made do very nicely as Toronto's city hall from 1890 till 1966 when a new civic building, spectacular but a trifle short on humanity, went up on the other side of Bay and the politicians and bureaucrats moved in. Since the move, Old City Hall has been given over to the Provincial Courts. They're the lowest on the rung of courts and the busiest in criminal cases. Provincial Court judges hear all the messy low-life stuff, and the lawyers who appear before them don't require gowns. I had on a shirt with fine vertical grey stripes and a plain maroon tie. I set my face in an expression to match my wardrobe. Sincere.

I walked the fifteen minutes it took to get from my front door to Old City Hall. A breeze was blowing up from the lake and there was a hint of fish in the air. I knew James Turkin would be in the holding cells in the basement on the northeast corner of Old City Hall. He would have been brought in in a yellow police van that morning from the West End Detention Centre with a bunch of other guys who couldn't make bail and were waiting out the time until their day in court in the gracious custody of the Province of Ontario. I rapped on the thick wooden door to the holding cells, and it was opened almost immediately by a policeman who was holding a plastic cup of steaming coffee in his right hand.

"You got a villain in here, Crang?" the cop asked.

He knew me from many villains past. His name was Moriarty, and he was built like a linebacker who'd gone to seed, six four and close to three hundred pounds. There were dark sweat stains radiating from the armpits of his blue policeman's shirt and grumpiness radiating from his flushed policeman's face.

"Warm enough for you, Moriarty?" I asked.

"Which is yours?" Moriarty turned to pick up a clipboard on a chair inside the door. He spilled a small stream of coffee on his shirt.

"Shit," he said without much expression.

"Kid named Turkin," I said.

"Black or white?" Moriarty asked. "Got most of the niggers in number one cell. Rest of them are in two."

"A whiter shade of pale," I said.

A young cop with a moustache standing behind Moriarty laughed.

"What's with you?" Moriarty asked him.

"The man made a funny," the young cop said. "See, there used to be a rock group—"

"Shut the fuck up," Moriarty cut him off. He looked at me. "Fucking heat."

"Turkin," I said.

"Yeah, yeah." Moriarty put his coffee on the flattened green cushion that covered his chair. Drops ran down the edges of the cup and made a wet ring on the cushion. Moriarty would be delighted when he noticed. He flipped through the pages on the clipboard.

"Turkin, Turkin," he said. "Over there, number two cell, and don't mess around. I already had five of you lawyers in here this morning."

I stepped through the door and Moriarty slammed it behind me. Inside, the air was ripe.

"Like a rose garden this morning."

"One of those assholes threw up," Moriarty said.

I crossed the ten or twelve feet to number two cell. It was a space no larger than twenty feet square, all bars on the side facing into the room. Twenty or twenty-five men leaned against the back wall or sat on benches on the other side of the bars. Nobody talked. James Turkin was easy to spot. He had the looks of an earlier James: sulky and white-faced, with light brown wavy hair and a wiry body, he was a throwback to James Dean.

He saw me and stepped close to the bars. I said hello. He stared at me. It wasn't the stare of some of the wackos I get for clients. There was a flavour of the cool to James Turkin rather than a suggestion of the catatonic.

"Your parents aren't coming down," I said.

"Figures."

"When you go upstairs, I want to say something to the judge that will make him look kindly on you."

The kid shrugged.

"Otherwise it's the reformatory."

"I thought about it already," he said in his flat voice.

"Maybe you thought the wrong things. I know you've got some brains. The pre-sentence report says you passed grade twelve."

"Big deal."

"Says you were brilliant in maths."

"So?"

Behind me, I could hear Moriarty cursing the spilled coffee on his green cushion.

"This may not interest you, Jimmy," I said, "but for the hell of it, I'll tell you I've acted for a thousand guys in the same situation as yours and I think I know how to help you in front of the judge this morning."

"James."

"Never Jimmy?"

"James," the kid said. "And I don't give a shit who you acted for."

His eyes looked into mine without a blink.

I said, "You got any suggestions about what you'd like me to tell the judge?"

"Such as?"

"Ambitions," I said. "What do you have in mind as a sequel to your splendid career hitting on cab drivers?"

"I want to be a real good break-and-enter man."

I contemplated smacking the kid's chalky kisser.

"Why?" I asked instead.

"Computers suck."

Maybe we'd established a basis for communication.

I said, "I'm not keen on the age of electronics myself."

James Turkin leaned closer to the bars and his voice dropped to the confidential level. Lower volume, same monotone, more voluble.

"Any creep can screw money out of a computer if they know how to punch into it," he said. "All these fourteen-year-old kids at school, the ones with the glasses, those wimps, they got their systems worked out. I did it myself. So what's the deal? But, like, one night this spring, I figured my way into the Canadian Tire store up Yonge Street, right past the alarm, no noise, no tipoff, nothing. I walked around in there a couple hours. Nobody knew. It was a total high."

"What did you take out when you left?" I asked.

"VCR for my sister."

"That's all?"

"All I could think she needed."

What was I dealing with? The Pale Pimpernel?

"I felt real raced up," Turkin said. "Getting in that store, not anybody could do it. It's what I'm meant for, break and enter."

"If you're such a smarty," I said, "how come you mixed in this little contretemps in the underground garage that's going to send you to the slammer, barring an act of God?"

"It was the girl's idea, the one who brought the cab down the garage," the kid said. His voice had lost the zest it displayed during his celebration of the art of breaking and entering. "Not my idea," he said. "I helped her out because we were—involved."

"You were what?"

"I was banging her."

The kid wasn't a hopeless cause, just had a slightly twisted sense of chivalry.

"Upstairs," I said, "call the judge 'sir' when he speaks to you and stand up straight in the prisoners' box. Small details help."

"I got excellent posture."

It was true. "See you in court," I said and turned away.

Moriarty had vacated his post at the door.

"He's gone to wipe off his shirt," the young cop said.

"My guy's coming up in Twenty-one Court," I said. "You mind taking a look who's sitting there today?"

The cop lifted the clipboard from Moriarty's chair and leafed slowly through the sheets of paper, one sheet for each courtroom in the building.

"Twenty-two's got Robertson," he recited. "Twenty-one's got— hey, you hit it lucky."

"Not Bert?"

"His Honour the old softie."

I knew James Turkin wasn't going to jail.

The young cop unlocked the door to the corridor. I walked up the stairs to the first floor whistling a happy tune. From *The King and I.* Bert Ormsby was a judge who led his own version of the Children's Crusade. Confronted by a teenage accused, his heart bled, his eyes watered, his brain turned mushy. If Jack the Ripper were an adolescent, Ormsby would give him probation. He wouldn't put eighteen-year-old James Turkin inside, not even if I told him Turkin had the nerve of a fifty-year-old second-storey man and the morals of a slug.

It was twenty minutes to court time. I wandered down the hall to the front of the building. Two scrawny, animated men in their early twenties came through the big wooden doors and up the steps into the high, airy lobby. One had a package of Camels rolled in the sleeve of his wrinkled orange T-shirt. The other had Rambo tattooed on his right biceps. The guy was the size of Sylvester Stallone's thigh. He and his buddy looked like they subsisted on a diet of hot dogs and white bread. They found a place on one of the benches that line the corridor outside the courtrooms along the east side of the building. A black man with his hair in greasy dreadlocks sat at the other end of the bench talking to an overweight girl in a halter top and tight pink jeans that squeezed the fat out over her waistband. A Canadian Indian stood motionless by the wall, not touching it. He had a long scar on his right cheek and a hangover that made him squint his eyes against the light. In my line of work, you run into a lot of interesting folks.

Twenty-one Court is on the first floor directly over the holding cells. When I walked in, James Turkin was sitting behind the wire mesh of the prisoners' box on the left side of the courtroom. He was in between a man with mussed hair and a stained white jacket and a kid in a ripped Blue Jays shirt. In his pressed khakis and clean white dress shirt, Turkin cut the nattiest figure in the box. The judge arrived promptly at ten o'clock and everyone in court rose while he settled on the bench. Bert Ormsby looks like the guy Central Casting would send over to play Gramps in a TV sitcom. He's in his early sixties, apple-cheeked, kindly-faced, grey-haired, and rumply. Up close, his eyes probably twinkle. It took him fifteen minutes to process eight requests for adjournments, a bail application, and two other guilty pleas.

"I'll hear number twelve on the list, James Turkin," he said.

I stood up at the counsel's table.

"Good morning, Mr. Crang," the judge said.

"Your Honour."

"Your client has pleaded guilty," he said, "and I note from the pre-sentence report in front of me, Mr. Crang, that he's eighteen years old."

I said, "You might also note, Your Honour, that Mr. Turkin has a previous record, one conviction for possession of a small amount of marijuana and another for theft under two hundred dollars. I emphasize that neither offence involved violence, Your Honour, and though the matter presently before the court is an assault, I would suggest that

Mr. Turkin made the error of allowing himself to be influenced by his companion in the crime. He acknowledges and regrets the incident, and he'd like to assure the court that he'll never again permit himself to be drawn into such a misadventure."

Where have you gone, Clarence Darrow? If Bert Ormsby ached for youngsters to be rescued, I'd give him James Turkin in self-recrimination and remorse.

"What does the crown attorney say?" Judge Ormsby asked.

The crown attorney was a pretty woman with streaked blonde hair and a frown.

"Your Honour, this was a heinous crime," she said.

"I thought you crowns reserved heinous for the Supreme Court," I said to her, not loud enough for the judge to catch.

The crown attorney's frown lines tightened.

"The prisoner used force to rob the taxi driver," she said to Judge Ormsby. "I submit the sentence should be commensurate with the violence of the act."

"Your Honour," I said, "there's been restitution of the money by my client."

The crown snapped, "A term in reformatory is called for."

"May I suggest, with Your Honour's indulgence," I said, "that jail would work to the detriment of my client's prospects. He has behind him an excellent scholastic record and I submit it promises a positive future."

Judge Ormsby aimed a grandfatherly smile at Turkin in the prisoners' box.

"Have you considered community college, young man?" he asked.

My kid turned his sullen face in my direction.

I said, "My understanding, Your Honour, is that the accused has ambitious career plans."

Judge Ormsby beamed another smile and said reformatory seemed inappropriate in the circumstances. The crown attorney's frown deepened into a scowl and she made a display of tossing her file on the counsel table. Judge Ormsby put Turkin on probation for two years.

He told Turkin to report to his probation officer every month, find a job, avoid evil companions, and stay out of underground garages. Fifteen minutes later, after Turkin had signed some papers and arranged his first probation meeting, he and I sat on a bench on Old City Hall's front lawn.

"Thanks," the kid said. The word seemed to give him serious pain.

I said, "I trust I won't see you in court again."

"Fucking right."

"Does this mean you're going to tread the straight and narrow?"

"It means I'm not going to get caught."

"That's what Murph the Surf said."

"Who's he?"

"Infamous jewel thief and convict before your time."

"So laugh at me," Turkin said. Something earnest was struggling to break through his sullen expression. "I can already do any lock on the market. Shutting down alarm systems, shit, that's a touch. And I met this old geezer when I was in the West End, guy about forty, he told me the real professional stuff about checking out a place before you go in."

"What was this forty-year-old geezer doing in the West End?"

"He made a little mistake."

"James, isn't that a lesson?"

"Yeah, he told me his mistake. I won't make it."

The kid shook my hand and walked away until he disappeared into the crowd of shoppers crossing Queen Street to Simpsons. He was probably right. He wouldn't make that mistake.

12

I **RODE UP AND DOWN** the elevators in City Hall, the new sky-scraper version, until I found an office that gave out the addresses of the Metro dump sites. Most were in the suburbs, and I drove around to four of them with my watch and notebook. At five-thirty, I knocked off the tour until next day, when I visited four more dumps. The story was the same at all eight. The guys inside the weigh offices took longer to do their operations with Ace trucks, between twenty and forty seconds longer per truck. That piece of information was confirmed and reconfirmed for whatever it was worth. At a dump in the east end, I came across the two men in the pink Cadillac: Solly the Snozz Nash and his boxer sidekick in the straw hat. I took my notebook back to the office and let it sit on the desk. Rereading my notes inspired unease but no deep thoughts.

Mrs. Reid had been in and left a memo. Matthew Wansborough had called three times, Tom Catalano twice. My client was getting antsy. It was four o'clock. I dialled the number at McIntosh, Brown and asked for Catalano.

"Wansborough wants a meeting," he said as soon as he came on the line.

"What happened to hello?" I said.

"Hello," Catalano said. "It has to be in a couple of hours."

"Is that his timetable or yours?"

"His," Catalano said. "He's at a political meeting at the Albany Club and he can slide over here at six before he goes to a cocktail party at the Toronto Club."

"So just like that you squeeze him into the appointment book," I said. "He must be a big-money client."

"Not that big, but old," Catalano said. "The firm started doing his family's business right after the first McIntosh was called to the bar, 1880 or something."

Outside my office, fresh developments were shaping up. I watched a pink Caddie stop and double-park.

"What're you going to have for us, Crang?" Catalano said on the phone. "You've been on this thing for a week."

"Six days."

The man in the straw hat got out of the driver's side, and Sol Nash climbed from the passenger side. He had on a light grey suit that looked shantung from my distance. His tan was deep and his nose was in the Jimmy Durante class. The guy with the straw hat was built like a ring post.

"So what have you got?" Catalano asked.

"Nothing conclusive so far," I said, "but enough to keep Wansborough interested."

The two men down below crossed the sidewalk and disappeared from sight. I could hear them opening the door off the street and starting up the stairs.

Catalano said, "I know you're not the kind of lawyer who'd stall around just to pull in a big fee and then produce nothing."

"Big fee?" I said. "That's the first time anyone has mentioned the magic words. Now I'll go into my major-league stall."

Nash and his driver had reached the top of the stairs and were coming down the hall.

"Just be here at six," Catalano said and hung up.

The man with the straw hat opened the door to my office. He was wearing a white-on-white shirt with the top three buttons undone and grey sharkskin trousers. His nose was flattened at the tip and he had scar tissue over his eyes. He wasn't tall, about five nine, but he was wide all the way down. The straw hat looked out of place on his head. Every man to his affectations. He glanced around my office, stepped inside, and held the door back for Sol Nash. Nash seemed about fifty years old. His black hair had grey at the temples, and even against the tan I could see deep lines around his eyes and mouth. He sat in a chair across from me. The guy with the straw hat closed the door and stood in front of it with his arms crossed.

"You know me, Crang?" Nash said.

"Your reputation precedes you, Mr. Snozz."

The guy at the door uncrossed his arms.

"Never mind, Tony," Nash said without taking his eyes off me.

I said, "And Tony's your interior decorator."

"What's he talking about?" Tony said. His voice had a thick rasp. Too many punches to the throat.

"Offices are his specialty," I said to Nash. "He rearranges the decor."

"Oh yeah, I get it," Tony said. He seemed to take my little joke as a compliment.

"Far as I know, Crang," Nash said, "you got no beef with me personally and you got none with the company I work for."

"Lovable me? I'm without enemies."

"So I want to know how come your face keeps coming up in my business."

"I'm thinking of a change of career," I said. "Garbage strikes me as a field with infinite possibilities."

I leaned back in my swivel chair and hoisted my Rockports on to a corner of the desk. That'd show Nash what a cool customer he was dealing with. Unless he thought Rockports looked wimpy. Mine were light brown canvas and leather. Maybe I should have left them on the floor.

"You assaulted one of my drivers," Nash said.

"Hey, that's a fancy word for what happened," I said. "Your driver and I went a couple of rounds. But I'll tell you straight, Sol, Tony here ought to give the guy a couple of pointers on style."

Nash stared at me. The colour of his eyes was as close to black as eyes get.

"On the other hand," I said, "Tony may not be the man for the job. From the look of his kisser, style isn't his long suit in the ring."

Tony made rumbling noises from his post at the door.

Nash said, "You're beginning to piss me off, Crang."

"Just when I thought we were getting along famously."

"You been hanging around the dumps," Nash said. "Tony and me spotted you twice and a couple weigh-masters said they seen that fag car of yours."

"What is it with you Ace guys?" I said. "All of you scorn my convertible's sexual orientation."

For the first time since he had sat down in the office, Nash looked somewhere besides at me. He turned to Tony and nodded his head. Tony stepped up to the desk. He stood within left-jab distance of my head.

"Here's your choice, Crang," Nash said. His eyes were back on mine. "Tell me what you got on with Ace or Tony's gonna punch your lights out."

I slid my Rockports off the desk.

"What makes you think Tony can accomplish your objective?" I said.

"He's younger'n you by twenty years," Nash said.

"Ah, but youth is only one attribute," I said. "I have a quicker brain and a nature that's wily."

"Make up your mind, Crang," Nash said. "I'm getting tired of this crappy office."

Crappy? Modest, okay, but crappy was harsh.

"You've made your move too fast, Sol," I said, "and I think you know it. If I'm interested in Ace, it's on behalf of a client. You want to find out who the client is. Sic Tony on me and I won't tell you. I guarantee. Let me alone and maybe you'll learn the client's identity in due and natural course."

I felt sweat dampening the armpits of my shirt. Peddling a line of patter to Judge Bert Ormsby took one skill. Trying out evasive verbal tactics on Sol Nash was a dicier proposition. Nash wasn't restricted by court decorum or a warm heart. He also possessed a more acute bullshit detector.

"Whatever's at stake, Sol," I said, "could blow over with no concern for anyone, you, my client, your people at Ace. You made a mistake tossing my office the other night, definitely premature, Sol, and you made another mistake coming in here with Tony's fists. Your play right now is to stay calm and let me and my client reach a decision."

Nash kept his ray-gun stare on me, and Tony hovered at my desk. His arms were at his sides and he was clenching and unclenching his fists. He made heavy-breathing noises with his mouth, the kind a fighter makes before he steps into the ring. The breathing noises were the only sound in the room. Except for my heartbeat. Tony and Nash couldn't hear it, but I could. It was up around one hundred.

Nash stared and Tony heavy-breathed for thirty seconds. It felt like thirty hours. Nash broke the tension with another nod of the head at Tony. Tony gave his fists one more clench and turned back to the door. He opened it, and Nash stood up abruptly and walked toward the open door.

"Besides," I said as Nash walked through it, "I'd bet me on a TKO over Tony, name the odds."

Tony slammed the door behind him and Nash, and my framed Matisse poster rattled against the wall. I watched Nash and Tony through the window. Tony pushed aside a skinny kid in American army fatigues who was leaning against the pink Cadillac's front fender. The kid stopped whatever he was going to say when he saw Tony's face. The two men got in the Cadillac and drove away.

As soon as the car had passed out of sight, I went down the stairs and along Queen past the Rivoli to the Horseshoe Tavern. I ordered a double vodka on the rocks at the stand-up bar. What the bartender poured didn't have the hit of Wyborowa and it tasted like perfume.

It was made in Alberta, but there was alcohol in there somewhere.

I wouldn't have bet on me against Tony. I hadn't the nerve to fight him. I just had the nerve to bait him. Two different things. I asked the bartender for another double and waited for my heart rate to drop below eighty.

13

AFTER FIVE-THIRTY in the afternoon, parts of downtown Toronto turn dulcet. The buildings empty, the bankers, brokers, and their minions head down to the subways and over to the expressways, and the streets are left to the strays. I walked south between the office towers on York Street and watched the setting sun bounce off the glass of the Stock Exchange Building. A good singer named Tommy Ambrose once wrote a song about Toronto. He called it "People City." Sometimes I like it better without the people.

At King Street, I went east. McIntosh, Brown's offices are in the black and daunting Toronto-Dominion complex, the only Mies van der Rohe buildings in the city, maybe in the country. I signed in with a security guard who sat behind a bank of buttons and TV monitors in the lobby and rode an elevator almost to the top. McIntosh, Brown occupies three floors. Tom Catalano works out of the floor in the middle and he was waiting for me under a Tom Thomson painting in the reception area. On the opposite wall there was a David Milne and a Christopher Pratt. If all the law firms on Bay Street got together and opened a gallery, they'd put my neighbour the Art Gallery of Ontario out of business. Catalano led me down a silent corridor to a small conference room. It had four Harold Town prints.

"Am I supposed to be overwhelmed by the display of good taste?" I said. "Is that why all you big-ticket law firms go crazy for art?"

Catalano shrugged. "I suppose it makes our rich clients feel like they're sitting in their own living rooms."

Tom Catalano has tight curly black hair and a long melancholy face. He plays squash. Plenty of lawyers in firms like McIntosh, Brown play squash. They can fit it in at seven o'clock in the morning at the Cambridge Club. Back in law school, Catalano was known as a cagey guy around the poker table; now he just works too hard.

"Fix yourself a drink," he said. "The booze's in the cabinet. Ice too. I'll go and greet our client."

"I thought juniors attended to the night doorman's duties."

"I dispatched my juniors to the library," Catalano said. "If they got a look at you in those jeans, they might be tempted to defect."

The Scotch in the cabinet was Johnnie Walker Black, the gin was Tanqueray, the vodka was domestic. Some kind of anti-communist conspiracy seemed in operation. I poured two ounces of the vodka into a tall glass, added ice and soda water, and sat down at the conference table. It was polished oak, and at each place there was a small white pad and a sharpened yellow pencil. I sketched two stick men boxing. If the vodka didn't soothe my unease, maybe doodling would.

My drink was a third of the way down the glass when Catalano returned with Wansborough. He had on another three-piece suit, chocolate brown this time. It was without a crease and his cordovans had a high shine. I'd be willing to wager his undershorts were pressed.

"You know Crang of course, Matthew," Catalano said.

Wansborough tilted his head in my direction but didn't offer his hand.

"I'm keen to have your report, Mr. Crang," he said.

Catalano said, "Something from the bar before we start, Matthew?"

Wansborough asked for a Scotch and soda. His eyes didn't leave my face as he spoke. It was my day for being stared at.

"Something's not right at Ace," I said, "but I can't tell you what it is."

I described Charles Grimaldi's bloodlines, my discoveries at the Metro dump sites, and the recent visit from Sol Nash. I added the punch-up on Bathurst Street for flavour.

"I didn't expect violence," Wansborough said. The remark was addressed to Catalano. He put Wansborough's drink in front of him.

Catalano said, "I'm sure Crang knows what he's doing. He usually does."

"To hit a man as Mr. Crang did," Wansborough said to Catalano, "I don't wish the family to be associated with such behaviour."

"Let's call it self-defence in this case, Matthew," Catalano said.

"Yoo-hoo, fellas," I said. "Why not discuss my talents after I've left. There are a couple of other points I have for the agenda."

Wansborough turned his attention back to me. His face was a mix of worry and distaste.

He said, "I would like a guarantee there won't be any further hooliganism."

"Mr. Wansborough," I said, "my scuffle with the driver ranks near the bottom of your concerned list."

Wansborough did an elaborate throat-clearing.

"You say Charles Grimaldi is connected to the, ah, underworld," he said.

"Intimately," I said. "Through his dad."

Wansborough said, "Well, simply because Charles' antecedents are involved in criminal pursuits doesn't establish that Charles himself is party to anything improper. Not as it relates to Ace Disposal at any rate."

Wansborough didn't sound as though he were convinced of his own logic.

"Let's go with what we're reasonably certain of, Mr. Wansborough," I said. "There's something at Ace that Sol Nash and by extension his boss Grimaldi are wary about me uncovering."

"Which is what?" Tom Catalano asked.

"I'm not sure," I said, "but I'd like to talk to Alice Brackley."

Wansborough hadn't touched his Scotch.

He said, "What makes you think my cousin would be of any assistance in this deplorable affair?"

"She works at Ace," I said. "That gives her a head start in the information department. Whatever isn't on the square at the office, she might provide me with leads. It's a cinch nobody else is going to dish out secrets."

Wansborough took his first taste of Scotch and looked at Catalano. His expression wore a question mark.

"I see no harm in Crang talking to your cousin, Matthew," Catalano said. "He may not always seem it but he can be discreet."

Wansborough didn't speak. I held my glass up to Catalano. It was almost empty. He pointed a finger in the direction of the liquor cabinet, and I made another vodka and soda. Catalano was drinking straight tonic water. The non-conversation stretched out in the room. Wansborough brooded. Catalano and I waited. Catalano decided to prime Wansborough's pump.

He said to me, "Have you got a guess about what's going on at these dumps? Why the extra time in handling the Ace trucks? And the visits of this Nash character to the weigh people, what do they mean?"

"Ace has something happening under the table with the weighmasters," I said. "That's how it looks to me. But that is, in your word, a guess. I'd like to try out the guess on Alice Brackley."

"Very well." Wansborough had done with the brooding. "Go ahead and have your discussion with Alice, Mr. Crang, but I wish confidentiality observed."

"You mean," I said, "you don't want me to tell Ms. Brackley I'm acting for you."

"Exactly," Wansborough said. The take-charge tone was back in his voice. "There are good and sufficient reasons for secrecy."

"Such as?" I asked.

"Very privately, gentlemen," Wansborough said, taking in both Catalano and me, "I've had cause to question the nature of the relationship between my cousin and Charles Grimaldi."

"Oh-oh," I said, "they playing footsy around the office?"

"Don't be vulgar, Mr. Crang," Wansborough said. "It's simply that they may be spending more time together socially than is strictly necessary in business. Or so I'm informed by my wife's friends."

"What are we talking about here?" I said. "Something more than working lunches? That kind of thing?"

My questions were making Wansborough uncomfortable.

"I concede it's hearsay, Mr. Crang," he said. "But twice, different friends of my wife have reported seeing the two of them, Alice and Grimaldi, dining out around town."

"Twice isn't much."

"Alice was observed holding his hand."

"Well, well, handsy can definitely lead to footsy."

"Whatever it is," Wansborough said, "it wouldn't do for you to create an upset within the family by revealing too much to Alice."

"There might be an upset down the line."

"Not if all of us handle our tasks with due precaution."

I swallowed the rest of my drink and ripped the doodle off the small white pad in front of me. As I left, Tom Catalano was talking soothing words to Wansborough. I walked down the hushed corridor and out of the building.

An affair between Alice Brackley and Charles Grimaldi? This was more like it. Not just the suspicion of crime at Ace but the chance of romance, passion, seething emotions.

14

ALICE BRACKLEY was one of those women who have a tremor in their voices. She sounded like Loretta Young on the other end of the line. I called her at the Ace offices on Wednesday afternoon. After I'd introduced myself, and told her I was a lawyer and wanted to speak to her on a matter that concerned a client of mine, she added a note of defensiveness to the tremor.

"What is it in relation to?" she asked.

"I'd rather discuss that when we meet."

"I see," she said. "I don't know you."

It was a statement, not a question.

"I'm as cute as the dickens and I promise to be charming, Ms. Brackley."

"I haven't the time to waste on frivolous conversation."

"Meet with me and you won't find it unrewarding."

There was a blank from her end of the line.

"Crang?" she said. "Your name was Crang?"

This time it was a question.

"It's still Crang," I said.

"Yes, all right." She seemed to want me off her phone. "But it won't be here at the offices. I'll meet you in the bar on the first floor of the Four Seasons Hotel at six o'clock this evening. Do you know it?"

"The bar's called La Serre." I wasn't what you could call a regular. She put down the phone without saying goodbye.

I dressed to match the tasteful opulence of the meeting place. Charcoal-grey trousers, a cream-coloured double-breasted summer jacket, a blue buttoned-down Brooks Brothers shirt that I bought the year I took Annie to the Kools Jazz Festival in New York City, navy blue tie with red polka dots, and shiny black unadorned loafers. I looked in the full-length mirror on the hall door outside my bathroom and whistled. Too much elegance to waste on Alice Brackley. I phoned Annie and got her answering machine. I told it that if its owner wanted to be swept off her feet she should show up in the Four Seasons bar at seven o'clock that evening.

A pianist plays Rodgers and Hart after nine in La Serre. Until then, patrons make do with the decor. It runs to the kind of look that makes me feel comfortable in a bar—dark wood, exposed brick, dim lighting. A forest of ficus benjamina grows out of the planters scattered among the tables. Martinis cost five dollars.

I arrived fifteen minutes early. The hostess perked up when I dropped Alice Brackley's name and showed me to a table in a private corner beside the windows that overlook Yorkville Avenue and a posh antiques store. The hostess had auburn hair and carried herself like a runway model. I ordered one of the five-dollar vodka martinis. It came cold and very dry. The hostess put it down on a square paper coaster done in white and gold. She brought a dish of mixed nuts. I picked out the almonds.

Alice Brackley came fifteen minutes late. She was wearing an avocado-green jacket and skirt and a lot of gold. She had a gold chain made of thick links around her neck, gold earrings shaped like tiny seashells, a clunky gold bracelet on her right wrist, and a small gold Rolex on her left wrist. She had no rings on her fingers, gold or otherwise. She knew where to draw the line.

The hostess pulled out Alice Brackley's chair and Ms. Brackley thanked her. She called the hostess Miriam. Miriam went away without inquiring after Ms. Brackley's preference in beverage.

"You come here often?" I said. It was my customary snappy opener with strange women in bars.

"I live near by, Mr. Crang," Ms. Brackley said. Her voice had the tremor.

Miriam returned with a drink that looked like a Rob Roy. It came with a cherry. Miriam replaced the dish of mixed nuts with a fresh supply. Terrific, more almonds.

Alice Brackley was about forty. She had long dark hair and a face that received plenty of pampering. Her lips were thin, and there were the beginnings of fine lines on her cheeks. I felt a faint breeze of tension coming from her side of the table.

"What is this about, Mr. Crang?" she asked.

"Don't you want to wait for the greetings and preliminary remarks from the chair?"

"What I'd prefer is that you not be oblique."

"Right to the point," I said. "I have reason to deduce that things at Ace Disposal are not entirely aboveboard."

Alice Brackley opened her handbag. It was white leather. She took out a package of Vantages and tapped a cigarette from the package. I picked up the book of Four Seasons matches from the ashtray and suavely snapped one into flame on my first try, but I wasn't fast enough. Alice Brackley had already lit the cigarette from her lighter. It was a Hermès and gold.

"Nonsense," she said.

"Granted," I said, "but somebody's probably making a dishonest buck from the nonsense."

"Are you being deliberately offensive, Mr. Crang?" Alice Brackley said. She blew cigarette smoke through her nostrils and did her best to look stern. "If that's the case, you're succeeding admirably. I'm developing a severe antagonism to you."

"I'm not the enemy, Ms. Brackley."

"I wasn't aware there was a war."

"Could be I'm expressing myself badly."

"Clearly you are."

I fingered around in the dish of nuts until I came up with an almond.

"Let me build my case," I said. "Sol Nash and his chum in the straw hat are not what I'd call businessmen with MBAs from the University of Western Ontario."

"Their duties hardly require that sort of background," Ms. Brackley said. "Sol and Tony are very effective at their assignments."

"No doubt," I said, "as long as we're agreed that the assignments include shaking down the weigh-masters at the Metro dumps."

"We're agreed on no such thing," Ms. Brackley said. Her eyes had narrowed. I couldn't tell whether it was the cigarette smoke or part of the stern look.

I said, "Mighty peculiar how that little old pink Cadillac makes its rounds to the dumps."

Ms. Brackley stubbed out her Vantage. It was only half smoked. Miriam the hostess arrived to replace the ashtray.

"And what about your boss?" I said. "Charles Grimaldi is no stranger to shady stuff."

"You've gone way too far, Mr. Crang," Alice Brackley said. Her eyes became very wide. "Charles Grimaldi is a respected businessman and I'm not going to tolerate another word of your insinuation and slander."

"Charlie knows how to turn a profit," I said. "I'll give him that."

Ms. Brackley took another cigarette from her package. Before she raised it to her lips, I had a match lit. She looked at me and blew out the match. So much for gracious gestures. She snicked a light from the gold Hermès.

"Let me ask the questions, Mr. Crang," she said. "Who retained you to approach me with these insults?"

"That's confidential," I said, "but it's not someone who wishes you harm."

Alice Brackley gave her first smile since she sat down in the bar. It wasn't bad even with the thin lips.

"You know, Mr. Crang," she said, "I could make a few educated guesses about your client and his motivations."

"I'd be delighted to hear them."

"And you're not entirely unknown to me yourself."

"I didn't **imagine** I was."

Ms. Brackley dropped the smile.

She said, "What do you mean by that?"

"Nothing special," I said. "Just that it wasn't difficult for me to make an appointment with you."

"Perhaps I was curious."

"Perhaps you heard my name around the office."

Alice Brackley's head lifted. Her expression flashed surprise and a touch of alarm before she got her composure back in order. She was looking over my shoulder. I turned in my chair.

"Why, Charles," she said. "How nice."

The man approaching our table was all teeth and suit. Both were white and gleaming. He was handsome, if your taste is for Latin lounge lizards. The suit was linen and double-breasted and came with white shirt, tie, and shoes. The teeth were all his and blinded everything in their path. His skin was naturally bronzed and he had hair as sleek as Remington Steele's.

"I'm Charles Grimaldi," he said. He stuck his hand out and grabbed mine in the forthright manner that my grandfather used to call a good Presbyterian handshake. Miriam appeared behind Grimaldi and moved a chair into place. Grimaldi ordered a gin and bitter lemon. Alice Brackley fussed.

"I thought you'd gone home from the office, Charles," she said to Grimaldi. To me she said, "Charles has a wonderful house out in the Kingsway, one of the old Gooderham places."

Grimaldi paid no attention to Alice Brackley's chatter. He focused on me.

"And you're the busy Mr. Crang," he said.

"You mean I don't have to introduce myself?" I said.

Alice Brackley spoke quickly. "I'm forgetting my manners. Charles, Mr. Crang is a lawyer."

"A criminal lawyer," Grimaldi said.

"You recognized my style," I said. "Very flattering."

Grimaldi said, "You've been calling on my associates, Mr. Crang."

"Not exactly," I said. "Some of them initiated the get-togethers."

"Alice didn't," Grimaldi said. He turned his smile and all those radiant choppers on Ms. Brackley. She put out her cigarette and went into the Vantage package for another. Grimaldi picked up the Hermès and flicked it into action. Alice accepted the light with a smile. Wansborough might have been right about Alice's feelings for Grimaldi passing beyond a business connection, but I couldn't tell much from what was going on in front of me. Miriam arrived with Grimaldi's drink. I asked for another martini mixed just like the first. Sometimes there was virtue in vermouth.

"You're right," I said to Grimaldi. "I invited Ms. Brackley for a drink. We have mutual interests."

"I can't imagine what," Alice Brackley said. She sounded shocked.

"Correction," I said. "It's Ms. Brackley and my client who have mutual interests."

"Who's your client?" Grimaldi asked. He had a voice without a hint of thug. Must have practised since his days in his dad's grocery store.

"Isn't that funny," I said. "You're the second person who's wondered about that in the past half-hour."

"What was the answer the first time?" Grimaldi said.

Attentive Miriam arrived with two drinks, my martini and the Rob Roy that Alice Brackley didn't need to order.

"Somebody's got to give that girl a large tip," I said.

Grimaldi said, "Never mind her, Mr. Crang. Tell me who you're representing. It's my company you been hired to nose around in."

"You've heard of solicitor-client privilege, Chuck," I said. "I'm invoking it."

"Mr. Crang is a very exasperating man," Alice Brackley said to Grimaldi.

"Just attentive to the people who pay my bills," I said.

"You got an unhealthy attitude, Crang," Grimaldi said. His voice seemed to have dropped an octave.

"You know us lawyers, Chuck," I said. "We're taught two ways of talking, devious and blunt."

Alice Brackley busied herself with the Rob Roy and a cigarette. Grimaldi looked like he was blowing steam out his ears. He asked me about my client and the client's interest in Ace Disposal in four different ways. He didn't get straight answers. On the other hand, neither did I, and I was the smarty who'd arranged the meeting with Alice Brackley in my single-minded quest for information about Ace. As a sleuth, I wasn't stacking up. I looked at my watch. Seven o'clock. I peeked through the ficus benjamina beside my chair, and, right on cue, Annie B. Cooke made her entrance.

She had on cotton jersey leggings and a backless rayon turtleneck. Both were black. Her shoes were light green leather and had sling backs. Annie had cinched her hair with a white beret. She walked up to the table and smiled. Grimaldi liked what he saw. He motioned aside Miriam and held out a chair for Annie. I performed the introductions all round.

"Great," I said. "Four for bridge."

Annie asked for a glass of white wine.

"Are you a lawyer too, Miss Cooke?" Alice Brackley asked sweetly.

"Annie," Annie said. "No, I write about movies and review them on the radio."

"How fascinating," Alice said. She checked in Grimaldi's direction to see if he thought it was fascinating. He thought Annie was fascinating all by herself. Alice might have looked miffed at the attention Grimaldi was paying Annie. Or maybe I was reading her wrong.

Alice said she adored Fred Astaire. She had a VCR at home, and almost every weekend she rented an Astaire film. *Follow the Fleet* was her favourite. Annie said Fred and Ginger made ten movies together. Alice said, Really? She counted nine. The ladies worked it out that the movie Alice was missing was *Carefree*. Annie and Alice carried on like sorority sisters. Annie told Alice to steer clear of *Ghost Story*. Fred didn't sing or dance and it was a dud, even though Melvyn Douglas was in it too. Alice said Fred didn't sing or dance in *The Notorious Landlady* either and it was a charmer, even though Kim Novak was in it too. Alice had loosened up. Her frequent glances at Grimaldi were the only sign she might be roping herself in.

"How about you, Chuck?" I said. "What's your choice in movies? *Little Caesar?*"

Alice Brackley sucked in her breath.

"You trying to aggravate me, Crang?" Grimaldi said.

"Isn't he a kidder?" Annie said to Grimaldi. She was laying her ambassadorial smile on him. "Terrible in polite company."

"Just a searching discussion among us film aficionados," I said.

Annie got her white wine and there was another Rob Roy for Alice. She steered the movie conversation back on track. Annie responded and Grimaldi chipped in. He liked Goldie Hawn. No telling people's tastes. He waxed lyrical about *Private Benjamin.* Alice stayed relaxed as long as Grimaldi was talking and distracted. Annie was enough distraction for him. He directed most of his remarks to her. When he ran out of Goldie Hawn lore, he stood up and said he had an appointment. He beamed fondly on Annie and left. Alice trotted after him. Nobody said anything about the bill.

"That's one edgy lady, your friend Alice," Annie said.

"And I just thought she talked like Loretta Young."

"She's nice," Annie said. "Classy in the way that money helps. Pleasant woman. But she's plenty, plenty nervous."

"She was steaming along in imperious form until the Man From Glad arrived."

"Dazzling he is."

"Wansborough thinks Grimaldi and Alice might have something going."

"Different types," Annie said. "But, what the heck, opposites attract."

"That's only in the physics laboratory."

"I detected tiny vibes between them," Annie said. "Mainly from Alice's side. Might be one of those crazy mixes, you know, fear and sex and fascination. I've seen it before."

"In movies."

"Real life too."

My martini glass was empty. I fiddled it between my fingers. It made a rich, tinkling sound on the top of the table.

I said, "Uncanny how Grimaldi showed up at old Alice's gabfest with me. La Serre is way off his territory if he lives out in the Kingsway."

"What are you telling me, Crang?" Annie asked.

"Either Grimaldi wants to keep Alice on a short leash or he's got his eagle eye on me," I said. "Doesn't really matter which. I'd say his main concern is to separate Alice and me."

Miriam arrived with another martini.

"I ordered?" I said to her.

"I'm sorry, sir," she said. Her smile was in the Grimaldi league for candle power. "You tapped the table."

Girl didn't miss a trick.

"So I did, Miriam," I said. I gave her my expansive look.

Annie stood pat with her wine. She didn't give Miriam any kind of look.

Annie said, "I wouldn't blame Ms. Brackley if she felt frightened of that Grimaldi man. Under the Mediterranean charm, he's actually menacing."

"Notice how I stood right up to him?"

Annie ignored the opportunity to compliment my dash and pluck.

"Go back a bit, fella," she said. "What was that part about him keeping an eagle eye on your good self?"

"His heavies paid a visit to me," I said, "and I can't believe Grimaldi didn't order it."

I described the meeting in my office with Sol Nash and wide Tony.

"Crang," Annie said, "the quicksand is at about the level of your upper thighs."

"Not too late for someone to haul me out."

"Never mind someone hauling you out. I mean there's still time for you to pull out on your own."

Miriam set down another paper coaster and placed my martini on top of it. She took away the empty glasses.

Annie said, "Personally, me, if I were standing beside the quick-sand with a board in my hands, I'd use it to bop you over the head."

"Strong language," I said.

"So far," Annie said, "you've been caught shadowing a truck the size of a house, come close to getting beat up by a man who apparently knows how to do it, and you've intentionally alienated the two top executives in the company you're supposed to be checking out."

"You haven't cottoned on to my modus operandi," I said. "I'm needling the bad guys into submission."

Annie asked if we could eat. I let her choose the restaurant. That was my idea of living dangerously. Once, Annie led us to a vegetarian place run by devotees of an Indian mystic. I was starved before we made it back to the parking lot.

"Great," Annie said in La Serre. "We're going to Brasil."

"Long way for dinner."

"This Brasil," Annie said, "isn't spelled with a zed. It's that Portuguese restaurant in Kensington Market that we went to a few months ago."

I put my American Express card on the table and Miriam was instantly at my side. "The bill has been taken care of, sir," she said. Her smile was beatific. Somebody had given her the large tip. My guess was Ms. Brackley.

It pays to make friends in high places.

15

I **WOKE UP** Thursday morning with a headache and the beginnings of a plan. The sun shone through a space in the curtains and I lay watching motes dance in its beams. A cloud passed over and blocked the sun. I was gingerly getting out of bed. A cup of coffee eased back the headache. The plan remained in the starting gate.

I sliced a banana over a bowl of Harvest Crunch and ate it while I read the *Globe and Mail*. Jay Scott had a long piece on the films of Ron Howard. Scott is a witty and perceptive movie writer, and that afternoon he and Annie were getting together over a Nagra tape recorder. Annie was preparing a twenty-minute item for a CBC radio arts program on whither film in the late 1980s. She had an interview laid on with Vincent Canby of the *New York Times*. She said she was nervous about interviewing Canby. Not about interviewing Scott. Annie said Jay's a pussycat.

Harry Hein was part of my nascent plan. I dialled his number from the phone in the kitchen. The line was busy. Harry Hein is a chartered accountant who practises by himself. Two years earlier, he was a chartered accountant who almost didn't practise by himself or in anybody else's company. A slick con man named Tony Holmes had unfolded a cockeyed scheme for Harry. Surefire moneymaker, Holmes told Harry. Couldn't miss. Holmes said he had a shot at two hundred thousand dollars' worth of municipal bonds that the Mafia in Buffalo had accepted in return for gambling debts and wanted to unload at forty cents on the dollar. According to the Holmes tale, he also had Arab purchasers who'd take the bonds off his hands at ninety cents on the same dollar. All he needed was a stake to make the buy from the mob in Buffalo. The suckers formed a line at Tony Holmes' door. Harry Hein was one of them. He socked in twenty grand. Trouble was it was a client's money. Harry knew he'd got himself shafted when Tony Holmes told him and the other investors that, oops, sorry, the bonds he said he scooped up from the Mafia were lost when the Learjet carrying the bonds to the Arab purchasers in Cairo ran out of fuel and ditched in the Mediterranean. Holmes had a smooth way with words and all the suckers but one swallowed his explanation and took their losses. Harry was the exception. He brought the story to me and I told Holmes that I'd hit him with a civil suit and drop a word in the ear of a contact on the Metro Police fraud squad unless he chose to ante up Harry's client's twenty grand. It was ninety-nine per cent bluff, but Holmes came through in twelve hours. I accepted the money, covered Harry's tracks, and phoned my fraud squad connection. Holmes got four years. Harry said if the Institute of Chartered Accountants had found out what he'd done, they would have hung him out to dry.

The second time I called, Harry's line was free. He said he'd be in to me all morning. I left the house and walked up Beverley Street and cut through the university grounds. Harry Hein's office is on the second floor over a sleek Italian furniture store on Bay Street north of Bloor. It was a sunny, benign day made for an aimless walk. I crossed the front campus toward University College. The University of Toronto doesn't have much to boast about in the architecture line, but University College fits near the top of the short list. It goes back a century or so, with time out for one historic fire, and it's a handsome hybrid of a bunch of European styles. Canadian architects used to go in for hybrid. A dash of Romanesque, a pinch of Byzantine, some Tudor, a sprinkling of Italian palazzo. Stir, and fill with people. I walked under the Hart House tower, up Philosopher's Walk, and east along Bloor past the upscale shops.

Harry Hein's office occupies three rooms. He has a secretary, an accounting student, some leather furniture he got on sale downstairs, and a computer. The computer terminal stands beside Harry's desk.

"Long time no see, Crang," Harry said.

"Couple of years," I said.

"You think I don't remember."

Harry shook his head and sucked in air with a faint whistling noise. The head was balding, and Harry's face was a mix of jowls and bags and creases. He was in his shirt sleeves and had his tie loosened around the collar. He wore crimson suspenders. His desk was a clutter of print-outs from the computer. Harry was in his early fifties and he'd never made much money. We sat in chairs in his office.

He said, "What can I do you for?"

"I want you to listen to a story, Harry," I said. "It may be an accounting story."

"Shoot."

I told Harry about my investigations of the Ace Disposal operations. He listened very attentively. Practice was making me efficient at doing my Ace routine, and I had the story down to about ten minutes, start to finish.

"One guess," I said, winding to the end, "is that Ace is leaning on the weigh-masters. Shaking them down somehow."

"That doesn't make sense," Harry said. It was his first interruption since I began my recitation. His voice had authority.

"Tell me why," I said.

"Leaning on someone," Harry said, "means that the someone is paying out to people who are doing the leaning."

"That's the usual definition."

"But from what you've told me about the way the dumps run," Harry said, "the weigh-masters would have no reason to pay out to a company like Ace."

"Other way around maybe," I said. "You mean Ace has no reason to make the weigh-masters pay."

"Right," Harry said. He snaked his thumbs under the crimson suspenders. "It would be much more probable if the two sides were working in concert, Ace and the weigh-masters."

"Harry," I said, "I knew there was a reason for consulting you."

"The weigh-masters could be doing a favour for Ace," Harry went on. "Supposing they're giving Ace a break on the weight of the truckloads."

I said, "That'd account for the extra time it takes to weigh the Ace trucks going into the dumps. The weigh-masters need the time to rig the weights."

"If they weigh the trucks in light," Harry said, "then Ace doesn't have to pay as much to Metro for dropping their loads in the dumps. Lighter the loads, the smaller the fees."

"And in return for that piece of shiftiness," I said, "Sol Nash drops around and makes a little payoff to the cheating weigh-masters."

Harry had a question. "Didn't you say," he asked, "it also takes longer to weigh the Ace trucks out of the dumps?"

"That's what I said."

"So the weigh-masters weigh the trucks out heavy. Get it? The weigh-masters make sure the trucks are lighter going in and heavier coming out. That cuts down the dumping fee Ace has to pay Metro at both ends of the transaction."

"Neat," I said. "I like it. Only thing is it's all theory."

"Pretty damned tidy theory," Harry said. He was running his thumbs up and down under the crimson suspenders.

"I need to document it," I said. "My client expects something in the way of hard numbers."

"Yeah," Harry said. "I understand."

I kept quiet and let Harry figure it out.

"You want me to document it," he said after a moment of reflection. "You want me to look at this company's books. Ace's books."

I didn't speak.

"I owe you a favour," Harry said.

I said, "It crossed my mind."

"Okay, you weren't going to mention it," Harry said. His thumbs were moving more rapidly under the suspenders. "You didn't need to. I know I'm indebted. So, what else, I'll go over the books."

"Thanks, Harry," I said. "But going over Ace's books is the job. Something else is the favour."

"Crang, you're going too fast for me."

I said, "Ace won't be keen on you examining its financial records."

"The hell, I didn't think they'd exactly invite me in."

I said, "Fact is, Ace isn't going to know you're examining the records."

"But I thought probably you had access to their papers . . ." Harry said. His voice trailed off and he stopped rubbing his suspenders.

I said, "The favour is, Harry, that you trust me."

"So you're bringing the documents to me?" Harry said. He was sitting very still in his chair.

I said, "I'm going to take you to the documents."

"You are?"

"Of necessity, Harry," I said, "this will be a night job."

16

I **NEEDED THREE CALLS** from the phone in Harry Hein's office to locate James Turkin, the fledgling break-and-enter man. Calls number one and two were to his mother. She hung up the first time. I rang back and applied the old Crang persuasion.

I said, "Mrs. Turkin, I'd hate to feel obliged to ask James' probation officer to visit you and your husband."

She said she thought James was living with his married sister in Regent Park. She didn't know the address. Did she know the married sister's name? "My own daughter?" Mrs. Turkin said. Her voice squawked. "I should think I know," she said. "We're close-knit." Yeah, like J. R. Ewing and clan. The married sister's last name was Gruber.

The phone book showed a Gruber on Sackville Street, and I dialled the number. The woman who answered said James would be back from work at five-thirty. The woman had a pleasant voice. Was I a friend of James? His lawyer, I told her. She thought that was wonderful and looked forward to meeting me. I didn't ask what James was working at.

Regent Park lies south of Gerrard and east of Parliament. It's a housing development for low-income and welfare families that sprawls over several discouraging blocks. Not long after the end of the Second War, bulldozers went into the area and levelled the one-storey houses and shanties where Toronto's poor Irish made their corner of the city. A planned community went in in its place. The plan produced brick low-rises and fourplexes done in institutional squares and rectangles. Grassy patches define the areas between the buildings, and there's a battered recreational centre for kids. Regent Park has never been a neighbourhood calculated to produce tomorrow's stalwart citizens.

At six o'clock I parked on Gerrard and walked down Sackville to a two-storey building that was split into four apartments. Two little boys were playing with a G.I. Joe on the scarred brown lawn in the front of the building. The G.I. Joe was short one arm. Both little boys were Vietnamese. A card with the Gruber name was inserted in a slot under the apartment mailbox on the lower left. I pushed the buzzer and James Turkin answered the door.

"Am I in trouble?" he asked.

"Not yet," I said.

"My sister told me you phoned."

James stood inside the door and held it open about a foot. The perfect host.

"I'm here to talk business," I said. "Your business."

James kept his deadpan expression in place.

"Invite the gentleman in, James," a woman said from behind Turkin. I recognized the pleasant voice from the phone.

James opened the door and stepped back. He was wearing a short-sleeved red shirt with the words "Home Hardware" sewn in yellow across the breast pocket.

The woman inside had a smile to match her voice.

"You must be Mr. Crang," she said. "I'm James' sister, Emily Gruber." We shook hands.

"Would you care for some refreshment, Mr. Crang?" Emily Gruber asked.

Odds were Emily didn't run a Polish-vodka household.

"I've two things cold in the fridge," she said. "Beer or Diet Pepsi?"

Best definition I'd heard of the space between a rock and a hard place.

Emily weighed fifty pounds more than was healthy. The skirt of her white dress ballooned over her stomach and rode up at the hem to show an inch of beige slip. Her brown hair was held back from her face with bobby pins that glinted in the light. Her face was chubby and full of eager welcome. She appeared to have cornered the social graces in the Turkin family. Lucky her.

"Beer would suit if somebody's joining me," I said.

"Oh, my husband's the only drinker in the family, Mr. Crang," Emily said. The smile made dimples in the fat of her cheeks. "James doesn't indulge and I don't like the taste."

James had taken up position in an armchair that was covered in a purple and orange floral pattern. The front door opened directly into the living room. On the wall over a fireplace there was a painting of a nineteenth-century sailing ship crashing against a craggy shore. The fireplace was occupied by an electric heater. Next to it stood a television set with a VCR. New, and courtesy of Canadian Tire. Emily left the room down a hall to the right and I sat on the sofa. It was covered in yellow corduroy.

I said to James, "You moved fast on the job market."

"A hardware store," he said. "I got my reasons."

"Dare I ask?"

James shrugged.

"I need to put together a good kit," he said. "Blank keys, saw blades, a real good screwdriver, stuff like that. Hardware store's the best place to swipe from."

"Sensible career-planning."

"You gonna tell my probation officer?"

I said, "Would it divert you from the break-and-enter business if I did?"

"It's what I got a vocation for," James said. "I can tell."

"A vocation. My, my."

Emily Gruber returned with my beer. She had poured it into a tall glass and it was on a tray beside a smaller glass of Diet Pepsi. She offered my beer with a little bow and did the same with the soft drink for James.

"My husband likes his supper soon as he comes in from the plant, Mr. Crang," Emily said. "I'll be in the kitchen if you want anything."

She waited until I tasted the beer.

"Very refreshing, Mrs. Gruber," I said.

Emily dimpled her face and went back to the kitchen.

"So?" James Turkin said. "You telling the probation officer or what?"

I said, "The proposition I've got for you, I don't think your probation officer wants to hear about."

"Yeah? For me? What kind of proposition?"

"I hire you to open a few doors that the owner prefers to keep shut."

"You want me to get inside a place and steal stuff?" James asked. His voice lost some of its flatness. It sounded as close as James Turkin could approach to incredulity.

"Just get inside," I said. "No stealing."

James contemplated his Pepsi.

"You trying to set me up?" he said.

"Paying job, James," I said. "One hundred dollars for a night's employment. I'll lead you to the building, you apply your arts to guide another gentleman and me past its locks and alarms."

"It's against the law."

"Exactly why I thought of you."

James wiped his mouth with the back of his hand and rubbed the hand against the front of his Home Hardware shirt. It left a small, damp smear.

"One hundred dollars?" he said.

"Cash money," I said. I'd finished half of the beer. It tasted like Lifebuoy.

"When?" James asked.

"It has to be after midnight," I said, "and it has to be soon, probably tomorrow night."

"I'd want to look at the place first, whatever it is, an office building you're talking about?"

"Small office in the suburbs," I said. "Got a fence around it, gate with a padlock I think. Don't know about the door into the building. I haven't been that close."

"I need to see everything," James said. He put the glass of Pepsi on an end table beside the chair with the floral pattern and shoved himself forward to the edge of the chair. "Wire fence, padlock, all that, I got to see for myself."

"Case the joint."

"Huh?" James obviously hadn't seen enough Edward G. Robinson movies.

"I'll drive you out after dark tonight," I said. "What's good? Ten o'clock?"

James and I arranged to meet up the street at the corner of Gerrard and Sackville. I told him I'd be in a white Volks convertible.

"What's this deal about?" James asked.

"It's about one hundred dollars," I said. "That's all you need to know."

Emily Gruber came into the living room from the kitchen. She had put on a frilly blue apron over her white dress and was carrying an unopened bottle of beer and a bottle opener. The beer was Miller Lite. Could have fooled me. I declined the second beer, and after a friendly handshake, she instructed James to see me to the door.

"How did your sister acquire the good manners?" I asked James when we were on the porch.

He said, "Emily's weird, all right."

I drove home and ate two ham sandwiches with a shot of vodka. Was I corrupting a teenager's morals? Hardly. James Turkin's morals had found their home in a nether region long before I appeared on his scene. If he was hell-bent on a life of crime, better he should perform in a worthy cause. Getting Harry Hein and me into Ace Disposal's offices qualified as a worthy cause in my book. Nothing I or a probation officer could say would dissuade James from exploring the career option of breaking and entering. It would take a couple of stretches in prison to cure him of his predilections, and in the meantime, as long as he was operating under my thoughtful supervision, he had a better chance of avoiding arrest. I poured another shot of vodka and admired my gift for rationalizing awkward moral dilemmas.

Me and Immanuel Kant.

17

I LEFT EARLY enough to drop in on Annie for an unannounced visit before my date with James. Annie's apartment was five blocks due north of the Gruber homestead. The five blocks defined the distance from chic Cabbagetown to glum Regent Park. Something like the difference between the two Germanys. Without the Wall.

"Guess who's come to dinner?" Annie said.

She was whispering in the hallway outside her apartment door. I'd knocked first. Always the gent.

I said, "Not Richard Gere."

"If it was him," Annie said, "it'd be for naked lunch."

From where I was standing, I couldn't see into the apartment. Blue air drifted out. Whoever was inside was a heavy smoker.

"The shade of Ed Murrow?" I said.

"Alice Brackley," Annie whispered. "She phoned this afternoon. I asked her over."

Alice was sitting behind a bottle of Cutty Sark at the table in the front window. Annie must have made a rush trip to the liquor store on Parliament Street. Scotch wasn't a staple in her booze cabinet. Empty plates had been shoved to the end of the table. They'd eaten chicken breasts with some kind of tomato sauce. My stomach lurched in envy. Alice was using one of Annie's cobalt-blue soup bowls for an ashtray.

"Am I trespassing on your time with Annie, Mr. Crang?" Alice asked me. She was wearing her gold and a smile that anybody would call winning.

"It's me who's making the surprise visit, Ms. Brackley," I said. "Nice to see you."

"Nice?"

"Honest."

Alice looked at ease. Maybe the Scotch. Maybe the absence of Charles Grimaldi.

Annie said to me, "We've been talking more movies."

Annie looked at ease too. With her, I knew it had nothing to do with Grimaldi or Scotch. She was drinking red wine sparingly.

"And talking about you, Mr. Crang," Alice Brackley said.

"Alice was frank," Annie said, again to me. "She wanted to know if she could trust you."

"With what?" I asked.

I meant the question for Alice. She didn't answer directly. She said, "The impression you made at La Serre, Mr. Crang, was mixed."

"Smiling Charlie wouldn't say so," I said.

"I wasn't speaking for Charles," Alice said.

"He thought you were a smarty-pants," Annie said. "I didn't blame him."

Annie's tone was light, but she was letting me know there was a point to be made in the room.

"Whose side you on?" I said to her.

My tone matched Annie's for lightness, but I was letting her know I wanted someone in the room to get on with the point.

"I hope I'm not presuming too much," Annie said, turning from me to Alice and back to me, "but I think Alice might want to consult you, Crang."

"Is that what the thing about trust is all about?" I said.

Annie had candles on the table. In their glow, Alice's face looked soft and rosy. She reached into a bowl of ice, dropped three cubes in her glass, and poured Cutty Sark on top. Soft and rosy and tiddly. On her at that moment it wasn't a bad combination.

"Do you know anything about the disposal business, Mr. Crang?" Alice asked.

"I'm picking up on it fast."

"In disposal," Alice said, "there's no quarter given."

"Especially tough for a woman, I'd imagine."

"It's sexist," Alice said, "but so are many businesses."

"Many businesses aren't also crooked."

"Crang," Annie said, "you're going too fast."

Alice said, "One takes the edge where it's offered. That's what I've learned at Ace."

It was Alice's dance. I'd follow her lead. But as tangos went, it was mighty leisurely. I was sure to step on her toes before we got off the dance floor. Either that or I'd OD on my own metaphors.

"What else have you learned at Ace?" I asked Alice.

"The president's office is the place where you find the only real satisfaction," she said.

Where was the woman going with this line of palaver? I knew where I should be going. My watch said eight minutes to ten. Eight minutes until my assignation with James Turkin.

"What you just said," I said, "sounds like something they teach at the Harvard Business School."

"Mr. Crang, I'm in the business world," Alice said. "I know where power resides."

"And how it's wielded?"

"Sometimes a line is crossed," Alice said.

Alice may have expected me to understand. Rosy in the candlelight, safe in Annie's company, comfortable in the Scotch. I couldn't be sure whether she wanted to spill some beans or was merely high and loose on the ambience and the liquor. It might take another hour to find out. I made a swift weighing of priorities. My meeting with James won out.

"Let's get together, Ms. Brackley," I said. "Take lunch. Have your machine call my machine. Pencil in a date. All those other things you guys do in the executive suite."

"Don't pay attention to the flip stuff, Alice," Annie said to Ms. Brackley. "You can rely on Crang."

"I'll be in contact," Alice said to me.

"But will we touch base?"

Annie went to the door with me.

"You shouldn't tease the woman," she said in the hall. She was whispering again. "I think Alice might be on the verge of saying something important."

"She's treating it like the Geneva arms talks," I said. "We don't have the space for prolonged negotiations and other tap dances."

"Well," Annie said, looking back into the apartment, "she's welcome to stay here and talk for as long as she wants."

"Keep her mainlining the Cutty."

"Crang, I'm not going to pump the woman. Just lend an ear to someone who's got problems."

"Come up with deep-throat material," I said, "and I'll stick the bottle of Scotch on my expense account."

"That's my guy. All heart."

I kissed Annie on both cheeks, went down to the Volks, and drove around the corner to Sackville and Gerrard. James was waiting in front of a variety store. He had on a long-sleeved black shirt and black jeans.

I said, "I like a man who dresses for the occasion. Except, James, tonight isn't the occasion."

"I know what I'm doing," James said.

He was carrying a cloth whisky bag. I hesitated to ask what was in it. It wouldn't be whisky.

I went out the Queen Elizabeth Way with the top down on the Volks, cut north at Kipling Avenue, and drove past the muffler outlets and body shops to Ace Disposal's quarters. A bright spotlight illuminated the sign at the front, and all the lights inside the one-storey office building had been left on. There wasn't an indication of human activity on the premises. I pulled into the parking lot on the south side of the bar and restaurant across the street. The lot was three-quarters full, and sounds of happy revelry came from inside the club. The exotic dancers who were its advertised feature must have been in full terpsichorean flight. Or maybe the food was just awfully good.

"That the place over there?" James said. He was twisting around in the front seat looking at the Ace building. "Can't see much from here."

Two cars came up the street and parked in the lot. Three young guys in T-shirts that read "University of Toronto Engineering" piled out of one car and a man in a business suit got out of the other. They went into the club. It was called the Majestic. "No G-Strings," a hand-painted sign over the door proclaimed.

"We'll get a table inside that looks out on the street," I said. "Less conspicuous than the parking lot."

We entered the Majestic. It was crowded and smoky and dark. Loud rock music came from two speakers mounted on the stage that ran along most of the back wall. There were stand-up bars on either side of the stage, and tables with customers at them spread across the floor in front of it. Pink lights were directed at the stage. A young woman danced in the lights. She wasn't wearing a G-string or anything else.

Two or three of the tables at the back of the room were empty, and James and I sat at one that was up against a window. A waitress asked what it'd be. She was wearing high heels and a shortie jacket that proper girls put on only at bedtime. James asked for a Coke and I ordered vodka. When the waitress turned away, she flounced her jacket and offered a flash of pale buttock.

James reached into the whisky bag in his lap and took out a pair of small binoculars. He turned the focusing dial and raised the binoculars to his eyes. They were pointed through the louvred window blinds at the Ace building. The kid was all business.

There was a break in the thump of the music, and the young woman on the stage gathered up a small pile of discarded clothes she'd left at one corner of the stage. She held them in front of her as she descended the stage's stairs. She managed to look decorous.

"Alarm box's over the door," James said. He was leaning forward and pressing the binoculars against the window.

The waitress brought James' Coke and my vodka. I gave her a ten-dollar bill and got back a handful of change. The waitress paid no attention to James and the binoculars.

"Take me maybe five minutes on that box," James said.

The rock music thudded back to life, and a well-built woman climbed up the stairs to the stage. She was dressed in a nurse's uniform: white dress, white cap, white shoes with laces and low heels.

"You want to see what I mean?" James said.

He handed me the binoculars. Above the metal and glass door in the brick wall of the Ace building, beside an overhead light, there was a square box with wires leading from both sides. The wires ran down the edges of the door and disappeared into the brick.

"That's your burglar alarm," James said. His voice had the sound of expertise. "What I'm gonna do is rig in another wire that bypasses the box. That way, it won't ring when I go through the lock on the door."

"If it rang," I said, "where would that be? Police station?"

"Ring like hell in the building over there," James said. "And in two other places. Police station is one, security company's the other. Cars from both'd be here in five, ten minutes."

"The security company installed the alarm?" I said. "That's what you mean?"

"Put the binoculars on the door," James said. "Little sticker on the corner, see it? That's the security guys. Alarm rings in their office and at the police station."

I moved the binoculars over the glass pane in the door and found a sticker in the lower right-hand corner.

"Not worth shit," James said. He took back the binoculars.

The nurse onstage had divested herself of the white cap and dress. She was wearing high-cut gym shorts and a formidable white brassiere. Not for long. She danced to the heavy thump of the rock and took off the shorts and brassiere. Directly in front of the stage, eight or nine men seated at two tables that had been pushed together were pointing their fingers to one side of the stage and shouting something at the dancer. The shouting solidified into a chant. "Shower," the men pleaded. There was a shower stall at the rear of the stage closest to the stand-up bar on the right side. It had clear glass walls and an intricate arrangement of nozzles and tubes. The woman stepped into the stall. A cheer went up from the front tables.

"That padlock on the gate, I saw ones like that a hundred times before," James said. He had the binoculars back on the Ace property.

"Add up the time for me," I said. "How long will it take you to open the gate and get through the door into the building?"

"The padlock, that's a wire job, twenty seconds," James said. He was looking through the glasses as he talked. "I go across the path they got there and work on the box over the door. Three, four minutes for it, putting in the bypass wire. So that's only the lock on the door that's left. I don't know, couple more minutes. I can't tell what kind of lock it is."

Water sprayed over the woman in the shower stall onstage. She held a nozzle in her hand and aimed the shooting water at her breasts. Her face was raised to the ceiling and her expressions let the fans at the front tables know she'd achieved a higher form of ecstasy. Her breasts shone in the water. I estimated her brassiere size at 38C.

"What'd you think?" James asked.

I said, "I think if she performs that shower routine four or five times a night, she keeps squeaky clean."

"About the job," James said. He had an annoyed edge to his voice.

"You're talking seven minutes," I said. "Is that too long to be exposed out there?"

"Won't be exposed to anybody after this joint's closed down and everybody's gone home," James said. "No reason for traffic at night around here."

"True," I said. "What about night patrol cars? Do the security people who put in the burglar alarm check up on their customers' property?"

"How 'bout we stay here and watch?"

"How 'bout we do?"

The woman stepped from her shower and dried herself off with a small blue towel that didn't seem adequate to the task. She retrieved her nurse's whites and left the stage. Her place was taken by a woman in a long diaphanous gown and a panty girdle.

James and I had two more rounds of Coke and vodka, and in the forty-five minutes we sat at the table, no patrol cars cruised past Ace's property. Traffic in and out of the Majestic's parking lot remained brisk. So did the parade of young women on and off the club's stage.

"Nothing's happening," James said at eleven-thirty. We finished our drinks and walked out the front door.

Outside, away from the pounding music and the thick cigarette smoke, the night was still and sweet. We turned the corner of the club and stepped into the parking lot. One row of cars over, two men were standing beside the white Volks. A tall guy in a jean jacket had his hands in his pockets and was listening to the other man, who was talking and waving his arms. The talker had a thick beard and a bulky build. It was the Ace driver I'd defeated by a TKO on Bathurst Street. I took James' arm and stepped behind a maroon Volvo.

"Those two guys by my car," I said, "go over and tell them the car's owner is inside on the pay phone."

James looked across the lot.

"Sure," he said.

"Tell them something's spooked the guy on the phone and he's calling a cab and wants it fast."

"What if they ask how come I'm telling them this stuff?"

"Say you've got a beef with the guy," I said. "And tell the bearded guy you know it's him the guy on the phone's trying to steer clear of."

James walked across the parking lot to the two men by the Volks. My former adversary stared at James. He heard James out, and as he listened, his jaws began to work. Froth at the mouth and drool in his beard ought to follow any minute. The guy was aching for a return bout with me. He turned away from James and took a step in the direction of the club. The guy in the jean jacket grabbed his shoulder and pulled him back. Jean-jacket did the talking. He held the floor and the bearded guy listened. Jean-jacket switched his line of patter to James. He was firing questions. James answered. He looked assured. Nothing moved except his lips. No fidgets, no nervous body language. James stood his ground. The tall guy in the jean jacket and the fat man with the beard looked at one another and walked away from James. They broke into a run and cut behind the back of the Majestic.

"Nice," I said to James when I reached the Volks. "Lot of finesse, James."

"The tall guy didn't go for it at the first," James said.

"He went for it at the last," I said.

I turned the key in the ignition, switched on the headlights, and backed the car out of the parking slot.

James said, "Those guys are pissed off at you."

I drove down the row of cars to the front of the lot and stopped to let two cars go by on the street.

"Not both guys," I said. "The guy with the beard."

I turned right. The front door of the Majestic banged open. I had the Volks in low gear. Someone was running from the Majestic toward the street. I pressed the accelerator.

"Here comes the tall guy," James said.

I said, "Didn't fool him long enough."

The tall man in the jean jacket was going full tilt. At the rate he was covering the ground, he'd reach the road before I was past the Majestic. I had two options, stop or step on the accelerator and risk smacking into the tall guy. He slid into the street and threw up his arms in front of the Volks. There went option number two. I stopped.

"You see the other guy?" I said to James. "The fat one with the beard?"

"Just coming out the front door," James said.

The tall man stood in the lights of the car and looked back toward the Majestic. He was waiting for his friend. I couldn't wait. One guy I might have a chance of handling if James pitched in. Not two.

The top was still down on the car and I shouted at the tall man over the windshield.

"Hey you, stringbean," I said, "you want some of what I gave your fat pal the other day?"

With my left hand I turned the handle on the door and opened it a crack.

"You're asking for a broken head, asshole," the tall man said. He walked out of the headlights toward my side of the car.

I said to James, "Where's fatso now?"

"Halfway to us."

The tall man reached my door. His hands were set to grab me. I swung the door open fast. It caught the tall man in the right kneecap and just below his ribs. He fell on the road. I slammed the door shut.

"Fat guy's coming quick," James said.

The tall man rolled over on the pavement. He didn't know whether to grab his kneecap or his stomach. He was moaning.

I pushed the accelerator and the rear tires squealed.

"Fat guy's gone crazy," James said. His voice was louder.

I glanced to my right and saw the guy with the beard launch himself at the car. His arms were stretched in front of him as if he were diving, and his feet had left the ground. I pulled the steering wheel hard to the left. The man with the beard thudded into the door on James' side. I straightened the steering wheel and the car kept moving.

"Bet he left a dent," James said.

I looked back. The bearded man was on his knees watching the Volks drive away down the street. He had his hands on his hips. The tall man was still rolling on the pavement.

"Now," I said to James, "both guys are pissed off at me."

18

I DROVE ANNIE out to the airport Friday morning. Her appointment with Vincent Canby for the CBC radio item on movie critics was set for Canby's office at the *New York Times* that afternoon. Annie was excited but a shade weary. Alice Brackley hadn't left her place until almost two.

"You may be right about a romance between Alice and Mr. Grimaldi," Annie said in the car.

"It was Wansborough who raised the possibility," I said. "Actually Wansborough's wife. No, scratch that, it was Wansborough's wife's friends. Two of them. Separate occasions."

"You finished?"

"Run with it."

"Okay, Alice didn't give names, not Grimaldi's anyway," Annie said. "But she made it clear she was involved with a man no one she knew would consider appropriate. Certainly not her family."

"Don't see Alice making a guy like Grimaldi the centrepiece at a Wansborough-Brackley gathering."

"I thought Wasp families were supposed to be loosening up these days."

"From my small intercourse with clan Wansborough," I said, "I'd judge a pound of gelignite wouldn't loosen them up."

"Well, she's obviously troubled by the relationship."

"What'd Alice want from you?" I asked. "Just a sympathetic ear?"

"Seemed so," Annie said. "I guess she doesn't feel her friends would understand the situation and I made a safe alternative."

"Yet she stopped short of telling you that Grimaldi is the forbidden love she holds in her breast?"

"My, aren't we poetic," Annie said. "No, she didn't say Grimaldi was her beau, but I think it's possible to read between the lines. The whole time she was talking, God knows it was hours and hours, I automatically read the name Grimaldi into the script."

"Alice make a pretty deep dent in the Cutty Sark?"

"Drank half the bottle."

"Half doesn't look right on the expense account."

"The whole thing?"

"Call it twenty bucks."

"Good golly, what a prince you are."

"What was this other line of chatter Alice was pursuing?" I said. "The one about trusting me?"

"That was the early part of the evening, before you came by," Annie said. "Alice wondered about legal advice, something she said she needed before she made a decision that had to do with her work."

"Elliptical talker, that Alice."

"She's feeling her way."

"Slowly."

"Well, I sympathize," Annie said. "She's got a romantic crisis, a business crisis, maybe a drinking crisis. Lot to balance at one time."

"Did you draw the conclusion the crises were linked?"

"Wouldn't surprise me," Annie said. "The talk about the love affair seemed to flow naturally from the talk about the job decision."

"Doesn't take a great leap of the imagination to say that Grimaldi might be common to both."

"And he could drive a girl to drink."

Annie had the Nagra tape recorder on her lap, and a stuffed shoulder bag sat on the floor of the Volks. She planned to stay overnight in New York and come back on the noon plane Saturday.

"You keeping out of trouble tonight, buster?" she said.

"There's a nurse I wouldn't mind looking up."

"Not that kind of trouble," Annie said. "You haven't mentioned what you're up to on the Ace front."

"Loose lips sink ships," I said.

"You're holding out on me, Crang."

"Just waiting until fresh developments turn up," I said. There was no sense in alarming Annie with my plans for that evening at the moment when she was leaving town. Crang, the fount of wisdom and cowardice.

I was going to the airport by way of Highway 427. I turned off it onto the crisscross of roads that led to the two airport terminals. Annie was flying American Airlines. Terminal One.

Annie said she'd be higher than a kite when she got back next day. Manhattan did that to her.

"The air must be thinner down there," she said.

"Rarefied," I said.

I pulled the car into a gap between two taxis in front of the American Airlines entrance. Annie kissed me on the lips, got out of the car, and swung down the sidewalk, the Nagra in her right hand and the bag over her left shoulder. I watched until she disappeared through the pneumatic doors. Lady had a great ass.

Back downtown, I laid on arrangements for the evening. Harry Hein was a trifle sticky. I told him on the phone I'd pick him up at his office at twelve-thirty. The nighttime twelve-thirty, I said. He wanted to know how he should explain the nocturnal absence to his wife. An all-night poker game, I suggested. Harry said he didn't play poker. I told him to invent. Harry fretted on the phone. Chartered accountants aren't accustomed to inventing.

James Turkin took my call with aplomb. I bet he didn't know he possessed aplomb. He was speaking from the Home Hardware store where he worked and looted. Twelve-fifteen at the corner of Gerrard and Sackville, I said, and he said he'd see me. Brevity and aplomb, that was my James.

Later in the afternoon, I walked over to the Sheraton Centre on Queen Street and rented a black Dodge Dart from the Avis outlet in the hotel. Compared with my Volks, it felt as broad as William the Refrigerator Perry. I parked it in back of the house and whiled away the evening. Heating tomato sauce from a jar and eating it on fettuccine from a package took care of a half-hour. I watched *Miami Vice* and the local news, and just about the time a sensible lawyer would hit the hay, I went down the stairs and drove away in the Dodge Dart.

James was standing in front of the same variety store on Gerrard. I leaned across and opened the passenger door, and he climbed in to the back seat. He had his cloth liquor bag and a kitchen stool. The stool had chip marks in its white paint but looked sturdy and about two feet high.

"A stool?" I said.

"You'll see," James said. He didn't talk while we drove over to pick up Harry Hein outside his office on Bay Street.

Harry was nervous. He got in the front seat, carrying a small briefcase, and acknowledged James when I introduced the two. One sweating man and one teenager. My team.

"Crang," Harry said, "you know how many years I can get in prison for this?"

"Look at it another way, Harry," I said. "With me defending you, you'll have a lawyer who's truly involved in the case."

I drove down University Avenue and out the Gardiner.

"This is crazy anyway," Harry said. "The amount of time I'm going to put in on these people's books, I can't do any kind of systematic analysis."

"You got till Ace's morning shift comes on, Harry."

"They work Saturdays?"

"Not till after the sun comes up."

I passed the old Seaway Hotel and crossed from the Gardiner onto the Queen E.

"Car smells new," James said from the back seat. He wasn't nervous. "You trade the Volks for this thing?"

"Rented it," I said. "The Volks was growing familiar to our friends in the west end."

The traffic was light, some tractor-trailers and a few late-nighters driving back to the suburbs from a hot time downtown.

"Besides," I said, "all rented cars smell new. Comes from a spray patented by Mr. Avis."

The lights were out in the Majestic and the parking lot was empty of cars. I parked the Dart at the rear of the lot under a tree with over-hanging branches that were thick with leaves. It would be tough for anyone passing by to spot a black car.

"Now what?" Harry said.

"Across the street," I said, "that's our destination."

A white handkerchief was fluffed out of the breast pocket of Harry's jacket. He had on a business suit and shirt and tie. He looked over at the Ace building and used the handkerchief to wipe the perspiration off his forehead.

"Place looks like the *Queen Mary*," he said, "all those damned lights."

"Okay, James," I said into the back seat, "do your stuff."

I got out of my door and pulled back the seat to let James exit with his bag and stool. He was wearing his black outfit from the night before and he trotted with deliberate speed across the parking lot and over the street to the people gate in the chain-link fence around the Ace property. The bag was in his right hand, the stool in his left. He dropped both on the ground in front of the gate and took a short, thin wire out of the bag. He leaned over and applied it to the padlock on the gate. In half a minute he straightened up and yanked at the pad-lock. It opened. James pulled the gate toward him and stepped through it with his bag and stool. He put them on the path inside the grounds and pushed the gate back into position. He left the padlock dangling loose and open.

"The kid's fast," I said to Harry.

"You think that's going to make me relax?" Harry said.

"And he's slick," I said. "You should appreciate slick."

Across the street, James scooted up the cement path to the door into the Ace building. He took a pair of pliers out of his bag and another piece of wire. This wire was of the thick industrial variety and about three feet long. James positioned his stool on the ground under the alarm box over the door. He stood on the stool.

"Planning ahead," I said. "You like that, Harry?"

"Just let him get the hell on with it," Harry said.

James balanced himself on the stool, reached up, and used his pliers to clip off the wire leading into the alarm box from the left side. With a roll of black electrical tape that he took out of his back pants pocket, he bound one end of the piece of industrial wire into the loose strand on the top of the door. He ran the wire over the alarm box and performed the same operation on the right side of the box. Clipped the wire leading out of the box and taped in the industrial wire. If James had things correctly doped out, the alarm box was now neutralized and out of commission.

I looked at my watch.

"Four minutes and fifteen seconds," I said.

Harry grunted.

"Was that approbation?" I said.

"Oh, shit," Harry said. He was ducking his head and pointing toward the street.

The headlights of a car cut through the darkness from somewhere down the road beyond the Majestic.

"Red alert," I said.

I tapped the horn once and lightly. It was enough to catch James' ear. He looked out to the street. My view of the car with the headlights was blocked by the Majestic. James scooped up his stool and bag and scuttled toward the corner of the building away from the approaching car.

"Must be about a block up the road," I said to Harry, "and not coming fast."

Harry said, "It doesn't matter how far up the car is if whoever's driving it saw the kid doing all that suspicious stuff."

"It's not suspicious," I said. "It's criminal."

The headlights grew brighter and the car came into sight around the outline of the Majestic.

"Damn, damn," Harry whispered. He crouched in his seat below the level of the window.

The car on the street was a yellow cruiser. Two cops sat in front. The cruiser was moving at not much more than twenty miles an hour, and as it pulled even with the Ace building, James disappeared around the back corner out of the cops' range of vision. Their range of vision seemed limited anyway. The driver was talking and the cop in the passenger seat nodded his head and laughed. Both were looking straight ahead. Swell watchdogs. The talk and laughter carried from the cruiser's window across the parking lot. It made a companionable sound in the late night. The cruiser moved out of my sight down the street.

"Start breathing again, Harry," I said.

I got out of the Dart.

"When I signal," I said to Harry, "give the horn a soft honk."

"Crang, for chrissake, my hands are shaking," Harry said. He held up both hands. They were shaking.

"Use your foot," I said.

I walked across the lot to the edge of the road. The cruiser's rear lights were drifting away, growing fainter as I watched. When the lights were the size of a couple of glowing cigarettes, I raised my hand to Harry. The car horn gave a harsh blare that echoed off the wall of the Majestic. James stuck his head around the rear corner of the Ace building. I held up my arm to him in a stop motion and looked back down the road. Two or three minutes went by and there was no sign of a returning cruiser. I waved at James. He came out from behind the building with his bag and stool. I walked back to the Dart.

"I'm not cut out for this, Crang," Harry said. His hands were making knots with the white handkerchief.

"You're doing fine, Harry," I said. "Little heavy on the horn, but that's not your specialty."

"Hardly touched the damned thing," Harry said, "and it went off like that."

James was hunched over the door into the Ace building. His body cut off the view from the Dart of what he was up to. After three or four minutes he straightened up. He had a small implement in his right hand, another toy from the cloth bag. James turned in our direction and flapped the hand without the small implement.

"We're on," I said to Harry.

"Wait a minute," Harry said. "He hasn't got the damned door open."

"He wants his audience."

Harry and I crossed the parking lot and went through the gate into Ace and up the paved walk.

"I'm done," James said. If he was feeling triumphant, his face wasn't ready to give it away.

"Turn the knob, James," I said.

"Hold it," Harry said. He looked at James. "You positive the alarm up there isn't going to ring?"

"I bypassed it," James said.

"Yeah," Harry said, "well, how do you know there isn't a backup alarm?"

"No more wires," James said. Along with aplomb and brevity, James had patience. My own wasn't unlimited.

"Harry," I said, "when we get inside, James isn't going to second-guess your accounting techniques."

I nodded at James. He reached out, turned the knob on the door, and pushed. Harry made a loud swallowing noise and held his brief-case to his chest. The door swung open and bumped against the inside wall. The bump was the only sound in the night. No clanging alarm broke the silence.

"Textbook job, James," I said.

James grinned. The grin was part smirk and part snigger. James' face wasn't built for grinning. Or maybe he was out of practice.

19

ACE'S ACCOUNTING DEPARTMENT occupied a double office that looked out the back windows of the building. Harry liked that. No one passing in the street could see him at his clandestine labours. The department consisted of several desks, a medium-sized computer, and a wall of filing cabinets. Harry opened his briefcase and took out three sharpened pencils, a pad of foolscap, and a pocket calculator that ran on batteries. He laid out his tools of the trade on one of the desks and walked over to the filing cabinets.

"You want us to give you a hand?" I asked. James and I were standing at the door into the accounting area. I didn't feel useful.

"No," Harry said. He pulled open one of the drawers in the wall. A row of brown file folders filled the length of the drawer. Each folder had an indicator tag sticking out of the top at the left side. Harry flipped through the folders, stopped, and looked back to James and me.

"No, for chrissake, Crang," he said. "Bad enough in here without you guys hanging over my shoulder."

James and I stepped into the hall.

"You're on guard duty," I said to James. "I'll snoop."

I posted James at a window that gave him a view of the street.

"Anything fishy," I said, "let out a shout."

"What's fishy?"

"You'll recognize it."

I walked down the hall past the accounting department. At the end of the building, two roomy offices faced one another across the hall. The office on the street side was Alice Brackley's. It had a blonde wood desk and armchairs with chintz covering. On the desk there was a photograph in a silver frame of Alice and a man with grey hair who looked old enough to be her father. He probably was her father. Same thin lips.

The office on the other side of the hall didn't display any personal photographs, but the ambience announced Charles Grimaldi. Its furnishings were heavy and masculine. Oak desk, leather sofa and chairs, a LeRoy Neiman drawing on the wall of a halfback crashing through the line. In one corner, a rectangular silver machine that stood waist high gleamed at me. I went over and patted it. It was a photocopier.

At the desk in the accounting area, Harry was intent over an opened file folder. A sheet of foolscap at his right showed a list of one-word notations with numbers opposite the notations. The fingers of Harry's left hand danced on the keys of the pocket calculator, his right hand held a pencil and jotted on the foolscap. Harry's handwriting made up in speed what it lacked in legibility.

"Harry," I said, "a copy machine in the boss's office. That in the usual line of executive furnishing?"

"You want me to get through this stuff," Harry said, "don't interrupt."

"How you making out?"

"This is going to be strictly a sampling," Harry said. "Anything definitive, I'd need four, five days."

"All I'm asking is hints," I said. "Trends."

"One thing I can say already, General Motors doesn't keep books the way these people do it."

I turned back to the door.

"The answer to your question is negative," Harry said from his desk. "It makes no sense for the boss to put a photocopy machine in his personal office."

Two short flights of stairs led from the first-floor hall down to the building's basement. At the bottom of the first flight, I looked through the window in a door opening on to Ace's back property. Two hundred trucks waited in their spaces. In the silence and shadows, they took on anthropomorphic features—ominous, skulking creatures at temporary rest. Another minute and I could have worked myself up for the Robert Redford role in *Out of Africa*. Herd of beasts out there, Karen, dangerous when roused.

A time clock jutted from the wall of the landing just inside the door. Rows of cards in slots covered the rest of the wall space. The cards were light brown and each had a name and an employee number printed at the top. There were twenty-six cards in the line of slots along the bottom row and I pulled every one of them. Made for exciting reading, times punched in to work, times punched out after work. Some employees came on at eight a.m. or a few minutes thereafter and left at six p.m. or a little earlier. Some worked noon till eight or nine at night. And some had a shift that brought them to Ace at six in the morning. Those early birds better not catch the burglars.

Down the second short flight of stairs, the basement was given over to a locker room. Beat-up grey metal half-lockers ran lengthwise along two sides, and in the middle of the room there were two groupings of wooden tables and chairs. One table had a deck of cards on it, and a *Playboy* calendar hung on the back of a closet door. Miss July bore more than a passing resemblance to the nurse on duty at the Majestic. The locker room seemed the preserve of Ace's drivers. They must come in from the yard through the back door, change clothes, play cards, shoot the breeze between trips on the monsters outside. There was a shower stall off one end of the room, and an electric kettle, some mismatched mugs, and a jar of instant coffee sat on a rickety table in a corner. I made three cups and carried them upstairs. Harry took his black, James wanted double sugar.

At three-fifteen, Harry spoke.

"Make yourself useful, Crang," he said.

On his desk, Harry had organized papers and documents into three orderly piles. The tallest pile was of file folders from the wall cabinets, the smallest was his own stack of notations on the sheets of foolscap. The medium-sized pile seemed to be made up of waybills and invoices. Harry pointed to the third collection.

"Them, I want copies of," he said to me. "Use that machine you found in the boss's office, whatever his name is."

"Grimaldi."

"And keep the papers in the same order I gave them to you," Harry said. "That way, I know exactly what file to put them back in, and nobody's going to know we've been looking at this stuff."

"What are these papers I'm copying?" I asked.

"Could be your smoking gun."

The nervous Harry of earlier in the night had been replaced by the confident accountant.

I made three more cups of coffee at four o'clock. Thirty minutes later, Harry sent me back to the photocopier with a second bundle of documents. At five o'clock a thin line of yellow dawn showed across the eastern sky. Time to urge on the troops. When I suggested to Harry that we close down operations, he said he'd reached the limits of immediate information. He began returning the file folders to the cabinets and packing the copied documents in his briefcase. At five-thirty, James walked down the hall.

"Cops out there," he said.

"Son of a bitch," Harry said. He dropped a folder from his hand and the papers inside spilled across the floor. While he hastily gathered them, I went back down the hall with James and peeked through the window. A yellow cruiser was parked across the street in front of the Majestic. Two policemen sat in front talking to one another.

"Same cops that came by when I was doing the alarm," James said in his best matter-of-fact voice.

"You recognize them?" I asked.

"Not the cops," James said. "The numbers. I saw the numbers last time and this car's got the same."

The numerals 3148 were printed in blunt black on the side door of the cruiser. The driver got out of the car and raised his arms in a leisurely stretch. The other cop came around from his side of the car.

He was smoking a cigarette. The driver reached through the cruiser's window and brought out a brown paper bag. He opened it and offered a sandwich to his partner the smoker. The smoker shook his head and the driver bit into one of the sandwiches. He was a methodical chewer.

Harry joined James and me at the watch. He carried his briefcase in both hands. It was much fatter than when we'd arrived.

"Why in hell don't those cops get on with their business?" Harry said.

"They've settled in for a fuel break," I said. "Is it breakfast if that guy's eating a sandwich?"

James said, "I'm gonna need ten minutes to take my wire off the alarm box and hook up the system the way it was before."

I looked at my watch. Almost five-forty. The sun was above the line of buildings to the east.

"By six o'clock," I said, "we'll see traffic out there."

"What're you talking about?" Harry said.

"The guys who drive Ace's trucks," I said. "Six is starting time for some of them."

"Jesus, we're cooked," Harry said. The nervous Harry had resumed ascendancy over the confident accountant. "A goddamned employee's going to come through the gate before those cops move off."

"Something might hurry them on their rounds," I said. "Maybe a disapproving taxpayer."

I went downstairs and opened four of the half-lockers until I found what I was looking for. Inside the fourth locker there was a dirty maroon windbreaker with "Ace" written in yellow across the back. The lettering was the same as on the sign in front of the building. I put on the windbreaker and a John Deere cap that was hanging on the hook underneath it. The windbreaker made a tight fit. A wooden box with a handle lay across the top of two adjoining lockers. It held a collection of wrenches and hammers and soiled rags. I used one of the rags to give my hands and face a wipe of grease. The tool box was heavy, but I hoisted it in my right hand with a jaunty swing and walked upstairs.

"Master of a thousand disguises," I said. James said nothing. Harry's eyes rolled back in his head.

I opened the front door and started down the path, trying like hell to look like I belonged to the tool box. The cop with the cigarette nudged the cop with the lunch. He was working on an apple. Both followed my forthright progress along the path. At the gate, I lifted out the padlock, stepped through, and locked the padlock in place. I tested it with an authoritative yank.

"Hey, you guys got the soft life," I said to the two cops when I was partway across the street.

The cop eating the apple stopped chewing.

"What're you doing around here this hour, Jack?" he said.

I said, "Working, which is more than I can say for you and your buddy."

I let the tool box drop to the pavement. The cop with the cigarette flinched at the bang and the jangle of the hammers and wrenches.

"Working?" he said. "At what?"

"Couple of trucks needed servicing before they go on the road this morning," I said. "Took all fucking night."

The cop threw the cigarette on the road and butted it out with his boot.

"How'd you get here?" he asked. "Car or what?"

"Parked over there," I said. I pointed at the Dart under the trees in the Majestic lot. "I came on around midnight and the only key they gave me is for the lock in the little gate. That satisfy you hotshots? I had to leave my car outside."

Both cops thought over my answer.

"Ask more questions, why not?" I said. I put my hands on my hips and worked my mouth into a lopsided grin. "Make you feel real big-time, hey guys?"

The cop with the lunch put his half-eaten apple in the brown paper bag.

"That lip's gonna get you run in one day, Jack," he said.

"What for?" I said. "Doing my job like an honest citizen?"

The cop who'd been smoking took a turn.

"Don't lean too hard," he said to me.

"So radio in," I said. I was grinning like a fool. Let the law know it had a crazy on its hands. "Tell the dispatcher you got an innocent bystander needs his ticket punched."

The cop who'd been eating tossed his paper bag through the cruiser's window. He motioned to his partner with his hands, palms up, thumbs pointed out. The gesture had its own eloquence. It said the morning was early, the shift was almost over, and a loudmouth was hassling two tired cops. Time to toss in the towel.

"Your lucky day, fella," the first cop said to me. He opened the door on the driver's side. The other cop walked around to his side.

"Look at me," I said. "Trembling in my boots, Officer."

The driver started his engine and squealed his tires as he pulled down the road.

"Hey," I shouted after the car, "have a nice day."

James and Harry came out of Ace's front door on the run. Harry ran like Danny DeVito. They reached the gate.

"You're absolutely nuts, Crang," Harry said.

"Only in emergency situations," I said.

James applied his thin wire to the padlock and sprang it open for the second time in six hours. I went through the gate with the tool box. Harry headed in the opposite direction with his briefcase, bound for the safety of the Dart. I returned the tool box, jacket, and cap to the basement locker room and cleaned my face and hands, and when I got back upstairs, James was standing on his stool and working on the alarm box. He untaped the wire he'd used to bypass the box and fit in new wires running into the box and leading out of it on the other side. It was eight minutes to six. A car drove up the street. James didn't hesitate at his task. The car kept moving past the Ace property.

"Anybody studies real close, they're gonna see what I did here," James said. He was taping the wires into place. The tape made a matching pair of lumps in the otherwise even line of the wiring.

"Not your concern, James," I said.

Three more cars passed in the street.

"Also," James said, "I left a couple of marks where I picked the lock on the door."

Two fine scratches showed where James' pick had missed the key-hole.

"Never mind the perfectionism," I said. "The job's done."

"Almost," James said.

He stood down from the stool. Cars were moving on the street in a regular rhythm of traffic. Four minutes to six. If I were Jimmy the Greek, I'd shorten the odds on an Ace employee showing up. James pulled the front door shut. No bells rang.

"Okay," James said. "The alarm's operational."

"Operational?" I said. "Any chance of putting me up for member-ship in your word-of-the-day club, James?"

James slung the cloth bag over his shoulder and picked up the stool. We were almost to the gate when a blue Cutlass stopped at the truck gate into the Ace property. The Cutlass's driver put on his handbrake and got out of the car. He was rotund and middle-aged and had a cigar in his mouth. He wore a security guard's uniform and carried a ring of keys in his hand.

"Hell of a great day for it," I shouted over to him. My voice resonated with the hearty sycophancy of Ed McMahon buttering up Johnny Carson.

The rotund man stared at us.

"You bet," he said. He had the look of an instinctively friendly old boy, but the presence of James and me was giving him trouble. We didn't belong to his daily routine. The signs of a small inner struggle showed on his face. Quizzical. That was his expression.

"Everything's shipshape inside," I said. James and I kept walking.

"Oh, hell, this shop turns over like a clock," the rotund man said. He took the cigar out of his mouth and gave us close scrutiny. He had piggy eyes.

James and I reached the pedestrian gate.

"What d'you think?" I called to the rotund man. "Lock this thing up or leave it for the others?"

"Office staff don't come in Saturdays," he said. "You guys office people?"

"Consulting job," I said. "One shot and we're gone."

"Yeah," the rotund man said. He was jingling the ring of keys in his hand. "Wondered why I didn't recognize you and the kid."

"In and out," I said. "That's the way it is in our game."

"Well, hell, you might's well lock the gate," the rotund man said. "I'm only supposed to look after this here one for the vehicles."

He pronounced it vee-hick-els.

I snapped the lock and waved to the rotund man.

"See you next year around the same time," I said. My smile was as radiant as Wayne Newton's. And as false.

"Where'd you say you two guys were from?" the rotund man asked. "Like, what company?"

The smile must have been too close to Wayne Newton's.

"Didn't say," I said.

"Maybe I better take a look at who sent you people," the rotund man said. He put the cigar back in his mouth, the keys in his pants pocket, and took a first step toward us. "I mean, what's the kid doing with that there stool anyway?"

A horn honked behind us. The rotund man turned. A pickup truck had pulled behind the Cutlass, and back of the pickup a bright yellow Honda Civic was stopping. The pickup's driver leaned out of the window. He was wearing a maroon and yellow Ace cap and a pair of wraparound sunglasses.

"You gonna jaw all morning, Wally?" he shouted. "Or you opening the fucking gate?"

Rotund Wally looked at the driver and back to us.

"Stay right there," he said to James and me. "Just my duty, you understand, but I gotta check who you are."

"No problem, Wally," I said. The grin made my cheeks throb.

The driver in the pickup sounded another blast of his horn.

"Hold your water," Wally said. He got the key ring from his pocket and unlocked the padlock on the truck gate.

"Soon as he moves his car," I said to James, "we walk over to the Dart."

Wally swung open the gate, secured it in place, and climbed back in the Cutlass.

"Now," I said.

James and I stepped between the rear of the pickup truck and the front of the yellow Honda. I gave a friendly flick of my hand to the man behind the Honda's wheel. He smiled back. Two more cars had joined the line waiting to get in the gate. James and I crossed the road and reached the Majestic parking lot. Rotund Wally had driven his Cutlass far enough into the Ace grounds to allow the following cars room to pull in and pass him. When he stepped from his driver's seat, dust stirred by the wheels of the cars whirled around him. By the time James and I got to the Dart, Rotund Wally hadn't spotted us.

"This is cutting it too fine, Crang," Harry Hein said from the back seat. The briefcase sat on his lap and he'd worked his white handkerchief into a damp ball.

I turned the Dart out of the parking lot to the right. Rotund Wally, his hands swatting at the cloud of dust that enveloped him, was looking left. We drove downtown into the rising sun. My eyes ached, and the rest of my body felt the way it should, like it'd been up all night. No one spoke in the car until I turned off the Gardiner at Spadina.

"Now we're all square, Crang?" Harry said.

"It's a saw-off in the favour department, Harry," I said.

Harry thought he'd need until Monday morning to sort out the data he'd lifted from Ace's accounting department. I let him out of the car in front of his office, then drove James to Regent Park, where I handed the kid six twenties. He raised his eyebrows.

"Bonus for efficiency," I said.

James walked away from the Dart without speaking. I went home and stood in the kitchen and drank a quart of milk from the carton.

20

I **T WAS DARK** and I answered the phone on the first ring. The small black clock on my bedside table read twenty past four. Annie moaned from under a pillow. She didn't wake up. Answering on the first ring wasn't bad for someone who'd devoted most of the previous early morning to breaking the laws against burglary. After I'd got back from Ace, I napped for a couple of hours and met Annie at the airport. In the afternoon, we'd wandered around the Saturday antiques market at Harbourfront and eaten dinner at a restaurant called Spinnakers. It was outdoors and had a view over to the Toronto Islands. I didn't tell Annie about the undercover operation at Ace.

"This better not be a wrong number," I said into the phone. I was whispering.

"Mr. Crang?" a woman's voice said. I recognized Alice Brackley. She slurred her words. Both of them.

"What is it, Ms. Brackley?" I said. I was still whispering. Annie didn't stir.

"I need t'see you," she said. She shushed the "s." "V'ry import'nt."

"I don't think La Serre is open at this hour, Ms. Brackley," I said. "How about noon? Noon today? Sunday? That convenient?"

"Life er death," she said on the phone.

"Whose?" I asked.

The silence on the line lasted long enough for me to suppose Alice Brackley might have gone for a fresh drink.

"V'ry import'nt." She was still with the phone.

"What's the address, Ms. Brackley?" I said, louder than a whisper. "I'll come by your house around noon."

"'At's right," she said.

The next sound from her end was the dial tone. I eased the receiver back on the hook.

"A client *in extremis*?" Annie said. Her voice was muffled.

"Sorry," I said. I felt for her shoulder. "Tried not to wake you."

"You almost made it," Annie said. She snuggled her back against my chest. "Who called?"

"Alice Brackley," I said. "She seemed to be keeping company with Rob Roy."

"Poor thing," Annie said. The snuggle was escalating in erotic degrees. "What'd she want?"

"An appointment."

Annie rolled over on her back and put her arms around my neck. She said, "I won't keep you but a few moments."

"We've got most of eight hours."

Annie and I surfaced from love and sleep a little after nine. The morning felt to me like wheat cakes. I made them from a box that said "jiffy" on the front. They came out lumpy, but Annie said they tasted just like the kind her mother used to whip up. I served the wheat cakes on the kitchen table with orange juice squeezed from real oranges by my own hand, slices of nut bread, some peach preserve I bought one Saturday morning at the St. Lawrence Market, and a pot of coffee. Annie said she was starved, and both of us ate without much talk.

"I've done it again," Annie said after a while.

"Which it is that?"

"The one where I over-research."

Annie went to the refrigerator and got out cream for her coffee. She was wearing a Boston Celtics sweatshirt of mine. It looked fetching with the silk panties. They weren't mine.

"The piece on the critics has to run twenty minutes," Annie said. "Absolutely not a second longer. What I've got is enough to keep the network humming for two hours. All golden stuff."

Annie's Friday in Manhattan had been full of surprises of the welcome variety. When she finished with Vincent Canby at the *Times* office, he offered to put her in touch with David Denby, the guy who writes movie reviews for *New York* magazine. Denby was free that afternoon. Annie interviewed him, and Denby directed her to a party Friday night where she met Molly Haskell, who does the *Vogue* reviews. Annie unloaded her Nagra and Haskell talked into it.

"The things she came up with were bang on," Annie said in the kitchen.

"Which is the trouble."

Annie said, "Every syllable I taped from Jay Scott and the New York people is terrific radio if I do say so myself."

"You're entitled."

"I'll be days in an editing room."

I told Annie I'd drive her to the CBC Radio building.

"No rush," she said. "I've checked. All the editing machines are booked until two o'clock."

I said my appointment with Alice Brackley was for noon. "If an appointment," I said, "is what I've got."

"Poor thing."

"That's what you called her this morning."

Annie leaned her elbows on the kitchen table and held the coffee cup between her hands. On the middle finger of her left hand she was wearing a ring with a rectangular piece of lapis lazuli.

"We're getting to be buddies, Alice and me," Annie said. "I seem to know more than maybe I should about her personal life and I like her. She's nice, nothing more spectacular than that, nice and quite bright and quite good-looking and I like her. And, well, she's got problems. I can't forget the way she was at La Serre that first time all of us met. Alice sat there, partly scared of Grimaldi and partly attracted to him. Or that's how it seems now, and it just strikes me as unfair."

"Very important is how she put it on the phone," I said.

Annie's coffee cup was three-quarters empty. I picked up the pot. Annie spread her fingers over the top of the cup.

"No more," she said. "I'm going to be practically injecting caffeine at the CBC."

I rinsed the dishes in the sink, put the peach preserve in the refrigerator, and took a new cup of coffee back to the kitchen table.

"Alice's call this morning," Annie said, "was it the first you've heard from the Ace people in the last few days?"

"They haven't come knocking on my door," I said. "But you might say I knocked on theirs."

"Anybody home?"

"As a matter of fact," I said, "no."

"That didn't stop you."

Annie's tone was bantering. But with another question or two, she would push me into telling her things she would not approve of. I knew the conversation was headed in that direction and Annie knew it. That would end the bantering.

"You remember Harry Hein?" I said.

"Your accountant client," Annie said. "But wait a sec, I'm not finished with Ace."

"None of us is, not you or me or Harry," I said. "I was able to put my hands on some Ace documents. Harry's analyzing them with his accountant's eye and maybe we'll see what sort of chicanery Ace is involved in."

Annie said, "You phrased that circumspectly."

"Circumspection and I are well acquainted."

Annie leaned back in her chair and stretched her arms over her head. She made small groaning noises and gave the Boston Celtics shirt an interesting workout. The shirt had number 33 on the other side. Larry Bird's number. Annie brought her hands back to her lap.

"Okay," she said. "You mind getting some more of that peach jam out of the fridge and another piece of the nice bread?"

While Annie chewed on her bread and preserve, I looked through the telephone book.

"Ms. Brackley?" Annie asked.

"There's an A. Brackley on one of the streets that run off Avenue Road north of the Four Seasons," I said. "Must be her. Only seven Brackleys in the listings."

Annie said, "Is the means by which you put your hands on the Ace documents likely to get you in trouble?"

"How accurately you remember my circumspect phrasing."

"Must be practice."

"Not now it isn't going to get me in trouble."

Annie reached for a paper napkin and wiped the preserve off her hands. She put a clean hand on the back of mine and squeezed gently. I turned my hand over and squeezed hers.

"Phone Alice," Annie said.

I dialled the number from the phone book and let it ring ten times. No one picked up the phone on the other end.

Annie said, "You thought she'd been drinking."

I put the receiver down.

"She'd packed away enough to make her lose the tremor in her voice," I said.

"She's probably sleeping it off," Annie said.

"Maybe."

"That sounds like a dubious maybe."

"Another thing she said on the phone this morning," I said, "was life or death."

"Was she being dramatic?"

"Possible."

"That's one dubious maybe and a very shaky possible."

I said, "I'll go by her house."

Annie went into the bathroom and turned on the shower. When she came out, she was wearing a towel. It was wrapped around her wet hair.

"Don't think I'm slow," she said, "but is there a connection between your possession of those Ace documents you were talking about and Alice Brackley's case of nerves?"

"I was pondering that one."

"How'd the pondering come out?"

"The connection's too remote," I said.

"But not utterly beyond question?" Annie said.

"First place," I said, "it'd take luck and some fast figuring by a very clever person for anyone at Ace to realize I have some of their documents. Copies of documents, to get specific."

Annie was rubbing her hair with the towel.

"Second place," I said, "it hasn't been established yet, not in black and white, that the documents prove anything crooked on Ace's part."

"That's Harry Hein's role?"

"Right."

"So how come Alice got herself tanked and phoned you out of business hours?"

"Alice is the weak link maybe," I said. I'd almost finished a third cup of coffee. "The rest of the gang at Ace, Grimaldi and the guy with the nose and the others, dirty stuff is old hat to them. But if the company is cheating at the Metro dumps and Alice knows it, she's more likely to run scared when someone comes poking into the operation."

"Namely you."

"Yeah," I said. I put my empty cup on the table. "Me namely."

Annie shook her hair. It was damp and sleek, and she was standing naked in the kitchen.

"Love your outfit," I said.

"Really?" she said. She vamped like Marilyn Monroe. "This old thing?"

I showered and shaved, then got dressed in the bedroom, where Annie had settled on the bed. She had on my terry cloth bathrobe and was surrounded by the Nagra, her interview tapes, and a notebook. She said she was going to play the tapes and make notes on passages that could be edited out when she got to the CBC.

"Tell Alice hello from me," Annie said.

I said I would.

21

SOMEBODY HAD ORGANIZED an anti-nuke demonstration outside the provincial legislature. I drove up University Avenue
straight toward the legislative building and swung the Volks
around Queen's Park Crescent. The demonstration had drawn a small
turnout, not more than a couple of hundred people. A young man carried a sign that read "Arms Are For Hugging," and a folk trio sang a
ragged version of "Blowing in the Wind" from the steps of the legislative building. A sunny Sunday in July didn't strike me as prime time
for a rally against nuclear disarmament. Schedule the same event for a
brisk Saturday in October and two or three thousand concerned Torontonians would show up. They might even find some politicians on the
premises.

I crossed Bloor and began watching for Alice Brackley's street on
the left. Her neighbourhood was in the eastern Annex, where the bat-
tle against encroaching developers was being waged in the front lines.
A handful of condominiums and some tacky reno jobs had insinu-
ated themselves among the Annex's dignified old homes, but the resi-
dents were showing stubborn resistance. The streets remained green
and the houses had a proud, cared-for look. Alice Brackley's street ran
one-way into Avenue Road. I went a block north and parked under a
chestnut tree. It appeared to be in sturdy health.

I walked around the corner to the Brackley house. It was on the north side of the street, a narrow and elegant two-storey townhouse built of red brick that had been recently sandblasted. Two brass lamps were mounted on either side of the front door, and the bricked-over yard had four large wooden tubs overflowing with deep red impatiens. Except for two kids six or seven houses down from the Brackley place leaning on their bikes and absorbed in their talk, the street was deserted.

No one responded to my first ring of the bell at Alice's front door. Two more rings and a rap of the knuckles didn't rouse any action. I looked through the small window in the middle of the door. The window had leaded panes, and I couldn't see much past the entrance hall. It had a floor tiled in black and white and no sign of life.

There was a walkway between the Brackley house and the house on the west that went to the back. I followed the walk and opened a high gate to a bricked-in backyard. Lady had something against green grass. There were more wooden tubs of flowers, geraniums this time, and a set-up of white lawn chairs and tables. A sliding glass door led from the yard into the house. The door was open, and someone had punched a hole in the glass next to the latch. The hole was big enough to reach a hand through, and the glass was sprinkled on the brick outside the door. I stepped over the glass and through the door into the living room.

Alice Brackley was in the living room. She was lying on the broadloom, face up, with her neck twisted at a very uncomfortable angle. In my limited experience, only dead people assumed Alice Brackley's posture.

I stood where I was and listened for noises in the house. A couple of minutes went by, and the strain of listening produced a small pain in my forehead. The only sound was of traffic moving on Avenue Road. If anyone was in the house, he was the sultan of stealth.

I turned and went back out through the sliding door and over the broken glass into the yard. A pair of monarch butterflies zigged and zagged among the geraniums. I sat in one of the white lawn chairs. The idea was to organize my thoughts and control my emotions. It might take a while. After three or four minutes, I realized that a phrase was running through my head. In for a penny, it went, in for a pound. Where had that come from? It made a perverse kind of sense. I'd been retained by Matthew Wansborough to look into possible dubious operations at Ace Disposal, and in the course of my investigations, admittedly of the ad lib variety, I'd committed a crime or two. It was too late to knock off the case even if someone—to wit, Alice Brackley—seemed to have been murdered. I got out of the lawn chair and stepped over the glass and through the door. In for a penny, it went in my head, in for a pound.

I knelt down beside Alice Brackley and felt the carotid artery in the right side of her neck. No beat. I thought about applying other medical tests but rejected the idea. Touching a corpse wasn't turning out to be much fun. Besides, Alice's neck told me enough. It felt cold and stiff. Ms. Brackley had been alive at twenty after four when she phoned me. Eight hours later, her body had no warmth and rigor mortis was right around the corner. She must have died not long after she got off the phone, and the likeliest cause seemed to be a broken neck. There was a high red mark on her right cheek that looked like it had come from a blow. It wasn't makeup. I stood up and shook off a small attack of queasiness.

Alice was dressed for an evening alone. She had on a quilted dressing gown and fluffy slippers with heels. One of the slippers had fallen from her foot. The gold Rolex was on her left wrist. She was lying on beige carpeting that went wall to wall, and around her the living room was furnished in pieces that glowed and shone. Silk fabrics on the armchairs and dark wood tables with a high polish. The paintings on the walls didn't go with the rest of the decor, stolid nineteenth-century landscapes and formal portraits of men with spade beards. Family heirloom stuff. Nothing in the room had been disturbed. Except Alice.

I went upstairs. The master bedroom was at the back of the house. Mistress bedroom. Powder blue was its dominant shade. There was a duvet on the bed, and it and the sheet underneath were lightly rumpled, not as if someone had been sleeping between them but as if someone had been lying in them reading or watching television. A glass filled with brown liquid sat on a bedside table next to a push-button phone. The phone was powder blue. I sniffed the glass. Scotch and not much water. Two video cassettes for the VCR across the room lay among the bedclothes. I leaned over to read the titles without touching the cassettes. The first was a Fred Astaire movie, *Funny Face*, not one of the ten with Ginger Rogers. Audrey Hepburn. The other movie was titled *Going Down on Stud Ranch*. Alice had a dirty little secret.

Two doors opened off the bedroom on the right side, one to the bathroom and the other to a dressing room. Whoever had done in Ms. Brackley seemed to have visited the dressing room and not tidied up afterwards. An ornate jewellery box had been knocked over and its contents dumped across the top of the French Provincial dresser. Some of the contents had probably departed with the intruder. The pieces on the dresser top were costume jewellery of the bauble sort that Alice would wear for slumming. There was no sign of the fabulous Brackley gold collection.

I opened the top drawer of the dresser. It held three smaller jewellery boxes. I looked inside one of them and thought the contents seemed intact. The box held mostly shiny earrings in many shapes and sizes and materials. None of the materials was gold. I shut the box and pushed it into a corner. The edge of an envelope peeked out from under the box. It was an envelope from the Eddie Black photography people, and inside it was a bunch of colour snaps. I shuffled through them. They'd been taken on the patio of a beach house, probably Caribbean judging from the vegetation in the background, and they showed two people. Charles Grimaldi and the late Alice Brackley.

All the photos but one had Grimaldi alone or Alice alone. Grimaldi wore a white swimsuit and tennis shoes. The rest of him was bare and tanned. He had more hair on his chest than Gene Shalit has on his head. Alice was in a yellow bikini. Good figure, and breasts substantial enough to get her a job at the Majestic. Grimaldi must have snapped the pictures of Alice and vice versa. The last photo showed Alice and

Grimaldi together. Maybe a passing tourist took it for them. Alice was giving Grimaldi a lovey-dovey look in the photo. Grimaldi was beaming into the camera.

I put the pictures back in the drawer, went downstairs, walked around Alice's body, and left through the opened glass door. The kids on the bikes down the street remained engrossed in their conversation, and unless someone was spying from behind a curtain, I fled the scene of the crime undetected. I stopped the Volks at a phone booth outside the subway station near the bottom of Bedford Road and dialled 911. The cop wanted to know what I meant by trouble at the Brackley address and who was I, sir? Trouble that went with a break-in, I said, and told him I was a concerned citizen and a very influential chap. The cop sounded like he doubted it. I hung up and drove home to tell Annie about the murder of Alice Brackley.

Poor thing, she'd probably say.

22

ANNIE CHANGED HER MIND about another cup of coffee. I opted for a large vodka.

"Most conspicuously," I said, "the burglary that went with the murder wasn't the kind that professionals commit."

Annie couldn't keep the small tremble out of her hand when she lifted the coffee cup.

She said, "You've just told me that Alice's gold necklace and bracelet and whatnot were taken."

"Or even that a sensible amateur would commit."

"You were there, Crang," Annie said. "You'll have to explain what you're talking about."

"Whoever bopped Alice rigged the house to look like a break-in after the deed was done in the living room," I said. We were talking in the kitchen and Annie had her feet tucked under her in the chair closest to the window. "The broken glass gave it away. It was on the patio side, which means our intruder punched out the sliding door from the inside. Obvious stuff. And, another item, if he was so intent on Alice's gold, why did he leave the Rolex on her wrist? Everything about the set-up smacks of contrivance. Not very sophisticated contrivance."

I was leaning against the kitchen counter. My body wanted me to pace, but no one paces anymore: Doesn't look hip. I settled for leaning and drinking.

Annie said, "Well, how did this intruder get into the house in the first place? If he was some sort of threat to Alice, surely she wouldn't open the door to him."

"Maybe intruder isn't the right description."

"It's not bad for characterizing someone who murders the occupant of a house."

"*Ex post facto* intruder," I said. "Alice let him in because he posed no danger. He was a friend, an acquaintance, a late-night date, and afterwards he turned nasty."

"Killed her, you're supposing," Annie said, "and then arranged the rooms to make it seem like the killing happened when Alice caught a burglar in the act?"

"But why was he so sloppy about the cover-up?" I said. "We don't need to summon Sherlock Holmes from 221B Baker Street to spot the flaws in the faked robbery. It was as if the killer were making a show of his arrogance."

"Or his panic."

I'd drunk three ounces of Wyborowa. It was beginning to kick in with a muzzy warmth in my chest.

"I choose arrogance," I said. "This guy showed the same disdain when he killed Alice. The way it looked to me, the mark on her cheek, the position of the body on the floor, he smacked her hard and he broke her neck and she died. Gave her the back of his hand, you might say."

Annie said, "I can't believe we're speaking like this."

"I'll talk, you listen," I said. "It helps."

The words came out more sharply than I intended. Annie's mouth tightened around the corners, but she didn't say anything. Instead, she reached for her coffee cup. Her hand was no longer trembling.

"Presupposing Alice's murder is tied in to whatever's going on at Ace," I said, "the company payroll has unlimited candidates for the role of murderer."

"May I speak?" Annie said. There was no anger in her voice, but plenty of firmness.

"Be my guest."

"In my book, the list of candidates wouldn't exclude Charles Grimaldi," she said. "If anyone exudes arrogance, it's Alice's boss."

"Even if they were lovers?"

"We don't know that for absolute certain."

"A packet of photographs in Alice's dresser drawer seems to confirm the romance."

"Oh, no."

"Oh, yes," I said. "And there's another problem with pointing at Grimaldi as the killer. On arrogance, okay you're right. But Grimaldi comes from a mob background. Death by smacking isn't how these people handle office problems. They get rid of annoyances with a bullet behind the ear, and the body's more likely to wash up on the shores of Lake Ontario next year, not on the broadloom next day."

Annie said, "You've just reopened the possibility that the killer isn't necessarily an Ace person."

"Nothing about the murder is professional, I'll go that far," I said. "But it's got to be Ace."

"Well, old sport," Annie said, "whatever the explanation is for all this horror, it's a horror that's been taken out of your hands."

"Not really."

"The police are involved now," Annie said. "They'll make the decisions whether Alice's killer is one of those creepy men at her company."

"Cops have no reason to suppose Alice's death and Ace are tied in," I said. "They'll light on the phony robbery fast enough, and down the line, middle of the week probably, they'll put it together that Charles Grimaldi is connected to the mob. But right now, up at Alice's townhouse, all the cops have is the body of someone who happens to be a businesswoman and got herself bumped off by person unknown."

"Unless some responsible party tells them better."

"Yeah," I said. "When Wansborough hears the news about Alice, he might be spooked enough to summon the cops and speak of his concerns about Ace's surprising prosperity."

"The responsible party I had in mind," Annie said, "was a criminal lawyer of my close acquaintance."

"Call me irresponsible."

I swallowed more vodka. Something was making me feel giddy, the vodka or the murder. Likely a combination of both. *Call me irresponsible.* Catchy melody. I hummed the first bars and took another swallow from the glass of vodka.

"*Call me unreliable*," I was half singing. Giddiness had gained the upper hand.

"Crang," Annie said from her chair, "don't you dare."

Her look had a warning in it.

"*Throw in undependable too*," I sang, none too tunefully. I was holding out my arms like Sinatra without the hand mike.

"You idiot," Annie said, "a woman's just died."

But Annie was beginning to show a small grin.

"*Call me unpredictable.*"

Annie's smile occupied more of her face.

"*Tell me I'm impractical*," I sang. It was more wobble than croon.

Annie got out of the chair. Her hands reached toward me in a choke grip.

"*Tell me I'm impractical.*" I was racing the words. "*Rainbows I'm inclined to pursue.*"

The last line came out strangled. Annie had her hands around my throat and she was laughing.

"Crang," she said, "you're disgusting."

"So now you're a music critic," I said. "Pardon, reviewer."

Annie and I hugged and swayed and laughed in the kitchen.

"Bet you don't know what movie the song's from," Annie said after a while. She was talking into my chest.

"I know Jimmy Van Heusen wrote it."

"*Papa's Delicate Condition*," Annie said. "Early 1960s. Jackie Gleason, Glynis Johns, I think Elisha Cook."

Annie leaned on the counter beside me and I put my arm around her shoulder. She was still wearing the terry cloth robe.

"You really aren't going to speak to the police?" she said.

"No, but I'm really going to speak to Matthew Wansborough," I said. "If he goes to the cops right away, my name will come up and that'd leave all sides distressed, me because I don't have any solid answers and the police because they'll conclude I'm holding out on them."

"Holding out what?"

"That's the point," I said. "Give me a couple more days and maybe I'll have explanations to deliver."

"Wansborough's bound to get word of Alice's death some time very soon," Annie said.

"Well, he's family," I said. "Somebody'll call him. Even if not, the murder's going to catch tonight's news for everyone to see and hear and feast upon."

"Imagine what the *Sun*'s going to do with the story tomorrow."

"Take a guess at the headline."

Annie thought for a moment.

"'Sexy Socialite Slain.'"

"The proper alliteration," I said. "Don't know about the sexy."

"We're talking about a newspaper that measures sexiness on the Sunshine Girl standard," Annie said. "By comparison, Alice Brackley is a knockout. Was."

"How about 'Annex Asks Action On Attacker'?"

Annie said, "That's for the follow-up story later in the week."

Annie was past the first shock of the news of Alice's death, and time, vodka, and the sneak attack of the giddies had levelled out the jumpiness I'd brought back from the scene of the crime.

"You're going to keep on playing the intrepid adventurer," Annie said. She was back sitting in the chair. "Okay, but one suggestion. For backup or support or whatever you legal people indulge in, another opinion, why not put Tom Catalano in the picture right away?"

"The sort of job this is," I said, "the law society doesn't smile on."

"Just because one lawyer may get himself disbarred, no sense making it a double disbarment," Annie said. "Is that what you're telling me?"

"Something like that."

23

THE WOMAN ON THE PHONE spoke in the language peculiar to Rosedale matrons. She doubled up on the vowels. Matthew came out "Ma-ah-tthew." The woman was Mrs. Wansborough and she could lay honest claim to the accent. The Wansborough address, when I looked it up in the white pages, was in deepest Rosedale. Very proper and establishment Rosedale is, with a British tilt to it. Mrs. Wansborough said her husband was playing golf. She didn't mind telling me the name of the club where he was playing, the Royal Ontario, but she had a warning.

"Ma-ah-tthew," she said, "dislikes intrusions on his golf match."

"Diphthong," I said.

"Pa-ah-rdon?"

"What you do with the vowels," I said, "I think they call that a diphthong."

"Thank you so very mu-uh-ch," Mrs. Wansborough said. I had no doubt she was truly grateful.

I dropped Annie off at the CBC Radio building on Jarvis and kept going north to the Royal Ontario Golf and Country Club. It was an old stomping ground of mine. When I was married to the beautiful and wealthy Pamela, her father enrolled me in the club. Family tradition, he said, all the males belonged, including quaint sons-in-law. Pamela's father paid my initiation fee, five thousand dollars back then, five times as much today. I went into the club with the notion that golf was an effete activity for snobs. I was half right. Royal Ontario thrives on snobbery, but golf is a sport that plays hard tricks on the mind and body. I couldn't get my handicap under twelve, and after Pamela and I broke up and her father nudged me off the membership rolls, I never played another round.

Royal Ontario is the last Toronto course that still lies inside the city limits. From the first tee, you can hear the big transports changing gears up on the 401. I turned the Volks into the parking lot. Made of white clapboard, the clubhouse is two storeys high and shaped in a U that faces inward away from the course. Around it there are stands of tall rowan trees and flowerbeds that are long on snapdragons. I circled the clubhouse to the lawn that looks over the course's first holes. The course drops gracefully into a valley and makes a wide sweep through the valley's floor until it begins to climb up the back nine toward the clubhouse.

On the lawn, three or four dozen people were sitting in wicker chairs. Stewards in white jackets moved among them serving drinks and tea. You got six fingers of buttered toast with each cup of tea. Ancient club rule. One of the stewards recognized me. His name was Will and he'd served at the club for half a century. Each morning, in season, Will raises the flag beside the clubhouse and lowers it at sunset. Will mourned the passing of the Union Jack. So did the members.

I stood at the edge of the crowd of wicker chairs and Will came over to me. He was slim and erect and had a clipped moustache from his days as a colonel's batman in the Great War. Will thinks all wars are great.

"We haven't had the recent pleasure of your company, Mr. Crang," he said. Will knew that Pamela's father had banished me. His code forbade the mention of such seamy details.

"Other duties, Will," I said. "Other obligations."

"There's something we can assist you with this afternoon?" Will asked.

"Man named Wansborough," I said, "I'd like a word with him."

"The gentleman is in Mr. Thompson's foursome," Will said. He had a quavery voice. "That would be our Mr. Thompson the banker."

"Of course."

"Not Mr. Thomson the architect without a 'p'. They teed off not long past eleven."

"That ought to put them about the fifteenth hole by now."

"Mr. Thompson likes his quick pace."

"Maybe the seventeenth?"

"I should think."

"I'll pick them up at the eighteenth green."

"The gentleman you spoke of isn't a member," Will said. It was an accusation.

"Wansborough?" I said. "Didn't think I remembered him from my time."

"A guest," Will said. He walked away with his tray.

I wandered over to the eighteenth green. Four men were finishing their round. A young guy in lime-green slacks crouched behind his ball and lined up the putt. "For all the marbles, partner," one of the other players said to him. The speaker had a broad, flushed face and was leaning on his putter at the side of the green. The young guy hunched over his ball in a stance that was part Jack Nicklaus, part vulture. He hit the ball with a firm stroke and it ran in a right-to-left curve and curled into the centre of the cup. "Not too shabby," the man with the flushed face said in a loud voice. He and the young guy gave one another polite high-fives and walked away with their two opponents. No one glanced in my direction. Probably took me for a greenskeeper.

One more foursome played through the eighteenth before Matthew Wansborough came into view. The eighteenth hole at Royal Ontario is a long par four, about 440 yards, made longer by its steep upward slope. Good golfers have trouble reaching the green in two. Wansborough wasn't a good golfer. He had a short, choppy swing. He was wearing red-and-green-plaid trousers, and the flaps on the pockets of his white golf shirt had trim of the same material. Wansborough shanked his third shot into a bunker to the left of the green. He needed two whacks at the ball with his wedge before he blasted out. He three-putted. An eight. It might have been my fault. Wansborough gave me a long look before he stepped into the bunker. The sight seemed to unsettle his concentration. Maybe it was my jeans.

Wansborough picked his ball out of the cup and walked to the back of the green where I was standing.

"Good heavens, man," he said in a low, harsh voice, "you're not dressed."

I said, "Any guy got up like Sir Harry Lauder isn't in the best position to pass judgment on taste in clothes."

Wansborough made a snorting noise and looked over to the other men in his foursome. One was putting out and the other two waited at the edge of the path that led to the clubhouse. The man who was putting was large and meaty and wore rimless glasses. I took him for our Mr. Thompson the banker.

"You damned well cost me strokes on this hole, Crang," Wansborough whispered at me. He was annoyed.

"I've got news that might cost you more," I said.

"Couldn't it wait until business hours?" Wansborough asked.

"Right now," I said, "I'm on business hours."

The man in the rimless glasses called over to Wansborough. "The last hole gave these boys the nassau, Matthew," he said. He had a score-card in one hand and was making notations on it with a stubby pencil. "We owe them, um, nine dollars apiece." The way he said it, it might have been his bank's reserve fund.

"You fellows go on ahead," Wansborough called back.

The banker and the other two men gave Wansborough looks that asked why he was spending time on someone who plainly belonged below stairs.

"I'll be right along," Wansborough said. "Order me a gin and tonic."

"Better make it a double," I said to Wansborough.

"Whatever are you talking about, Crang?"

"The kind of news I have," I said, "is usually followed by a double."

Wansborough steered me along the path from the eighteenth green. Where it branched toward the clubhouse, he turned us in the direction of the parking lot. We sat on one of the white benches among the snapdragons.

"Now," Wansborough said. His right leg jiggled. He couldn't wait to join his cronies at the nineteenth hole.

"This is about your cousin."

"My lord, Crang, is that all?" Wansborough said. "If something came out of your meeting with Alice, you could have phoned my office tomorrow."

The man was aggravating me.

"Something came out of the meeting," I said. "Alice's death."

Wansborough's leg lost its jiggle.

"Your sense of drama is appalling," he said.

I gave him an edited version of my early-morning call from Alice and my visit to the scene of her murder. Wansborough looked straight at me most of the time I talked. Toward the end, his gaze drifted away, and when I finished, he spoke in a slow, thoughtful voice.

He said, "We have four spaces left in the family plot at Mount Pleasant."

The guy knew how to home in on the core of a situation.

I said, "We've got more immediate concerns, Mr. Wansborough."

"Alice's funeral is immediate to me," Wansborough said. "Her mother is a widow. She'll be on to me about arrangements."

"Somebody else might be on to you," I said. "The cops."

Wansborough made a hmm sound.

He said, "It's my duty of course to tell the police whatever I know that might assist them in their inquiries."

"For the record," I said, "it's better that you don't know anything."

Wansborough straightened into his indignant posture.

"I know," he said, "that it was my misfortune to have been persuaded by my cousin to invest a good deal of family money in a company that is in unsavoury hands. Now my cousin is dead and my investment remains in the same unsavoury hands."

"Why not keep that summary to yourself for a few days," I said. "Rushing off to the cops isn't going to get back your investment in Ace."

Wansborough looked down at his golf shoes. They were two-toned, black and white, and had little black tassels. Wansborough's strict dress rules got a holiday on the golf course.

He said, "What are you suggesting?"

"Silence."

"You're an exasperating man, Mr. Crang."

"Passive silence."

Wansborough got off another hmm.

I said, "Don't go to the cops with the suspicions about Charles Grimaldi."

Wansborough started to say there were more than suspicions. But his heart wasn't in the objection, and he allowed me to talk over him.

"You're in violation of no laws," I said. "Police come to you with specific questions, fair enough, you answer. But I'm betting that'll be a couple of days. Until then, you concentrate on organizing Alice's place in the family plot."

Wansborough got his spacey look, the one that signalled deep contemplation.

He said, "Approaching the police would seem an unnecessary public fuss."

"Alice is going to be on the front pages tomorrow," I said. "No sense your name joining hers."

"There's something in what you say."

"Done." I stood up before Wansborough did more slow-motion thinking. "I'll get back to you within forty-eight hours."

Wansborough didn't stand up.

He said, "Mr. Crang, you haven't been entirely forthcoming about the nature of my cousin's death."

"Not much to be forthcoming about," I said. "Someone whapped her. With a fist, I'd say. Must have been a man. Guy with a heft behind his punch. Someone built along your lines."

"That last remark is personally offensive," Wansborough said with his old snap.

"I could get more offensive and ask where you were early this morning."

Wansborough rose from the bench. I'd been wrong about his height. He had two or three inches on me.

"I'll await your report," he said. "Wednesday morning is your limit."

"All I want," I said.

"It had better be all you need," Wansborough said. "If you have no satisfactory solution, I'll instruct Mr. Catalano to arrange other means of resolving this disgraceful business."

"Resolve," I said, "is a word that takes in plenty of territory."

"When I retained you last week, Mr. Crang," Wansborough said, "I was seeking information. I wanted to know why Ace Disposal was showing an inordinate profit and why Charles Grimaldi and my cousin were reluctant to furnish me with financial details. Those questions have now become irrelevant as far as I'm concerned. What I wish, Mr. Crang, is the return of my investment. By one means or another, I intend to be clear of Ace as soon as that can be managed."

"Plain speaking. Mr. Wansborough," I said.

"If there's nothing more, Mr. Crang," Wansborough said, "we'll excuse one another."

Wansborough had become more stiff and formal. At his best, he was as yielding as the Tin Man. I'd hurt him with the crack about his whereabouts at the time of Alice's murder. A mild apology might be in order. Wansborough didn't strike me as a prime suspect in the killing. My thinking was, whoever knocked her off had a more direct link into Ace.

Before I could say my sorrys, Wansborough spoke from three inches over my head.

"Last evening, Mr. Crang," he said, "we had friends in for two tables of bridge and a cold supper. I spent the remainder of the night in bed at my wife's side. What transpired in our bedroom is none of your concern."

24

TIME for another phone call.

I made it from a booth outside a Mr. Donut in a down-at-the-heels shopping plaza on Bayview Avenue south of Royal Ontario. A woman answered and called Papa Anderson to the phone. I didn't ask after his health. I knew it was rotten. I asked after wide Tony the boxer. Papa Anderson started training boxers around Toronto when Little Arthur King was drawing fifteen thousand customers to the Gardens. That was the 1940s. These days, Papa sits at home with lung cancer.

"Guy you're talkin' about," Papa said, "sounds to me like Tony Flanagan."

A couple of years earlier, Papa went on, a fight manager named Curly Snider hired him at a day rate to teach Tony Flanagan ring refinements. The lessons didn't take. Tony was a natural brawler. But he had guts, Papa said, and he wasn't a bad kid once you got past the bravado. Papa didn't say bravado. He said bullshit.

"The kid gets main events down east," Papa said. "They bring him in, Truro, Sackville, them five-hundred-dollar towns, Tony's the opponent, fights whichever's the local comer. Name looks good on the posters, y'know, Irish from Toronto. He doesn't lose all the time, Tony. The kid stands up."

Papa said Tony trained at a gym on the Danforth. "Place's got some swank lately, I hear," he said. "Barbells, machines, kind of shit tightens up a boxer's muscles. Marty's it's called, used to be a real nice rathole."

I thanked Papa and said I'd drop by soon and talk. Papa said sure, as long as I didn't make it next year.

I drove down Bayview and took the cutoff to Danforth Avenue. Past Broadview, Danforth blossoms into a corner of Athens. The restaurants and travel agencies and produce stores are Greek and so is the lettering on the top half of the street signs. Greeks own the businesses, but not many live in the neighbourhood. They got prosperous and moved out to the suburbs. Yuppies are buying up the roomy old turn-of-the-century brick houses. They're installing rock gardens on the front lawns, parking BMWs in the driveways, and striking a truce with the last of the working folk who've stayed on in the Danforth family homesteads.

Marty's Gym was in the fifth block east of Broadview. I parked on a side street outside a house that had been done over with metallic grey shutters and brick painted a raspberry shade. The gym was on the second floor over Koustopolos Video. Fifty per cent off on Irene Pappas movies. A double flight of stairs covered in worn linoleum led up to a large space, more loft than room, that smelled of sweat and last week's socks. There were peeling George Chuvalo posters on the wall and a hand-lettered sign that admonished patrons to mind their language and their valuables. A ring with thick ropes dominated the space, though it was getting competition from a silver Nautilus in one corner. The young man whose biceps were locked into the machine seemed more intent on attaining Mr. Universe's title than Thomas Hit-Man Hearns'. The other men at work, nine or ten of them, were pursuing more boxerly activities. Skipping rope, punching bags, shadowboxing, breathing through the nose.

Tony Flanagan stood out in the surroundings. He was the only white boxer and the bulkiest. The rest, skinny and black, were light-weights and welters, quick, bouncy kids. Tony was dogged and stolid and was administering vicious damage to a heavy bag. A grey-haired black man with a moustache like Count Basie's was holding the bag in place and offering encouraging words. Tony didn't need encouragement. His fists hit deep and solid into the bag. I admired from the sidelines until five minutes went by and the black man pulled the bag away.

"Enough, man," he said.

I stepped into Tony's line of vision. He took ten seconds to make the connection.

"Reggie," he said to the black man, "get that guy outta here."

The black man put his hand lightly on my arm. "Hey, mister, Tony say leave, best be you split."

I said, "Papa Anderson, you hear the name, Tony, Papa Anderson told me where to find you."

Tony frowned.

He said, "How's an asshole like you get off talkin' to Papa?"

"He trained me, too," I said.

The black man looked from me to Tony, took his hand off my arm, and began to peel away the small gloves that Tony wore to punch the heavy bag.

"College fighting, Tony," I said. "Not like you."

Sweat stood off Tony's face in hot little beads. He had on a grey T-shirt, purple boxing shorts, and black boots laced up to his shins. The T-shirt was dark at the armpits.

The black man said to Tony, "Can't stand around, man."

"I'll wait till you finish, Tony," I said. "All I'm asking is talk."

"You know Papa?" Tony said. He needed time to compute the information.

"Since I was nineteen."

The black man prodded at Tony.

"You want, stick around," Tony said. "I might talk to you. Might not."

"I'm a spellbinding conversationalist."

"Might put my fist in your face like Mr. Nash wanted me."

"Take my chances."

Tony skipped rope. He lay on a bench and caught a medicine ball that Reggie the black man tossed onto his stomach. He threw punches at the air in front of a floor-length mirror while Reggie chanted beside him.

"Jab, hook, jab, hook, bap, bap, bap." Reggie's voice had a light Caribbean lilt. "Upstairs, downstairs, chigga, chigga, chigga."

After thirty minutes of labours, Tony put a towel around his neck and went into a room that said "Men" on the door. I didn't see any women on the premises. Two black lightweights wearing head protectors as formidable as space helmets flitted around the ring tossing punches at one another in blurs. Float like a butterfly, sting like a bee. By the time I was beginning to grow impatient, Tony emerged from Men looking fresh and sleek. His hair was damp and his straw hat sat on top of it.

I resumed my Papa Anderson pitch. Tony brushed past me at a swift clip and made an abrupt gesture with his hand. The gesture said to follow him and it struck me as a trifle smug. I followed.

We crossed Danforth to a restaurant called the Willow. It had Stevie Wonder on the sound system and plants hanging from the ceiling. The guys leaning on the bar that ran along one wall looked more Waylon Jennings and hubcap decor. If the neighbourhood was a mix of yuppie and working class, the Willow had a foot in both camps. The menu was Tex-Mex.

"So what about you and Papa?" Tony said. There was no mistaking the tone in his voice. Smug.

I said, "Papa trained pros, but he used to pick up walking-around money at the university. He coached the boxing team in the winters." Tony and I sat at a table in the Willow's window. I went on, "I made the team, middleweight, and whatever I learned, it came from Papa. I got to the intercollegiate finals one year. Lost the decision to a left-hander from Queen's. The guy had this incredible reach. Jabbed me silly."

"Yeah," Tony said, pushing, "what else?"

"Not much," I said. "I liked Papa. Who doesn't? He must have seen something in me, and we've kept in touch ever since."

Tony spoke in a tumble of words. He said, "Nights when Papa's guys are on the card down the St. Lawrence Market, you're there, right? At the fights?" Tony looked like the cat that swallowed the canary. Better, the tiger that swallowed the crow.

"You astound me, Tony," I said. "Is mind reading your sideline?"

"I asked Papa on the phone," Tony said. "You think you're dealin' with some kind of dummy. Shit, listen to this, at Marty's they got a pay phone in the dressing room. I'm back there, I call up Papa and ask about this lawyer comes into the gym, wants to talk to me. I got you figured out, man."

Chalk up one for Tony.

The waitress brought menus and Tony ordered without consulting it. Mexican black-bean soup, something called Tijuana tamales, and Tony wanted a plate of nachos while he waited.

"The training table has changed since my day," I said.

"What I'm eatin'?" Tony said. Indignation had replaced smugness. "I got a good constitution."

I asked the waitress for a vodka and soda, and Tony asked me what I wanted with him.

"To save your hide," I said. Even to me, the line rang of insincerity, but I hadn't dreamed up a more convincing script. "You're up to your ear in fraud. Could be there's no way out of that. But the murder, it's where we might make room for negotiation."

"The fuck you talkin' about?" Tony said.

It was barely possible to get a reading among the collection of scar tissue, unhealed bruises, and broken veins that made up Tony's face, but he seemed to be registering disbelief that was genuine.

"What murder?" he said. "I don't do murder."

"Alice Brackley's."

"She's dead? I seen her Friday walkin' around."

"I saw her this morning lying down. Someone swatted her out with one punch."

"You sayin' it was me?" Tony said. "I never punched a lady in my life. It goes against my religion. Not hard anyways."

"The blow Alice took broke her neck."

Tony said, "Jesus, that's tough. Nice broad, Mrs. Brackley. I used to run into her a little around the office out there."

"How much else do you run into, Tony?" I said. "Payoffs to the weigh-masters at the city dumps? You want to talk about that?"

"What do I know?" Tony made himself busy with the black-bean soup. A thick island of sour cream floated on its surface. "Mr. Nash says drive the dumps, drive the office, drive downtown, I drive. Rest of the time, I sit in the car waitin'."

"Mister innocence."

Tony stopped slurping his soup.

"What is it they call you guys?" He said. "Shylocks?"

"Shysters."

"Yeah, right, shylock's a guy puts money on the street."

"Shyster puts words in people's mouths."

"That's what I'm gettin' at," Tony said. "You're lookin' for me to say somethin' bad about Mr. Nash. Stick his nuts in the wringer for you."

Tony might have been headed some place interesting. I kept my mouth shut.

"Listen, what I'll tell you, you ought to watch your ass as far as Mr. Nash goes," Tony said. "Kind of guy he is, he carries this big fuckin' cannon in his belt. Colt Mag or somethin', I don't know the name. Blow a guy's brains all over the wall. He tells me stories sometimes we're drivin' around the dumps. It's what Mr. Nash does, scare people, shit like that."

I asked, "Would he kill Alice Brackley?"

"For what? They was both at the garbage company."

"Business associates have been known to fall out, especially when it's monkey business."

Tony tried out an expression that passed for disgusted.

"You back to that?" he said. "You're a friend of Papa's, all right, I'm sittin' here talkin' to you. It's a favour. Thing about the dumps, I drive the car. Do what Mr. Nash tells me. Murder, that's news to me. Fraud, also."

Tony waited for a moment, not paying attention to his soup, thinking hard.

"You want somethin'," he said, "you should ask about the bikers."

"The guys who drive Ace's trucks?"

"Them."

Tony's thought processes were diverted by the arrival of his tamales. He soaked them in salsa sauce and ordered a piña colada to wash down the hot stuff. It came in a glass the size of the Seven Dwarfs' bathtub.

I said, "What about the drivers?"

"Huh?"

"Why did Ace hire a squadron of Hells Angels to man the trucks?"

"Yeah, see, thing is the drivers do other stuff. Collections, for instance. Customer's slow payin' his bill, okay, one of the bikers gets sent around, asks for the money, customer shakes in his pants, and, shit, he'll pay double to get that big sucker out of his office."

"Unpleasant all right," I said, "but nothing illegal."

"Well, it's muscle," Tony said, disappointed. "Thought that was the kinda thing you were lookin' for."

"You want to tell me about the hustling?" I said. "Deals the drivers make on the side?"

"You caught on, right, the day you followed the fat guy around in that wiener car you got," Tony said. "Jesus, that stuff's no sweat. Mr. Nash knows what's happening, he laughs. He lets those guys do their deals."

I said, "The driver picks up a load and takes it to a gypsy dump."

"Yeah, a little load, from a house or somethin'. The contractor, guy building the house, he pays the driver."

"Cash."

"Eighty bucks is as high as it goes, a hundred maybe, and the driver has to pay the guy who owns the dump half."

"The transaction never shows up in Ace's books."

"Mr. Nash says forty bucks, the drivers are entitled. Like tippin' a waiter, Mr. Nash says."

"Gotcha," I said. "Forty-buck tip for a collection, something more impressive for a murder."

Tony gave me his stormy look, the one calculated to strike terror into the hearts of the comers in the Maritimes.

He said, "You get out of my face about this murder shit, Mr. Lawyer, or you go drink with them cowboys at the bar."

"Think of this as practice, Tony," I said. "Alice Brackley's dead. The police are going to come around wondering why. Tell me what you know and when the cops ask the same questions, you'll have the answers down pat."

"What's the question?" Tony said. "You talk so much bull, I forget."

"A driver as Alice's murderer," I said, "does that fit?"

"You're asking, did a biker do it for sure, I don't know," Tony said. "But those guys, their morals is all up their ass, y'know what I mean."

I took Tony's splendid metaphor to indicate that murder wasn't unknown as one of the Ace drivers' talents.

"What about Charles Grimaldi?" I asked. "Your boss?"

"Not my boss," Tony said quickly. "I work for Mr. Nash personal. Mr. Grimaldi, he's around, I walk away."

"You don't like the gentleman?"

"Nuthin' to do with it, like or not like," Tony said. "Mr. Nash's a hard guy, that's what he's supposed to be, the way he earns his living. Mr. Grimaldi's a hard guy, he does it 'cause he likes it. There's fighters, certain kind of fighter, hits guys that are already fallin' through the ropes. Weirdos. Mr. Grimaldi's that kinda person. I told Mr. Nash once. I said Mr. Grimaldi's weird, and Mr. Nash told me never mind. That's it, I never mind."

Tony had fibbed when he said he knew nothing about Ace Disposal's wheeling and dealing at the Metro dumps. I'd bet my house on it. I'd make the same wager he was straight with me on the other items. He didn't kill Alice Brackley and he had no first-hand information on who handled the deed. But in his own assessment, he wouldn't rule out Sol Nash, worship the man as he did, or one of the drivers, maybe on a contract job. And there was more. Tony's pigeonholing of Charles

Grimaldi's character seemed to make him, in Tony's mind, another possibility as a murderer.

"You done?" Tony said to me. "You wanta watch me eat key lime pie?"

"Enjoy, Tony," I said. "Thanks for the time."

"I never said nothing against Mr. Nash."

"You didn't throw a right cross at me either."

"Papa Anderson made the difference."

"I'll tell him so."

Tony said, "You go round and see Papa much, him dyin' and all that?"

"I intend to."

"Me, I'm at his place, me and these other fighters, regular every Saturday."

Chalk up two for Tony.

25

THE ROOM ON THE FIRST FLOOR of the CBC Radio building where I found Annie B. Cooke had a high ceiling, no windows, and a machine for editing tape. The machine was large and homely, and when I opened the door to the room, it was playing a passage from one of Annie's tapes.

"Some people say if a movie works in the theatre, it'll work on TV," the voice on the tape, casual and masculine, was saying. "Sometimes yes. *Testament* does. Sometimes no. *Nashville* doesn't. And anyway, you do get the idea of the Mona Lisa when the lady is printed on a bath towel, but what kind of idea is that?"

Annie mouthed "Hi" to me. She pointed at the tape and mouthed "Jay Scott." Her face registered a high-satisfaction quotient.

"On the other hand," Jay Scott's voice continued, "who would order struggling parents with three kids to risk an expensive evening at the moving pictures when chances are about even that the picture in question will have been designed from inception to show up on what Judy Garland called 'the hell where all little movies go when they're bad.' Television. Better by far to rent *Trading Places* for five bucks and save fifty. And that's the real devastation accomplished by video."

Annie pushed a button on the machine that stopped the tape, then punched another button that sent it whirring in reverse.

She said, "Isn't the man a treat?"

"A wizard with words," I said.

"Didn't have to edit a damn thing in that section, which is more than I can say for my other heroes."

Annie was sitting on the edge of one of the two folding metal chairs in the room. The other chair was dotted with tiny pieces of stray tape. I made a motion to wipe them into an overflowing waste basket.

"Yo, Crang, no housekeeping," Annie said. She reached over and caught my hand before it touched the cuttings. "You almost threw out my verbs."

"Every journalist should have a collection," I said.

"Two of the New York people kept dropping them out of sentences," Annie said. She tidied the scraps of tape into rows on the chair. "Whole paragraphs without an 'is' or a 'was' or a 'will'. I had to go through the discards and find a bunch of pasts, presents, and futures of 'to be'."

"Those are the little darlings on the chair?"

"Tomorrow I'll clip them into the stuff I'm using on air. My keepers."

"Make the critics sound literate."

"Crang, these guys are superliterate," Annie said. Her voice bounced in her enthusiasm. "I want them to sound complete."

"With verbs."

"I'm fussy that way."

Annie looked at her watch. She'd been editing for seven hours. I said she needed a protein boost. Annie packed her tapes, and we drove downtown to Joe Allen's restaurant. Joe Allen is a smart cookie who came out of the U.S. Army and opened a New York restaurant that picked up on military dining. Basic chow in a stripped-down setting. The idea worked in Manhattan and Allen took it to Paris and Toronto. The restaurant in Toronto is long and narrow and has wooden floors, red-and-white-checkered tablecloths, paper napkins, and ketchup bottles on the tables. Its decor runs to framed posters and photos of showbiz subjects on the walls. Annie and I sat at a table halfway down the room under a movie still that showed a beautiful woman from the waist up. She was wearing nothing except wide red suspenders. The woman did more for them than Harry Hein.

The menu was chalked on blackboards that were nailed high on the walls. Annie asked the waiter for liver. "Pink but not raw," she said. I ordered a hamburger, and while we waited, we drank from a litre of the house red and I told Annie about my day.

"The way it sounds to me," Annie said when I was done, "it didn't take much silver-tongue treatment to keep your client from making a beeline for police headquarters."

"Wansborough made the right solid-citizen noises," I said. "Objected when I asked him to keep events at Ace under his hat. But two other items took precedence."

"Solving Alice Brackley's murder and what else?"

"Alice is a distant third," I said. "A threat to Wansborough's investment in Ace comes first, and a threat to the good family name is second. Or the other way around."

"All soul, your Mr. Wansborough."

"I don't have to fall in love with my clients to take on their problems."

"Man's gotta do what a man's gotta do."

Annie's liver and my hamburger came with fried potatoes in jumbo size. They'd been hand-cut. The hamburger was thick and dripped juices. I felt like I was entering seventh heaven.

"What was it like," Annie asked, "returning to the scene of your former glories?"

"Royal Ontario?" I said. "As nostalgia goes, it wasn't a blast from the past."

"Truly? All that money and privilege you once knew?"

"I always understood I had the perks on loan," I said. "My ex-wife and her father didn't let me forget who held the purse strings. Them."

Annie was eating the fries with her fingers.

She said, "I never asked before, why did Cynthia leave you?"

"Pamela," I said. "She didn't leave me."

"Pamela. Cynthia. What's the difference? Upper-crust names. So why did Pammie split?"

"You're not getting the hang of this," I said. "It's Pamela to everyone except the girls she went to school with at Branksome Hall."

"They call her Pammie?"

"They call her Pam," I said. "She's got a cousin named Buff and an aunt named Bun. Her mother's Cle. Rhymes with key."

"What's the clue here?" Annie said. "One-syllable names?"

"Yeah, but they need the right ring."

"Not a lot of Glads and Myrts in the Branksome gang."

"Kate's about as common as it gets."

"So," Annie said, "why'd Pam leave?"

"I called her Pamela."

"That's because you weren't eligible for Branksome Hall."

"The reason we separated," I said, after I'd cleared my mouth of hamburger and bun and mustard, "was a mutual decision that Pamela should return to her own kind."

"Migawd, Crang, you make it sound like a case study in Anthropology 101."

"When Pamela was young, when I met her," I said, "she had a rebellious streak."

"Oh, sure," Annie said. "Voted NDP once and married outside her class."

"You're the one who started this conversation," I said. "You want to hear it out?"

"Sorry," Annie said. "I promise to use my mouth henceforth for nothing except chewing liver and sipping wine. Both are divine, by the way."

I said, "Everybody else in Pamela's group was hooking up with guys who were going into their daddies' firms. Lot of bond dealers in there, a few lawyers."

"Not your kind of law, right?" Annie said, breaking her promise.

"Corporate takeovers, leaseback deals, condo mortgages. Law that talks on paper."

"Then what happened?" Annie said. "Pamela trotted you out to the family as a symbol of her tiny rebellion?"

"Not that crass," I said. "In the gesture department, I was a large cut above brassiere-burning. Pamela cared for me. Genuinely."

"Well," Annie said, "shows her innate good taste."

"Put it like this," I said. "It added a dash of piquancy to the love affair that I was the only man she brought home who didn't have his own boat over at the Royal Canadian Yacht Club."

"You had boxing gloves."

"Things went along, three, four years of marriage, and I seemed less exotic to Pamela."

"She must have met your clients."

"She ran out of rebellion," I said. "Her gang went to Lyford Cay for February, flats in Belgravia, walking trips up Kilimanjaro. I didn't fit in with the gang. Pamela stayed home with me out of loyalty, but she felt on the sidelines."

Annie put down her knife and fork and whistled the first bars of "April in Paris."

"Eventually she went," I said. "As the unattached spouse."

Annie touched my arm.

"Never mind, Crang," she said. "I'm prying too much."

"She had an affair with a Swedish guy she met at a hotel on Sardinia."

"Really? How'd you feel?" Annie asked. She was getting right back into it.

"Lousy," I said. "For about a day and a half. What made it less painful is I'd already been through the hard part. I knew the thing between Pamela and me had gone to its grave long before she admitted it to anyone. To me, anyway."

"Prescient you."

"Hardly," I said. "One time I remember, watershed event, Pamela flew to Acapulco with a woman named Sass, her first excursion without me. Sass told her what to pack. New bikini, Sonia Rykiel sundresses, a bottle of Joy. Get my drift? Sass was the bad kid in the gang, and when

Pamela came back, she was changed in ways that told me our marriage wouldn't last into the sunset years."

"What ways?" Annie said. "She cancelled her subscription to *Ms.*? What? Took Amnesty International off her list of charities?"

"Let's just say," I said, "I knew Pamela was on her way home to the family and all that that entails."

Annie picked up her paper napkin from her lap and wiped very slowly around her mouth. She was fighting the urge to ask me more specifics about the change in Pamela after Acapulco. She won the fight.

"Where's Pamela got to?" she asked. It was a neutral question. "Since you and she broke up, I mean."

"She married a guy named Archie. His daddy's firm, Archie's now, makes cellophane wrappers."

"The kind you put peanuts in? I don't believe it," Annie said. "For crackers? That kind of cellophane?"

"I didn't say the old family businesses had to do something distinguished."

"Lot of money in cellophane, I suppose," Annie said.

"It puts Archie close to Pamela's league," I said. "They've got a house in Ardwold Gate and a daughter at Branksome."

"What's her name? The daughter?"

"Cordelia."

"They slipped up there," Annie said. "The kid's buddies'll have to call her Cord."

I was using the fries to sop up the nice red stuff that had oozed out of the hamburger on to my plate.

"What about you?" Annie asked. "I know why old Pamela went into the marriage. How was it from your side?"

"Easy," I said. "She was beautiful, hell of a dresser, knew how to get off a great line, and I was crazy about her."

"Well, I asked, didn't I."

"There was something else," I said. "I was young and foolish."

Annie leaned on her elbows. Her face was about a foot from mine, and it had a sly grin.

"Now," she said, "you're up for somebody mature."

"Close call between you and Cybill Shepherd. You win."

Annie had something with whipped cream for dessert. I ordered another hamburger, never mind the fries.

"Your client might have made an apt second-time-around guy for Pamela," Annie said.

"Wansborough?" I said. "You just insulted Pamela."

"Yeah, I guess," Annie said. "Except for this cellophane blind spot, she shapes up okay."

Annie fiddled at the whipped-cream concoction.

"Fact is," she said, hesitancy in her voice, "about Mr. Wansborough and his gang and your involvement with them, I seem to be experiencing, as of today, this severe bout of ambivalence."

I said, "One guy you haven't met, you don't like the sound of. Wansborough. The other guy you have met, you don't like the looks of. Grimaldi. What's ambivalent?"

"You left out I think it's unnecessarily dangerous for you to get mixed up in any kind of violent nonsense."

"I rest my case against ambivalence."

Annie's upper lip had a line of whipped cream running from one corner of her mouth to the other.

She said, "Alice Brackley's been really on my mind. I met her only those two times, not enough to get tight with her, but I told you this morning, she was the kind of woman I wouldn't have minded seeing a lot more. Now she's dead."

I chewed my hamburger and waited for Annie to go on. She took her time.

"Supposing," she said, "just supposing you figure out what's going on at Ace Disposal, the illegal dealing or whatnot, maybe you'll point the police at Alice's killer at the same time. For me, that's definitely on the approved list as long as you don't do anything fantastically ridiculous."

Annie wiped the back of her left hand across her upper lip and looked at the residue of whipped cream.

"How long have you let me sit here with this fine mess on my face?" she said.

"Homey as Norman Rockwell," I said. "I like that in a woman. Shows you have no airs."

"Next you'll let me slaver in public."

I said, "The contenders for guilty party in Alice's murder come from a small group and not all that select."

"You deduce."

"My conversation with Tony Flanagan helped narrow the field," I said. "But pinning the killer is secondary to what I'm hired to get done."

"By me, it's all that counts," Annie said. "Who cares about a few hundred thousand dollars when the man who might lose them wouldn't notice anyway?"

"Wansborough notices," I said. "Rich men stay rich by noticing."

"And, by extension, so does his lawyer," Annie said.

"One step at a time," I said. "Tomorrow morning, Harry Hein should be able to tell me the nature of the scam Charles Grimaldi is working at Ace. That information may provide the leverage to squeeze Wansborough's investment out of Ace. Wansborough doesn't want to leave his money in the company, not when the reason for putting it there in the first place is dead and gone from her office."

"At last," Annie said, "we get to Alice."

"First the money, then the murderer," I said. "But you're right, the two must be tied in."

"You think you can handle both? Safely, I mean?"

"Package deal."

Annie reached across the table and shook my hand.

26

RAY GRIFFIN phoned before I left the apartment for Harry Hein's office.

"I bet Woodward and Bernstein don't get up till noon," I said.

It was just past eight-thirty. I was drinking a first cup of coffee and reading the *Globe*. It had a two-paragraph item in the Metro section about Alice Brackley's death. A murder-robbery, the story reported, and gave Alice's age, address, and occupation. No-frills journalism.

"Who's this Alice Brackley?" Griffin said. "The story says she worked at Ace and she's dead."

"See," I said, "you really can believe everything you read."

"This is too much coincidence," Griffin said. His voice had its speedy quality. "You come around asking about Ace and a few days later one of its executives gets murdered."

"Are you on the Alice Brackley story?"

"Not officially," Griffin said. "I don't cover routine crime. We don't say 'on' the story anyway."

"What do you say?"

"Assigned to the story probably."

"Okay, are you assigned to the story?"

"What's the difference?" Griffin said. "If there's something here, I'm going to speak to my editors and write it."

"Something's here."

"Yeah?"

"But I don't know what the something is or the location of here."

"You must have facts of some kind, Crang," Griffin said. As his voice got faster, its pitch moved higher. Hadn't noticed that before.

I said, "When I've stitched my facts together, you've earned whatever they come out to."

"If you don't phone me," Griffin said, "I'll phone you. I'm serious."

"I can tell."

"At home, at your office, I swear."

The coffee was gone from my cup. I wouldn't stay for another.

"Is that what Alice Brackley's murder is called down there at the fourth estate?" I asked. "Routine crime?"

"At the moment," Griffin said.

The morning traffic on Bloor Street was jammed back from Bay, and the first parking space I found in the indoor car park on Yorkville was up on the sixth level. It wasn't starting out to be my best day. Harry Hein's face did nothing to lighten the load. The arrangement of lines, folds, and creased skin looked familiar and unhealthy. But his manner was more upbeat than it had been when I'd last seen him by dawn's early light on Saturday.

"Exactly like I figured, Crang," Harry said. "And then some."

He was sitting behind the desk in his office, jacket off, red suspenders on display. I recognized the papers on the desk as the copies of invoices and other documents we'd taken from Ace Disposal's accounting department. Harry paid no heed to the papers. It was the computer that had his attention. He was stroking it.

"I punched in the numbers last night," Harry said. "Real incriminating stuff we got here, Crang."

"Harry, leave the lawyer talk to me," I said. "You stick to accountant's language."

"Well, in plain man's terminology, Mr. Crang," Harry said, putting a testy touch to each word, "somebody at Ace is a crook and very blatant about it."

"Line it up for me."

"It would be my pleasure," Harry said. He was doing a Ralph Kramden to my Ed Norton.

"All righty," Harry went on, "you remember we talked possibilities the first time you came to the office. I said it might be Ace was in cahoots with the weigh-masters at the dumps."

"I remember."

"Boy oh boy, was I correct."

"About the cahoots."

"The weigh-masters were, and still are, no doubt in my mind, weighing the Ace trucks in light and weighing them out heavy."

"You've got the numbers to establish that?"

"I'll show you," Harry said. He swung his chair around to the keyboard on the computer.

"Don't bother showing, Harry," I said. "Telling will do the trick."

Harry gave me a baleful look. Most of Harry's looks were baleful.

He said, "You're not making this much fun, Crang."

Harry was right. He went along on the Ace break-in. That won him the right to show off with the computer and its secrets.

"Watch the screen," Harry said. He was typing on the keyboard.

I knew what to expect. My eyes would hurt. I'd seen enough computers and word processors in action. Law firms use them, newspaper reporters, bank managers. Jug-milk stores would be next. White letters on shiny green backgrounds. They made my eyes sore.

"See this?" Harry said. "Isn't it a honey? All in black and white."

"Green and white," I said.

Numbers in long columns blipped across the screen, and Harry performed his guided tour. By giving Ace's trucks a lighter weight going into the dumps and a heavier weight coming out, the weigh-master at the Leslie Street dump saved Ace an average of twenty dollars per load on the fee Ace paid to Metro Toronto. Harry's numbers said so. They said Ace trucks took about two hundred loads to the Leslie dump each day, sometimes more, sometimes less. Two hundred loads at a saving of twenty bucks per load meant that Ace was taking Metro for four thousand a day at the Leslie dump. Spread that across eleven more dump sites and the figure came to a daily forty-eight grand. Harry's computer projected the fraud over a week, a month, a year. The numbers began to look like Wayne Gretzky's salary.

"Not all profit for Ace, you understand," Harry said. "They got their small expenses."

"The bribes Sol Nash takes to the weigh-masters."

"I don't know from this Sol Nash," Harry said. "But there must be bribes. How much, I haven't got enough data to say. My educated guess, based on some entries the Ace books list under Miscellaneous, I'd say the payoffs are on the humble side. Doesn't really matter. Must be nice to have something extra coming in in any amount if you're a weigh-master."

"Miscellaneous?"

"Much-used entry at Ace."

"The truck drivers have to be in on the scam," I said. "They can't be wheeling on and off the scales without knowing the weigh-masters are doctoring the weights."

"You're not going to convict these guys in court if that's what you want," Harry said. "I know, I'm not the lawyer in the room. But there's nothing in Ace's books that connects them with what's going on. No sign of payoffs, nothing like that."

I said, "They get other rewards."

"How so?"

I explained the deals that Ace drivers made on the side with small contractors.

"Yeah, that's a form of payoff," Harry said. "Other thing is, their salary structure is very high for your ordinary truck driver."

"These guys aren't ordinary, Harry."

I stood up from my chair.

Harry said, "You think I'm finished?"

"That's what I'm doing on my feet."

"Oh, please, Mr. Crang, take your seat," Harry said, back in his Ralph Kramden role. "The best is yet to come, yes it is."

I sat down.

Harry typed on the computer's keyboard. He muttered ho-hos and huh-huhs and filled the space around his side of the desk with an uncharacteristically radiant aura. Uncharacteristic for Harry.

"Have a look," he said.

The left side of the screen was taken up with a list of company names. Some I recognized as outfits that did business of various sorts around the city. Laidlaw Construction, a specialist in shopping plazas. Mor-Jim, another big building firm. Consumers' Brick, a large supplier of cement products. Other company names in the list didn't ring any bells with me. On the right side of the screen, opposite the names, were a series of figures. They covered a wide range, mostly from the low hundreds to the high hundreds. Three or four numbers poked over one thousand. The screen wasn't saying what the numbers measured. Currency? Tonnage? Number of goals scored in a lifetime? Harry wasn't saying, either. He clicked at the keyboard and the lists of company names and numbers marched up the screen. My eyeballs were throbbing.

"Very impressive, Harry," I said. "What are they?"

Harry was silent until the parade of names and figures reached an end. He shifted in his chair to face me.

"All the names you saw there, a hundred and forty-four of them, they're Ace Disposal customers," Harry said. "The numbers beside the names are the charges at the dumps for the stuff Ace hauled away for each customer during one day in June this year."

"Those numbers are dollars?"

"Right."

"Why didn't it just say so on the screen?"

"Don't get picky, Crang."

"Okay, those figures showed how much Ace billed the customers," I said, feeling like a fast learner.

"I didn't say that," Harry said.

I held my hands up.

"I surrender," I said.

"Those numbers you saw came from invoices in Ace's files," Harry said. He was talking very slowly. Maybe he'd concluded the learner he had on his hands was less than fast. "I took a sample day for June, pulled out the invoices the drivers brought back from the dumps, and tabulated them the way you saw on the screen."

"Those figures," I said, "are the result of the doctoring by the weigh-masters."

"They are," Harry said. "But that isn't what's relevant here."

I told myself to have patience.

Harry was back at the computer keyboard tapping out another sprightly tune.

"Yes, indeedy," he said and leaned back from the keyboard. "Look again, Crang."

Down the left side of the screen, once again, a list of company names ran in a continuous vertical column. Laidlaw Construction was in place, Mor-Jim, Consumers' Brick, all the rest.

"Same list as before," I said.

"Same one hundred and forty-four customers," Harry said.

Opposite the names, as before, were numbers.

"Is the computer on the fritz?" I asked Harry.

"It's working perfectly, my friend," Harry said. "What you see is what I found."

The numbers were all the same. For each company name, the screen showed the figure 837. I presumed it was dollars.

"The numeral," Harry said, "is what Ace actually billed all those customers for the test day in June I told you I picked out."

Harry kept the names and numbers shifting up the screen. The names changed. The number stuck at 837. Dollars.

I said, "It didn't matter how much Ace dumped for each customer. All of them were billed the same amount."

"That's it," Harry said. "Beautiful piece of trickery. If you worked out an average billing for the day, which I did, average for all the customers, it comes to just over 450 bucks. Ace billed 837. That's a very tidy profit when you're talking a hundred and forty-four customers."

"Where did the figure come from?" I asked. "The 837?"

"That's what makes the scheme so plausible," Harry said. "One of the invoices from the dump, the invoice for a customer called Weyman Iron, showed 837 dollars. It was genuine. The real goods. What somebody at Ace did was make copies of that invoice, the 837, and send them to all the customers along with the normal charge for each pickup. That's seventy-five dollars. Seventy-five plus the amount on the invoice."

"The invoice doesn't show Weyman's name on it?" I said.

"Course not," Harry said. "It's all garbage. The only thing that counts to the customer is he's got an invoice from a Metro dump that shows Ace hauled 837 dollars' worth of junk to the dump. He assumes the junk is his. Why not? These are customers with big businesses. Lot of refuse gets taken away. It comes to 837 dollars? Okay, pay the man."

The list of names on the screen reached its end.

"Ace does it every day," Harry said. "Picks an invoice in the high range, copies it, and sends it to all of that day's customers."

"Gorgeous," I said. "All of them get the same thing, same amount and same invoice number. Except who's to know?"

"I'll print all this stuff out for you," Harry said. "You can take it with you. The invoices and other papers on the desk, them too. Take everything."

Harry pressed some keys on the board and switched on a button at the back. The printer that was hooked into the computer went clackety-clack and an endless stream of perforated paper began to fold out of a slot in the front of the printer.

I talked over the racket.

"Harry," I said, "Ace is cheating at both ends."

"You win a cigar, Crang," Harry said. "That scheme they got on with the weigh-masters, they're chiselling the Metro government out of a million minimum every month. With the customers, I'd say they're taking down another million and a half."

"The first, the deception at the dumps," I said, "that's a kind of negative fraud. Ace is saving itself big money. The other, with the customers, it's pure profit."

"Simple when you know what's happening," Harry said. "Took some brains to set up in the first place."

I sat up in my chair, put my elbows on the chair's arms, and tapped my fingers in front of me. My Alistair Cooke pose.

"There's got to be a flaw," I said.

"What flaw?" Harry said. "At the dumps they probably worked into it gradually, took a little off Ace's weights at a time. Spread it over a few months and nobody up in Metro's head office would notice what the weigh-masters were up to."

"If any questions got asked," I said, "the weigh-masters could blame the drop on a fall-off in building sites in the city. Something like that. Or maybe say it was a seasonal decline."

The printer clacked to a stop. Harry tore the sheets of paper along the perforations and assembled them in neat order.

"On the other side," I said, "the only way the customers might catch on is if they compared charges and discovered everybody was paying the same."

Harry said, "Not a topic that comes up at cocktail parties, Crang."

"Yeah," I said. "But just suppose somebody at Laidlaw Construction or one of those other companies on the list noticed they were paying more than they used to for the privilege of having their garbage lugged away by Ace. Suppose that happened and the guy at Laidlaw with the sharp eyes phoned Ace and asked, 'What about the increase?'"

"Jesus, Crang," Harry said, "I gotta lead you through this by the hand? The guy at Ace would tell him Metro had raised the prices at the dumps."

"Oldest dodge in the books," I said. "Blame the third party."

"No customers'd pick it up anyway," Harry said. "Not likely at all."

Harry's zeal was on the wane. Now that he'd revealed his computer's findings, he wanted me out of the office. He'd enjoyed his performance, but it was time to put the world of fraud behind him. He gathered up the copies of the invoices spread across his desk and added them to the pile of computer printouts.

I said, "It isn't hard to come up with the answer to the ultimate question."

"What's the ultimate question?"

"Who makes the copies of the invoices that go out to the customers?"

Harry was standing behind his desk with the printouts and invoices and the rest of the documents stacked in front of him. It reached a foot high.

"Crang, let me put it this way," Harry said. His voice had become weary. Or was it caution I heard? "There must be a dozen people in Ace's accounting department. From the size of the operation, I'd estimate there's three, four people in accounts receivable, same in accounts payable, couple in the computer area, plus the chief accountant and the comptroller. From out of that crew, you're speculating exactly who knew what."

"Go on."

"There's a bunch of possibilities," Harry said. "You really want to hear it all?"

"Please."

"It could happen," Harry said, "somebody in the accounting department or maybe a couple of them in there working in partnership could be the ones doing the photocopying of the invoices. But I don't think that's the route this scam goes."

"Why not?"

"Gotta originate from higher up."

"Yeah," I agreed, "but wouldn't it at least come to the notice of some of the accounting people that weird things are going on in the billing process?"

Harry shrugged his shoulders.

"Well, it's possible one or two employees could be in on it," he said. "I mean, somebody down the rungs might notice, what the hell, these customers are getting billed the same amount and the invoice numbers are the same for all of them."

"But not necessarily?"

"That's what I'm saying," Harry said. "See, in accounting, people get used to a system and never ask any questions. The system at Ace, I'm speculating the way it went, one guy pulled out the invoice he wanted, one invoice every day, and he photocopied it a hundred and fifty times, however many copies he wanted. He took all the copies to the billing department, and they got mailed to the customers. No questions asked."

"People are used to dealing in Xeroxes."

"Sure," Harry said.

He was still standing behind his desk, shifting from one foot to the other. Harry was growing anxious to be rid of me. He picked up the stack of documents and held them out. "Come on, Crang," Harry said. "Take these."

I tucked the papers under my arm. They weighed four or five uncomfortable pounds.

"The mastermind who does the photocopying," I said, "that's the one person for sure who knows what's afoot."

"Afoot?" Harry repeated. "Sure as hell he does."

"Want me to say it?"

"This is your party, Crang."

"There's a photocopy machine at Ace in the president's office."

"Yeah," Harry said, "but there's a couple other copy machines in the building."

"You agreed," I said, "it was out of the ordinary for the president to have a machine in his own office. Now I think we know what he's using it for."

Harry was making shooing motions with his hands.

He said, "Far as my involvement goes, this is the end of the line."

"You were right, Harry," I said. "We got the smoking gun and it's in Charles Grimaldi's hand."

"Smoking you're saying?" Harry said. "The damn thing's still firing."

He came from his side of the desk and opened the door to let me out.

"Thanks for all this, Harry," I said.

"Don't mention it."

"Never again."

"That's what I mean," Harry said.

He shut the door behind me.

27

DRIVING THE VOLKS down from the sixth level of the car park made me feel like Mario Andretti at the Monaco Grand Prix. All loops and turns and not much straightaway. I jiggered the car through the traffic on Yorkville, past the outdoor cafés where morning tourists were taking their espressos, and turned south at Avenue Road. The documents from Harry Hein's office were locked out of sight in the trunk of the car, and my destination was Charles Grimaldi's office at Ace Disposal. Strike while the iron is hot.

I had the weapons to deal with Grimaldi. I'd offer him my data on Ace's double fraud in exchange for a refund of Matthew Wansborough's investment in the company plus interest, dividends, and other business charges. It was an offer Grimaldi couldn't turn down. Or so my immaculate reasoning went. Getting Wansborough's money in hand was priority number one. Next I'd tend to the other chores. Ferreting out Alice Brackley's killer, blowing the whistle on Grimaldi, covering my own hide.

The truck gate leading into Ace's property was open and I drove through, raising a jaunty arm to the man in the guard's booth. It was Wally, the rotund gent who'd lost track of James and me in the dust of Saturday morning. Wally didn't wave back. I parked the car beside the Ace office building and stepped out.

"Can't leave your car there, mister," Wally called from his booth. "And you gotta check in with me."

Wally didn't recognize me from our first encounter.

"Back in a flash," I shouted.

My voice must have triggered Wally's memory.

"I know you," he called.

His voice had a quiver, the sound of a man done an injustice, and he came striding out of his booth.

"You're the guy mighta got me in deep shit," he said.

"Hold that thought, Wally," I said.

I sprinted around the corner of the building, through the door, and down the centre hall toward Grimaldi's office. Secretaries, accounting people, and other workers at their tasks gave me funny looks, but nobody made a move to halt my sprint. I reached Grimaldi's door. It was open. I braced myself for the grand confrontation and stepped into the office.

It was empty. The desk was clear except for an organized pile of unopened mail in the centre, letters on top, fat envelopes, circulars, and magazines underneath. No indication of Charles Grimaldi's presence on the premises. Quel anticlimax.

"May I help you, sir?" a soft voice asked behind me.

The voice belonged to a tall young woman with black hair to her shoulders and a clingy mauve dress that accentuated lots of breast and thigh.

"I'm Mr. Grimaldi's secretary," she said.

Lucky him, I thought, but I said, "Mr. Grimaldi around?"

"Did you have an appointment? There's nothing in his book."

"No," I said, "but he's bound to welcome me with open arms."

"Mr. Grimaldi won't be in until this afternoon."

"I'll catch him at his house."

"Sir, I didn't say he was at home."

"Cagey you," I said and went back down the hall, not sprinting. I'd try Grimaldi's house. The iron was still hot enough for striking.

Wally the guard was standing beside the Volks looking aggrieved.

"You mighta got me in deep shit," he said to me.

"You did hold that thought."

"It's true," Wally said. His security man's outfit smelled of cigar smoke. "Comin' out of the office the way you and the kid did, early in the morning, the kid with the stool."

"Mr. Grimaldi would be glad to know you spotted me."

"That's the part woulda got me in deep shit."

"You mean you haven't mentioned my visit to anybody?"

"Hell, no," Wally said. "Think I want to lose this job? I been scared since Saturday one of the people inside was gonna say something's stolen from the office. I'd catch some of the blame, sure as I'm standin' here."

"Relax, Wally," I said. "The coast is clear."

"Who the hell are you, mister?"

"Zorro without the mask."

"Fuck off."

I took Wally's advice. I drove up to Dundas Street, stopped at a phone booth to look up Grimaldi's address, and followed Dundas east until it met Bloor. As Alice Brackley had mentioned, Charles Grimaldi lived in the Kingsway, and Bloor was the route into the neighbourhood. It was a short hop from the Ace offices.

The Kingsway is the oasis for rich folks in the west end. It lacks the age, tradition, and grandeur of Rosedale, but the money is everywhere in evidence. Most of the houses are products of the overstuffed school of architecture. They're ponderous and weighty. Stockbroker baronial. Charles Grimaldi's home sat along the line of mansions backing on a ravine that separated the Kingsway from the rest of the city to the east. The property had a stone wall across the front and a driveway that looped in a semicircle to the front door and returned to the street. The house, a dour mix of Tudor and French château, was set fifty or sixty feet back and was shielded by two towering oak trees that kept the lawn in permanent shade. There were three cars in the driveway, a bright red Porsche with the sporty fin at the rear, a Lincoln Continental in black, and Sol Nash's pinkmobile. I parked behind the Cadillac and walked up to the front door.

Sol Nash answered my knock and didn't blink his charcoal eyes when he found me on the doorstep.

"Yeah?" he said. A man of few words.

"I'm a Miss Manners representative," I said. "We go door to door offering lessons in etiquette."

Nash didn't shut the door. Nor did he open it any wider.

"Just a little sample of what we provide," I said, "you might have essayed something more gracious for me in the line of greetings."

"Mr. Grimaldi phone you to come out?" Nash asked.

"I came on my very own initiative. But I have a proposal that ought to fascinate your boss."

Nash favoured economy in all things. Few words and decisive actions. He pulled the door inward just enough to allow me to enter and pointed at a chair where I gathered he wanted me to sit.

"Wait," he said.

Nash sat in a chair on the other side of a walnut antique table from my chair. The chairs and table were set against the wall in a long entrance hall that began three steps down from the front door. On the floor of the hall there was a Persian rug that had a lot of greens and purples in it. No pictures hung on the walls and the only natural light came from two slit windows on either side of the front door. It wasn't a room designed to cheer Grimaldi's visitors.

Behind another door at the far end of the hall, voices were raised in louder than conversational tones. The voices were masculine, and after a while, I decided there were a mere two of them. I couldn't make out the words, but there was no mistaking the emotion. Anger.

A copy of the *Sun* lay on the table between me and Sol Nash. I flipped through it. "Heiress Slain in Negligee." Page three. The headline touched all the bases. Money, murder, and sex. But it wasn't as catchy as Annie's version. And it was inaccurate, unless Alice was wearing a negligee under the quilted dressing gown. I didn't consider discussing the subject with Sol.

Fifteen minutes went by. I was reading Allan Fotheringham's column on the *Sun*'s deep-think page when the door at the end of the hall opened and banged against the wall. Charles Grimaldi was first out of the room. He had on a pair of white flannels and a white V-neck tennis sweater without a shirt. The man behind him had a face that was an older and blurred version of Charles'. His skin was dark and his features coarse. He was wearing a suit that matched the colour of the Lincoln Continental outside. From his looks and style, I took him to be one of the other Grimaldi brothers, Peter the Second or John. Neither he nor Charles appeared to be in the mood for fun.

Both men gave me the once-over. Peter or John spoke first.

"This guy one of your people?" he said, nodding in my direction but questioning Charles.

"He's a lawyer, Pete," Charles said.

Aha, it was the senior member of the second-generation Grimaldis, the brother who ran the laundries in Hamilton.

"He don't look like a lawyer to me," Pete said. "Monday morning and he's dressed like some guy works in your yard."

"I didn't say he was a lawyer of mine," Charles said.

Sol Nash was standing and looking respectful. I stayed in my chair.

"What's your name, lawyer?" Pete asked me. He was in a foul mood and my presence wasn't soothing it.

"Crang," I said, "and it's a thrill to meet another Grimaldi."

"Never mind, Pete," Charles said. "What I got with Crang, it's private."

"Another private," Pete said, close to a shout. His voice bounced around the entrance hall. "Everything's private with you. Pop tells me to come over and ask, how come Charles's living in this big house, drives a fancy little red car a movie star belongs in, throws money around like Rockefeller? I ask and whatta you tell me? Business is good. Shit, you think I'm going back to Pop with that? And this broad at your office, she's in the papers, dead. I ask, what about it? You say must've been some crazy drug-addict burglar. I don't like all this. Pop won't like it. And here's this lawyer coming to your house. What about him? Yeah, I know. Private, you say."

My head swivelled from Pete to Charles. Here was a juicy piece of news. Pete and the rest of the Grimaldi clan weren't privy to Charles' operations at Ace. They thought he was running the company on the up-and-up as I guess he was expected to. Of the four people in the room—Nash, me, the two Grimaldis—Pete was the only fellow in the dark.

Charles stayed calm under his brother's outburst. He put his arm on the sleeve of Pete's black suit jacket and spoke soft words. Pete was sweating and agitated. He kept swivelling his shoulders. But Charles persisted, and control in the room passed to his side.

"Go back in the kitchen," he said to Pete. "Nice new coffee machine back there. Solly'll make you a cup. I settle with the lawyer here, and you and me talk some more. Quiet, I mean. We're brothers, Pete. You and me aren't saying goodbye till I make you happy about everything."

Pete was still swivelling the shoulders, but his anger had been banked. Sol Nash crossed the hall to a door in the opposite wall, and when he opened it, sunlight streamed in and I could see a white kitchen at the end of another short hall. The lure of the bright, sunny room ended Pete's struggle and he followed Sol out of the entrance hall.

"Whatever you're doing here, Crang," Charles Grimaldi said when the door to the kitchen closed, "you've made a mistake."

Grimaldi sat in the chair on the other side of the antique table. His face was set in a glower and he had his hands laid flat on the table. Annie had been right about him. He was actually menacing. When I met him at La Serre, my eye had been taken with his shine and gleam. I hadn't registered all of the menace.

"Call Pete back in here," I said. "He'd get a big kick out of why I've come calling. The whole family would."

"Your choice, Crang," Grimaldi said. "Make your point fast or I tell Sol and Tony to throw your ass on the street."

"I've come to deal," I said.

"You haven't got anything I'm interested in."

"The other day," I said, "you were keen to find out the identity of my client. That's where the deal starts."

"Wansborough," Grimaldi said. "I know already."

"He wants his money back," I said, "everything he put into Ace. Three hundred grand and change."

"That doesn't sound like any kind of deal to me."

"What you receive in return, Charlie," I said, "is the documentation I'm holding on activities at Ace that might give some people cause to feel concern. Your family for one group and the fraud squad for another."

My announcement didn't precisely shatter Grimaldi.

"You're blowing smoke," he said.

"You've got the weigh-masters at the Metro dumps on the take," I said. "That's number one. You're overbilling your customers. That's number two. One and two combined are bringing in better than two million every month."

The snappy speech left me short on breath. Concise, I thought, succinctly worded and irrefutable. I was breathing hard but feeling triumphant.

Grimaldi said, "You know, Crang, I don't like dicking around with guys like you."

"Here's the key word, Charlie," I said. "Documentation."

"You done?"

"Information on paper, Charlie. Invoices photocopied on the same machine you use to phony up the invoices that go out to your customers."

Grimaldi's face gave away nothing. Same gleam, same menace.

"The trade is," I said, feeling marginally less triumphant, "my documents for Wansborough's money."

"That reads like blackmail."

"It's probably a field you're familiar with, Charlie."

"Nobody calls me Charlie."

My trouble with Grimaldi was his reluctance to address the issues. He'd doped it out that Matthew Wansborough was my client. That probably wasn't difficult, not after a week of reflection and a little adding of two and two on Grimaldi's part. Besides, there was no reason for keeping Wansborough's identity under cover any longer. The worrying point was that Grimaldi seemed not to be daunted by my insider information. I'd just finished telling him I could prove he was a crook. The news didn't shake him. It didn't even interest him.

"Charles," I said, "you following me? I got the evidence?"

"I don't know what you're talking about."

Was I handling this wrong?

"Let me explain," I said. "Invoices. Copies thereof. The ones with the same billing and same number that go out to all your customers on any given day. Remember now, Charles? That's the scam I'm talking about. I walked into your office and took out the paper. I'm offering to deal it back."

I listened to myself and I heard babbling. The implacable expression on Grimaldi's face was unhinging my tongue. If he was trying to stonewall me, he was succeeding. I'd come to threaten him into an arrangement, and now I was the guy whose nerves were turning shaky.

Grimaldi slid his hands off the table and stood up from his chair.

"Get the hell out of my house," he said.

"No deal?" I said. Dumb question.

"Crang, the last couple weeks, you've been a pain in the ass," Grimaldi said. "Not a big pain in the ass. A little pain. From what you've said the ten minutes in here, you sound like a guy looking to graduate to major pain in the ass. If I were you, I wouldn't do it. That's my advice. Smart people take my advice."

Grimaldi walked across the Persian rug to the door that led to the kitchen, opened it, and left me alone in the entrance hall.

Bravo, I thought, what a performance.

I went out to my car. Two Japanese gardeners had parked their truck behind me. I had to wait for the two to put down their rakes and hoes and move the truck before I could back out of the circular driveway. The delay made me itchy. What was going through Charles Grimaldi's head? Didn't he believe I had the goods to prove he was a crook? He must. How else would I have been able to recite the nature of his crookedness? Did he want me out of the house in a hurry only because brother Pete was on the scene? Was that it? Would he deal later? Or did he have something else in mind? The gardeners spent five minutes shifting gears and stalling the truck until they moved it far enough to let me squeeze onto the street. I drove away.

Strike while the iron is hot. That's one motto I'd consider dropping from my escutcheon. In for a penny, in for a pound wasn't looking so terrific either.

28

AT FOUR O'CLOCK I bought Annie a drink at the bar across the street from the CBC Radio building.

"Down to thirty-two minutes and a bit," she said, "and still cutting and splicing."

I was of two minds about mentioning my call on Grimaldi. Clam up on the failure or discuss it with Annie in the hope that talk might lead to a more inspired approach? The choice became academic. Annie was so high on coffee and work that the topic of my adventures on the Kingsway passed only fleetingly through the conversation. Annie was giving herself a thirty-minute break from editing the tapes of her interviews with the movie people. She planned to stick with them till twelve that night and Tuesday night.

"Get another ten minutes out," she said. Her voice made her sound wired. "Better than a rough edit but not quite finished product, and Wednesday morning I'll play it for the show's producer. With all fingers crossed."

I cheered Annie on in her endeavours and at four-thirty I drove back to my house. It was quiet when I shut the front door behind me. I went up the stairs, turned to the living room and walked into a rousing welcome from Tony Flanagan.

He socked me on the jaw.

I lost consciousness for a couple of seconds, long enough to hit the floor and settle. I raised my head. Sol Nash was sitting in my armchair and had his shiny black loafers propped on a leather footstool. Pamela gave me the footstool the first year we were married. She thought a lawyer was someone who needed to put up his feet in the evening and smoke a pipe. She bought me a rack of pipes. Tony Flanagan was standing between Sol and me with his fists raised to deliver another haymaker. Tony was wearing his straw hat. I was on my back on the floor. Of the three of us, I cut the least dignified figure.

I said to Tony, "I thought we might have arrived at a non-aggression pact yesterday."

"This here's business," Tony said. "Get up."

"Are you going to hit me again?"

"Unless Mr. Nash says never mind."

I rubbed my jaw. It hurt when it moved. But conversation seemed a wiser alternative to standing up to Tony's hands of cement.

"Well, Solly," I said to Nash, "we're awaiting your instructions."

Nash said, "If he don't get on his feet, kick him."

He was talking to Tony.

I stood up and Tony fooled me. I expected him to lead with a straight right. It was the punch that knocked me down the first time when he had surprise in his favour. I stuck out a quick left jab and tucked my head inside my shoulder to avoid his right. Tony swung a left hook and it landed high on my right cheek before I could block it. Tony didn't need the element of surprise. I fell down again.

After a few seconds I sat up. My head was ringing.

I said, "How'd you guys get in here?"

"Two queers and a dog let us in," Nash said. "Get up."

"Hospitable, didn't you find?" I said, not moving. "The queers and the dog?"

Nash said, "Tony, this guy doesn't quit with the chatter and stand up, put your boots to his knees."

I held my sitting position on the floor.

Tony scrunched his face into a little-boy look.

"I dunno, Mr. Nash," he said.

"You nuts?" Nash said. He bristled in his chair. My chair. "Give the guy your foot and let's do the job here."

"I ain't no kick-boxer," Tony said. His voice had a wounded sound.

"You ain't Rocky Graziano either," Nash said.

"Get up, Crang," Tony said to me.

I said from the floor, "Safer down here."

"Kick him," Nash said.

"Shit, Mr. Nash, I box guys," Tony said. "Kicking people's for somebody had no training."

"Good point, Tony," I said. "Kicking isn't legit."

"Shut up," Nash said to me. To Tony he said, "Stick your shoes in the man. Make him hurt."

"Jesus, Mr. Nash," Tony said.

He turned to his left, addressing the plea to Nash in the chair. Tony's attention was diverted from me. So was Nash's. I reached for a leg of the footstool with my right hand and pushed off the floor with my left. My head was light and buzzing, but my legs and arms felt able to do their stuff. I lifted from the floor and swung the footstool at Tony's head. He turned toward me at the moment I swung, and the stool came at his chin like an uppercut.

The stool made a cracking sound when it connected with Tony's jaw. Tony looked shocked. His straw hat rose off his head and spun three loops in the air. Tony stopped looking shocked. His eyes shut and he fell against the small table beside the chair that Nash was sitting in. Tony landed on the floor. The table tipped over and came to rest on his shoulders. He didn't notice. Tony was out cold. He wouldn't be fretting over the morality of punching versus kicking in the immediate future.

The impact with Tony's jaw had snapped the footstool in two pieces. The larger piece flew across the room and thumped into a row of hardcover American novels on a shelf. I held the other piece in my hand, one leg of the stool. Not much of a weapon. I dropped it.

Nash had his left hand on the arm of the chair and was pulling himself forward while his right hand reached behind him. The man was going for the gun that spread people's brains on walls. Fore-warned is forearmed. Nash's gun was tucked in a holster at the small of his back. The motion of reaching for it flipped up his suit jacket. I leaned over Nash's shoulders and yanked the jacket above his head. My yank lifted his hand away from the holster. The hand came up empty.

"Fucking asshole," Nash said. It was a businesslike mutter.

I pulled until the jacket bent Nash's head level with his knees. A wallet fell to the floor from his inside pocket. I gave the jacket one more tug. It didn't tear. Good tailoring. Nash's head under the jacket developed resistance. It held firm a foot from the floor and began to rise up. He was strong, Solly the Snozz, and as his head and shoulders rose, his right hand was returning to the gun.

I threw a short punch with my left hand at where I thought Nash's face was located beneath the jacket. The punch caught his skull and stung my hand more than it rocked his head. Nash grunted and his right hand kept moving for the gun.

Nash chopped at my legs with his left hand. I grabbed it and twisted the wrist. It was as thick and rubbery as a bologna. My twist slipped in its flesh.

His right hand found the gun. I dropped his left wrist. He brought the gun out of its holster. I raised my left knee. Nash's head was still covered by his jacket. He reached up to shake it off with his left hand. The gun came around Nash's body. I pushed forward with my knee. Nash had the gun pointed to the left, moving toward my stomach. His head came free of the jacket. My knee was aimed at his right hand and I lunged hard. My knee caught his hand and the gun and pinned them both against the arm of the chair. Solly made a noise like it hurt.

"Drop the goddamn gun," I said. My voice sounded loud. It wasn't natural to scream in one's own living room.

My knee pressed deep into Nash's hand. He dropped the goddamn gun. I picked it up and stepped away from the chair into the centre of the room.

Sol Nash looked at me with the almost-black eyes.

"I got a message for you," he said. His suit jacket was rumpled, his black hair mussed, and his right hand looked red and sore. His sang-froid seemed to be intact.

I said, "CN Telegraph's still in business."

I had a firm grip on the gun and pointed it at Nash's chest. The gun didn't feel right. My acquaintance with handguns was limited to holding them in court while I examined and cross-examined witnesses. The guns were trial exhibits that the police had allegedly taken from clients of mine who were facing armed-robbery charges. I'd never pulled a trigger in anger or out of any other compelling motive. Sol Nash's gun, the one in my hand, seemed without the heft of the weapon that Tony Flanagan had described the day before. I put a tighter grip on it.

"Message is," Nash said, "Mr. Grimaldi says you should butt out. Permanent, he means."

"For that you need Tony's fists?"

"Make sure you get the idea."

"Maybe Grimaldi didn't get my idea," I said. "I put a transaction to him this morning of mutual benefit to all parties."

"You tried to squeeze him," Nash said. "Thing like that, Mr. Grimaldi don't take from nobody. You especially, guy like you."

Nash waved a hand as if something unpleasant had come to the notice of his ample nostrils.

"A guy like who?" I said.

"Guy doesn't show respect," Nash said. "Comes to a man's house, no appointment, nothing, man's brother's visiting, and shit, you're looking to jam Mr. Grimaldi."

Nash crossed his legs in the chair, as casual as if the gun in my hand was part of the furniture.

"Reason Mr. Grimaldi sent me," he said, "you forget everything you said about a deal. None of that bullshit, and Mr. Grimaldi wants the papers you said you took out of the office."

"Or what?"

"I'll slam you."

"That didn't work right here this afternoon."

"Slam you when you're not looking. Professional."

"Without Tony?"

Nash turned his flat gaze on the floor. Tony's chest heaved and little bubbles of saliva floated out of his slightly opened mouth. Eyes shut, fists clenched, he was as immobile as the end table that lay across his shoulders.

"Kid was a good driver," Nash said.

I clutched the gun and kept it aimed at Nash's breastbone. It still felt insubstantial.

"Something's wrong with your gun," I said.

"Safety's on," Nash said. "Won't fire that way."

I looked at the gun and back to Nash.

I said, "How come you haven't tried to take it away from me?"

"Figured you knew how to push it off, the safety."

"You figured incorrectly."

"Dumb fuck."

"You or me?"

Nash didn't uncross his legs. I held on to the gun.

Nash said, "What're you talking about, gun's got something wrong?"

"Too light," I said. "Tony down there told me you carry a cannon."

"Sometimes."

"Blows holes through people."

"That ain't it, gun in your hand," Nash said. "Forty-four Mag you're talking about." His voice had grown instructive. "It's for when I go see tough guys. Guys who I need to make an impression on, you understand what I'm saying."

I didn't know whether to feel insulted or relieved.

"That one you took off me, that gun," Nash went on, "it's for pussycats."

I said, "One thing about us pussycats, we land on our feet."

Nash shrugged.

"You got lucky," he said. "Gimme back the gun."

"You'll shoot me."

"Not till somebody says I should."

I turned the gun over in my hand.

"How do you unload this thing?" I said.

"Little switch at the bottom of the barrel, thing your hand's on, push it."

A clip of six bullets slid from the barrel. I flicked them out of the clip, put the bullets in my jeans pocket, and handed Nash his unloaded gun.

"You bluffing about the papers?" he said, returning the gun to its holster. "The ones Mr. Grimaldi wants back? You really got them?"

"I've got them," I said. "In a secure place."

"No place's secure somebody wants them bad enough."

Nash was right. The invoices and Harry Hein's computer printouts were still in the trunk of the Volks. I wouldn't call that secure. I could transfer them to a safety deposit box. Or maybe secrete them down the hollow in the third tree from the left in the park across the street.

"I'll tell you something," Nash said. "Mr. Grimaldi's screwing up here. Between you and me, there's too much commotion going on. You, shit, you're not worth all the jacking around."

"Sol," I said, "you can't keep buttering me up this way."

"I'm talking to you confidential," Nash said. He uncrossed his leg. "You oughta go away quiet on this thing. It isn't like you're arguing a parking ticket for some guy. This is something where there's serious money involved and certain people's jobs."

"Yours, for instance."

"Yeah."

"And part of your job was to take the documents back to Grimaldi."

"Yeah."

"You failed."

"For now."

As Nash spoke, he bent from the chair, picked up the wallet on the floor with his left hand, and came up fast with the back of his right hand. It was aimed at the side of my face. Nash wasn't quick enough. Maybe advancing age, maybe he'd underestimated me. I hadn't underestimated him. Instinct or fear had me suspecting a snaky move from Sol, and as he swung, I slipped inside the arc of the punch and it passed over the top of my head. I backed away and held my hands in front of me.

"Don't do that again, okay?" I said.

"Just so's you know this ain't over," Nash said. He was holding his jacket by the lapels and shaking it. "Fucking wrinkles." He buttoned the jacket and patted its pockets. Apparently our conference had concluded.

"What about Tony?" I asked.

"You put him to sleep," Nash said. "You wake him up."

He walked to the top of the stairs.

"Tell the kid he's fired," Nash said. His feet made thumping noises on the stairs and he slammed the front door.

I went into the bathroom and looked in the mirror. Same face, marginally smarter. I filled the sink with cold water and submerged my head. George Raft used to give himself the same treatment in the movies after somebody punched him. The cold water hurt the sore spots on my cheek and jaw. Or it might have been Jimmy Cagney who soaked his face. One of those guys I shouldn't pick as a role model.

I rinsed a washcloth in the water and spread it on Tony Flanagan's forehead. He was holding firm on the living-room floor. I lifted his head, slipped a pillow under it, and raised the end table off his shoulders. Tony's jaw looked whole and unbroken, but I didn't envy him the headache that would greet his awakening.

Out in the kitchen, I poured three inches of Wyborowa in a glass with ice and took it to the chair that Sol Nash had so recently vacated. I sipped, watched a vein throb in Tony's neck, and contemplated my lame try at putting pressure on Charles Grimaldi. I'd disturbed him sufficiently to send Sol and Tony on a mission to retrieve the invoices but not enough to make him cut a bargain with me. Hadn't nudged him close to a deal. The vodka nipped at the inside of my mouth. Tony's punches must have torn something in there. I'd take another crack at Grimaldi. Give him an irresistible reason to trade with me. This time out, I'd be sneaky clever. Somehow put Grimaldi in a corner. Tony gave off blubbering noises and opened his eyes. I swallowed a long tug of vodka. Tony's eyes were glassy, but he managed to fix his gaze on me.

"Here's the good news, Tony," I said. "Sol thinks you're a hell of a driver. The bad news is he fired you."

Tony got on his feet without a wobble.

"Fired?" he repeated.

"That's what the man said."

"Guess I should of kicked you," Tony said.

He asked for a drink of water, and when he finished it, he left my apartment. He was wearing his straw hat.

29

RAY GRIFFIN was as good as his threat of that morning. He phoned. The call came thirty minutes after Tony had made his exit and I was applying a cold compress to a small lump on my cheek. I gave Griffin a warm welcome. He sounded surprised at the reception. He was more surprised when I said I planned to invite him over for a drink that evening. Major matters to discuss. He said he'd make it about eight o'clock, as soon as he'd wound up an interview. Wonderful, I said. By the time he hung up, Griffin's surprise had acquired a tinge of suspicion. Perceptive of him. He didn't know I had him ticketed for a key part in my latest surefire scheme.

He arrived closer to seven-thirty than eight. Suspicious but eager. He was wearing white pants with bell bottoms and a black tank top that showed the pimples on his shoulders.

"Want a vodka?" I asked. I oozed solicitation. "Sorry, it's all I have in the place."

"Sure," Griffin said. He was carrying a notebook. "What've you got to go with it?"

"Ice."

"Seven-Up? Or Sprite? Something to give it taste?"

I made him a Bloody Caesar and sat him at the kitchen table.

"I'm going to ask two things of you, Ray," I said. "One, you make a phone call. Two, you wait a couple of days before you print anything."

"Print what?"

"They'll stop the presses for this one."

"Unions'd go bananas if anyone stopped the presses."

"Give you a National Newspaper Award then."

Griffin's mouth puckered when he tasted his Bloody Caesar. I'd gone heavy on the Tabasco.

"Who do I phone?" he asked.

"Your old sparring partner Charles Grimaldi."

"So," Griffin said, "the story I get at the end is what's going on at Ace Disposal?"

"Terrific guess, Ray," I said. "But after the phone call, you hold your horses on the article until I say go. No speculation on your own, no digging around at Ace, no requests for interviews."

"And you'll give me the whole picture?"

"Exclusive."

"What do I say to Grimaldi?" Griffin asked.

I slid a piece of paper across the kitchen table. It had three names written on it in my own round hand. Laidlaw Construction. Stibbards Wire. Soward Brothers Concrete. I'd culled the names from one of Harry Hein's computer printouts. Beside the names was the magic number. 837.

"When you get Grimaldi on the line," I said to Griffin, "tell him you're following up on your garbage series from last year. Say you've got fresh leads and want to check out your facts with him. Read off these names on the paper and ask if it isn't odd the three companies were charged an identical amount for a day in the third week in June. That's the 837. Quote him the figure."

Griffin listened, his mouth hanging a shade open.

"Let Grimaldi talk," I said. "He'll have some kind of explanation."

"A glib guy, all right," Griffin said.

"Wait till he's winding down," I said. "Then say, well, you think you might have access to invoices that'll make things clearer."

"After that, what?"

"Nothing," I said. "Grimaldi'll have heard his fill."

"You're not going to let me in on what these names mean?" Griffin said. "And the significance of the 837?"

"Just dollars."

Griffin studied the sheet of paper for clues.

"I could follow this up myself," he said. "The companies are customers of Ace's, that's easy, and something's wrong with them getting billed 837 dollars."

"It'd take you weeks to get past what I've put in front of you," I said. "My way, you get the complete bundle in a couple of days."

I was exaggerating. Maybe lying. I couldn't tell what Grimaldi's reaction would be. He might bluff it out. He might catch a plane for Brazil. He might send Sol Nash around for another visit. Do it to me professional this time.

"Where's the phone?" Ray Griffin said.

Grimaldi was at home, and after Griffin exchanged happy memories of past interviews with him, he popped the questions.

"Uh, Mr. Grimaldi," Griffin said, "I've got some names here I'd like to try out on you for background on the story I'm researching. Laidlaw Construction's one. Stibbards Wire. That's with two 'b's in the middle. And the last is Soward. S-o-w-a-r-d. A concrete company."

As he talked, Griffin kept the receiver cradled between his left shoulder and his ear. He wrote in the notebook with his right hand and held the notebook in place with his left. I sat across the table with the soggy vodka and ice I'd been nursing along most of the evening.

"All customers of yours?" Griffin said into the phone. "That's what I understood. Well, the thing is, Mr. Grimaldi, it's come to my attention, these three, kind of a coincidence here, they were all charged 837 dollars by your company for work done on the same day in June. Wonder if you could explain that for the story."

Grimaldi talked for five minutes without allowing space for Griffin to butt in. Griffin kept himself busy writing in his notebook. The writing covered six pages before Grimaldi took a break.

"Sure, it makes sense, Mr. Grimaldi," Griffin said. "Good business practice, yeah, like you say."

Griffin and Grimaldi alternated talking in spurts. I listened to Griffin's end. I could imagine Grimaldi's end.

"Well, anyway," Griffin said when he had a space, "I believe I have a backup on this. Nothing definite, but a source of mine might make available the relevant invoices, the ones for the three companies I mentioned a minute ago."

Grimaldi took a turn. He raised his voice loud enough for me to make out two of his words.

"Fucking nerve," Grimaldi said. He repeated it a couple of times.

"Just running down my leads, Mr. Grimaldi," Griffin said. He was good on the phone, guileless, and a dangerous hint of information held in reserve. "If I get the invoices, you know, it'll be a matter of nailing down the answers. Confirm what you've explained."

Griffin let the phone fall from his ear. Grimaldi had geared up to a shout.

"That's getting serious, Mr. Grimaldi," Griffin said when it came back to talking time for him. "Nobody's threatening your company. Any event, I can't reveal my contact. He hasn't said he'll definitely come through with the invoices. It's up in the air right now."

Griffin got off the phone and flipped his notebook shut.

I said, "You care for another Bloody, Ray?"

Griffin shook his head.

"The reason the figure is the same for the three companies," he said, "is a system they got at Ace that's a variation on equal billing. Kind of thing Consumers' Gas does with your monthly bill."

"That's what Grimaldi said?"

"Makes crazy sense when he's explaining it, but I don't swallow it," Griffin said. "He asked me out to the office for a look at his accounting system. He said it's state of the art."

"He didn't lie."

"He got abusive when I brought up the invoices," Griffin said. "Wanted to know who the guy was, my source. Made some noise about taking steps. That was his phrase. He said the person with the invoices would end up with his ass in a sling."

"Another one of his phrases?"

"It's you he's talking about, correct?" Griffin said. "Whatever these invoices amount to, you've got them."

I told Griffin he'd get the story complete to every detail as soon as the rest of the pieces had fallen into place. Griffin tried a few questions. I talked around them. He thrust. I parried. And after a while, Griffin said he had to leave for another appointment. I asked if it was with his clothes consultant.

"Sometimes I don't know what the hell you're talking about, Crang," Griffin said.

He left and I put a Lester Young album on the stereo in the living room. It was from the 1950s when his sound had grown thicker and more sombre. I sat in the dark and looked out the window at the park across the street for a long time. Charles Grimaldi would know it was me who'd tipped off Ray Griffin. That was the point. I wanted Grimaldi to know. But he'd also recognize I'd given Griffin only a taste of what I had. Three names and a figure in dollars wasn't the basis for a solid investigation even by a persevering chap like Griffin. But the invoices, if Griffin got his hands on them and took note that the invoice numbers were the same on each of the three, would launch him in directions calculated to make Grimaldi nervous. Had I developed a scenario that might persuade Grimaldi to deal with me on Matthew Wansborough's three hundred thousand? It struck me as a good bet. Scenario? As words go, it was as moronic as interface and relationship. I was developing lazy etymological habits.

I got up and turned over the Lester Young album. He blew "Wrap Your Troubles in Dreams" as if it were a dirge. Nothing was stirring in the park beyond the window. It was a fair trade-off, Wansborough's investment in return for the documents I'd purloined from Ace and a promise to clam up to Ray Griffin and everyone else on what the documents revealed. Grimaldi had too much to lose by not going along with the offer. Bringing Griffin into the picture showed him I meant business. Tough me. Grimaldi wouldn't want Ace's operations spread across several pages of copyright story in the *Star*. The longer I buzzed the idea around in my head, the more persuasive it shaped up. One hitch, I didn't intend to keep my promise to shield Ace. But Grimaldi didn't know that. Would he guess? Could be.

Lester Young moved on to "Skylark" and I kept watch over the darkness of the park. Scenario, interface, relationship. Impact was another, used as a verb. Pepsi commercials impact on the under-twenty market group. Canadian foreign policy doesn't impact on anyone. Charles Grimaldi might impact on my head. I had two more Lester Young albums from the 1950s. I listened to them until past midnight.

30

THE MESSENGER wasn't a kid on a bike or an aging hippie in a Purolator jacket. He had on a black suit and tie, a white shirt, and a black cap like the kind limousine drivers wear. He was about sixty-five years old, and when I answered his knock on my office door, he removed the cap and handed me an envelope.

"My instructions are not to wait for an answer, sir," he said. His accent was plummy, his manner haughty.

"Indeed?" I said. The messenger made me feel inadequate.

"But I am to confirm you are Mr. Crang," he said in clipped English tones.

"Want to look at my driver's licence?" I asked. I wished I had some Earl Grey in the office. Invite him in for a cup. Talk cricket scores.

"Your word is sufficient, Mr. Crang," the messenger said. "I was advised you would be the gentleman in the casual dress."

I changed my mind about the Earl Grey. The messenger left and I opened the envelope. It and the piece of stationery inside were as thick and substantial as parchment. Publishers don't print books on stuff that good. The letterhead announced that it belonged to a man named Frederick A. Lewis who was a vice-president at the Bank of Commerce. His signature was indecipherable, but the letter's one-paragraph contents were crystal clear. They told me that a cashier's cheque payable to Matthew Wansborough had been issued by the bank that morning in the amount of $324,592.17.

The paragraph didn't say from whose account the cheque had been issued. But it had to be Charles Grimaldi. He'd swung into action in speedy time. It was ten o'clock, not much more than twelve hours since Ray Griffin had called Grimaldi from my kitchen.

The phone on the desk rang.

"I want this done clean and immediate, Crang," the voice said on the line. "You got my bona fides."

The voice was Grimaldi's. With a phrase like bona fides, he wasn't kidding around.

"The letter from the man at the bank looks like the real goods," I said.

"It is," Grimaldi said. "I'm holding the cheque. You get it when I get the invoices."

"Last time we talked, you had no use for my little proposal," I said. "I admire a man who keeps an open mind."

"Don't stretch me, Crang," Grimaldi said. "We meet at my office. You bring the invoices. I give you Wansborough's cheque."

"At your office," I said. "Oh, sure. Midnight suit you? I'll drive on out in the dark and Sol Nash can whack me. Make it easy for you."

"Daylight, Crang," Grimaldi said. "Come here in an hour. Eleven o'clock. I told you I wanted this ended simple and right away."

"Eleven o'clock?"

"This morning."

"Sounds okay."

"What's your problem?" Grimaldi asked. "You haven't got the invoices?"

"In a secure place," I said.

"Eleven," Grimaldi said and hung up.

He'd thrown me off balance. I was hoping for a deal but I didn't expect it to come off so crisp and out front. The Ace Disposal offices wouldn't be my first choice for a meeting place, but mid-morning on a business day, the place full of employees, didn't appear to offer the potential for grief.

I phoned the head office of the Bank of Commerce, and after a ten-minute wait on the line, I spoke to an assistant to Vice-president Frederick A. Lewis who confirmed that a letter had gone out to my office from his boss that morning. Better still, he said a cashier's cheque payable to Matthew Wansborough had been sent by messenger to Ace Disposal. The cheque was for $324,592.17.

It was another day of sun and high blue sky, and again I left the top down on the Volks for the drive out the Queen Elizabeth. With any luck, this would be my last run to the west end and Ace's establishment. The landscape was beginning to pall. I drove past the Speedy Muffler outlet, the Rad Man's, and the body shops and came to the wire fence that surrounded Ace Disposal.

The scene did not look as it should. Rotund Wally wasn't on guard in the security man's hut. Nobody was. The truck gate into the property was shut. Beyond the fence, behind the office building, the slots for the Ace trucks were all occupied. Two hundred or more of the monsters sat silently in place. The garage was quiet, and no one moved on the grounds. The place seemed deserted except that the smaller gate that allowed office employees on to the premises, the gate that James Turkin had opened on the night of the great invoice heist, stood open. The door into the office building was also opened wide. Charles Grimaldi was standing in it.

I could have turned the car around and driven back to the city. I could have but I didn't. I was too close to a resolution of the case to shy away at what should be the penultimate moment. Following through seemed the natural thing to do. Or the brave thing. Or was it the foolhardy thing?

The Majestic's parking lot was empty. I turned the Volks across the road and parked at the front of the lot. By the time I opened the trunk, lifted out the documents, and walked back to the gate into Ace, Charles Grimaldi had vanished from the front door. He'd left it open, and I went down the path and into the building. It was silent inside. I held the pile of papers in both arms and headed in the direction of Grimaldi's office. I didn't pass a soul on the way. Grimaldi was sitting behind his desk waiting for me. He wore his customary grim face, but he'd eschewed the usual wardrobe. No whites today. He had on a dark blue suit, the same in a tie, and a light blue shirt.

I said, "The lovely lady who greets your visitors doesn't seem to be on call."

"Not today," Grimaldi said.

"Nor does anybody else."

"I gave the staff the day off," Grimaldi said. "Out of respect."

"For whom?"

"Alice Brackley's funeral is at two o'clock this afternoon," Grimaldi said. "I'll be there."

The slippery devil. Grimaldi had got me out to Ace at an hour when he knew we'd be on our own. Mano a mano. Slick.

I said, "We deal alone."

"Not quite."

Footsteps sounded in the hall outside Grimaldi's office. They were footsteps that went with people who walked hard. Probably walked tall too. Grimaldi didn't move in his chair, hands crossed in front of him on the desk. I looked around, and into the room stepped two guys who hadn't learned to love me. First came the fat Ace driver with the beard and behind him was his pal, the long drink of water I'd smacked with the car door a few nights earlier. Both wore smiles. I noted that the tall guy was limping but took little satisfaction from the observation.

"What's this?" I said. "Reunion of the halt and the lame?"

"Dump that stuff on the desk," Grimaldi said, pointing at the stacks of paper that were still in my arms.

"What about the cheque?" I said.

Mutt and Jeff had stationed themselves between me and the door. They kept silent but they were looking awfully pleased with themselves.

Grimaldi pushed an envelope across the desk toward me. It was of the same formidable stock as the letter I'd received from the snooty messenger an hour earlier. I deposited my papers on the desk, opened the envelope, and beheld a cheque payable to Matthew Wansborough in the amount I'd now committed to memory, $324,592.17.

"Great," I said. "Well, that'll make it time for me to run along. I expect you gentlemen have chores to do."

In the deepest place in my heart, I didn't believe I'd get off that easy. But it was worth a try.

Grimaldi said, "Put the cheque back on the desk."

"Of course," I said. "You'll want to review my documentation first."

I returned the cheque and took two steps in the direction of the leather sofa under the LeRoy Neiman art work.

"Not there," Grimaldi said. "Downstairs."

Grimaldi hadn't raised his voice from the moment I arrived in the Ace building. He conveyed authority with his tone. Low, husky, hard like nails. I was beginning to think Annie's adjective didn't come close to describing Grimaldi in his present state. He was more terrifying than menacing.

"I need ten, fifteen minutes alone with this stuff, Jerry," Grimaldi said. He was talking to the bearded guy. "You and Nicky take Crang downstairs."

Jerry and Nicky? What happened to Spike and Butch? As bad guys' names went, Jerry and Nicky didn't pack much punch. The thought didn't make me any less apprehensive.

Jerry led the way out of Grimaldi's office, I was in the middle, and Nicky brought up the rear. We walked along the hall and down the stairs past the time cards and the door to the outside and into the drivers' clubroom in the basement. Jerry was wearing jeans and a black T-shirt. This one had "Van Halen" printed across the front. Another puzzle. Was Van Halen the guy or the band? Or perhaps both? Nicky had on a lumberjack's outfit. Checkered shirt, thick brown pants, heavy boots. His face was gaunt and pockmarked. He was about as tall, though not as husky, as the average NBA point guard, about six three or six four. There was nothing about Nicky or Jerry that gave me comfort. The three of us sat at one of the basement tables.

"Well, fellas," I said, "what say we let bygones be bygones?"

Jerry laughed. Not a pretty sound.

"We're gonna bygone you, asshole," Nicky said to me. He had a high-pitched voice.

Jerry laughed again.

"That's good," he said to Nicky. "Bygone him. Bye, bye."

"Gone, gone," Nicky said.

I had Abbott and Costello for babysitters.

Ten minutes went by. Slowly for me. Jerry and Nicky tried more plays on words at my expense. None rose to the heights of the bygone routine. Nicky shuffled the deck of cards on the table. He had a nimble touch. He kept on shuffling until the action became mesmerizing and tedious.

Jerry got up and took two paper bags out of a locker. The larger bag had two submarine sandwiches. Power lunch. Jerry sat at the table and chewed on one of the subs. The second bag, much smaller, made a clunking sound when Jerry dropped it on the tabletop. Something heavy in there. Nicky ended his shuffling game and, almost idly, picked up the second and smaller bag and let the contents slide out.

I'd seen most of the contents twice before.

On the table, out of the paper bag, rested a gold chain made of thick links, a gold bracelet, gold earrings shaped like little seashells, a gold Hermès lighter. There was more jewellery, all of it gold and valuable. It was the late Alice Brackley's collection.

"Nice stuff, eh?" Nicky said to me. "Worth plenty."

"Yeah," I said. My voice was a croak. "Very nice, Nicky."

Something inside my head began to swim around, and for a moment I felt faint. These two clowns were killers. It was Jerry and Nicky who'd smacked Alice Brackley. I gripped the edge of the table and waited for the weak spell to go away.

31

GRIMALDI HAD THE PAPER I'd brought him separated into two piles on his desk. The division was obvious: copies of the invoices on one side, Harry Hein's computer printouts on the other.

"You got access to a computer, Crang?" Grimaldi asked me. "And if you don't, who was it analyzed the numbers on these invoices?"

The four of us had reassembled in the president's office. Grimaldi sat behind the desk, Jerry and Nicky flanked the door, and I stood in the middle. My position cast me in the role of the supplicant.

"I have many skills," I answered, inventing a new skill for myself on the spot. "Firing up a computer is only the most recently acquired."

"The concern I got," Grimaldi said, "is suppose somebody else worked this out for you, he knows what's in the papers."

"Nobody else," I said. I wasn't going to drag Harry Hein's name into the proceedings.

"Whose computer'd you use?" Grimaldi asked. "Sol said there's nothing in your office except Mickey Mouse stuff."

"Sol would put it that way," I said. "A friend's computer. He let me into his office on the weekend."

Under pressure, I could fib with the best. Sometimes without the pressure.

"What friend?" Grimaldi insisted.

"Irrelevant," I said. "He wasn't around while I computed."

"You print more copies?"

"Only what's on the desk in front of you."

"What about the diskette?"

"Not to worry."

"Don't give me that bullshit," Grimaldi said. "What'd you do with the diskette? The information still on it?"

"I wiped it clean."

Was that the right terminology? And what the hell was a diskette? Must be the vehicle in the computer that stored information. Made sense, but had I answered Grimaldi's question without revealing my technological ignorance?

Grimaldi took his sweet time considering the response I'd offered. I couldn't tell whether he was genuinely worried that someone else might be in on the computer analysis of his scam or he was merely letting me stew in my predicament. Either way, the conversation over the diskette and my usage of it was just the first and easiest hurdle. What about Jerry and Nicky, the murdering duo? Had they knocked off Alice Brackley on a caper of their own? Or had someone else directed the deed? Grimaldi for example? So many questions.

Grimaldi spoke up.

"If you're lying, Crang, screw it," he said. "Let's get down to business."

He gave his words a different ring. Same hard sense of authority but with a new tone that resounded to me of finality. The words seemed to be a signal for Jerry and Nicky. They moved up behind me, fat Jerry at my right shoulder, towering Nicky breathing on my scalp from the left.

I said, with more than a touch of haste in my voice, "The rest of the business is straight ahead, Charles. Keep the documents, fork over Wansborough's cheque, and I'm gone."

"The business I'm talking about," Grimaldi said, "is what Jerry and Nicky's gonna take care of."

Jerry snickered on the right.

"Let's be candid, Charles," I said, haste beginning to give way to panic. "The two creeps you're talking about, Jerry and Nicky, these guys are killers."

Nicky had his turn at making a risible noise. It emerged in the range between alto and soprano.

I kept talking to Grimaldi. "Alice Brackley's blood is on their hands." Overdramatic, but I needed something powerful in the way of effect.

"You shithead," Jerry said, meaning me.

"Hit home, did I, Jerry?" I said.

Nicky grabbed my left arm.

"They knocked her off and walked out with the jewellery," I said, still addressing Grimaldi. "Alice's gold is in a locker downstairs. It's time to act serious around here, Charles. You phone the cops and we'll put these two goofs in the slammer where they belong."

Grimaldi took my vigorous proposal in the phlegmatic manner I'd come to loathe.

Nicky didn't.

"Kill that broad?" he said. "It wasn't us."

He was gripping my arm with the force of an indignant Arnold Schwarzenegger. I tried to yank my arm free. Unsuccessfully.

Jerry chimed in from the right.

"Where's this bull comin' from?" he said.

The two voices pounding in my ears, one voice per ear, generated a load of outrage.

Nicky said, "Somebody needs to be banged on for sure, it's you."

"That other thing you're talkin' about," Jerry said, "we didn't steal the gold stuff downstairs."

"Mr. Grimaldi give it to us," Nicky said.

I stopped trying to wrestle my arm from Nicky's grasp. At the same time, he and Jerry ran out of shouts. Behind the desk, Grimaldi was showing the first smile I'd seen on his face for a while.

"Light go on in your head, Crang?" he said.

A light the size of the beacon on the CN Tower.

"You killed Alice," I said.

The words came out involuntarily.

Grimaldi seemed to be enjoying his smile.

"You found out she phoned me Sunday morning," I said to him.

One part of my brain warned I was foolish to say anything more, another part wanted to get it all out, everything that was rapidly becoming more or less clear.

"She must have phoned you too," I said. "The booze loosened her tongue."

"A drunk is all she was," Grimaldi said. He overflowed with disdain.

"My God, Grimaldi, the woman was your mistress."

"Good lay," Grimaldi said. "But a drunk."

I didn't have time to linger over the man's attitude to Alice Brackley. It was the murder that counted.

I said, "You got nervous about what Alice might tell me."

My mouth had taken over from both parts of my brain.

"Alice knew something about the system you worked out at Ace," I said. "Pillow talk maybe. She probably didn't know everything, but enough to scare her when I came snooping around. She was going to spill it to me, whatever she suspected you were up to."

Grimaldi's smile had run its brief course.

"When she told you what she intended to do," I said, "you went to her house and broke her neck."

"Enough already," Grimaldi said.

I knew I'd finally got it right.

"What'd it take, Charlie?" I said. "Just one punch?"

Grimaldi's expression, like a piece of Arctic landscape, told me I'd goaded him enough. Too far. He wasn't going to say anything more about Alice's death. But I wasn't ready to quit.

"You made it look like a murder committed by jerks," I pushed on, talking fast, maybe a little hysterically. "And you passed the jewellery along to Heckle and Jeckle here, a couple of world-class jerks by anyone's definition."

My last remark caught the full attention of Jerry and Nicky. Nicky loosened his grip on my arm. He and Jerry were concentrating on Grimaldi. Jerry's jaw had gone slack.

"What's happening?" Nicky asked Grimaldi.

"Nothing's happening," Grimaldi said. "Crang's pulling a number."

"What's he saying?" Nicky asked Grimaldi again. "You looking to set me and Jerry up?"

"You believe that, you got piss for brains," Grimaldi said. His face was showing red through the tan.

Jerry's head had been working on another puzzle.

"You really bump that broad?" he asked.

"Who the fuck cares," Grimaldi said. He was scaling new peaks of annoyance. "Yeah, I bumped her. You satisfied? Now let's do the deal."

He couldn't be talking about the deal I'd come to the Ace offices to consummate. He meant a deal that Jerry and Nicky were apparently privy to.

"Hold on, Mr. Grimaldi, okay?" Nicky said. "The jewellery's like a first payment, right?"

"Melt it down," Grimaldi said. "I told you, it's worth twenty grand on the market."

I'd become the forgotten man in the discussion. But the let-up in concentration on me didn't seem to offer any advantages apart from the chance to recover from the threat of panic and hysteria. If I tried to run for it, Nicky and Jerry would be on me before I reached the door. And I didn't fancy a plunge over Grimaldi's desk and through the window. I needed something else. A diversion. It was a cinch the cavalry wasn't going to rescue me in the last reel.

"Afterwards," Jerry was saying to Grimaldi, "after the job, we get the rest? That's what you mean?"

"Another twenty grand," Grimaldi said. He bit at the words.

"Cash," Nicky said.

"Yeah, cash," Grimaldi said. Bad temper oozed from every pore. "If you assholes got no more questions, let's cut it."

"You gotta understand me and Jerry's position, Mr. Grimaldi," Nicky said. He sounded apologetic. "Crang talks about us killing the broad, the jewellery's hers, whatever the hell, we just kinda wondered."

"Right," Grimaldi said. He had no further use for gab.

Grimaldi took a key from his jacket pocket and fit it into the lock on the top centre drawer of his desk.

"You shoot the guy," Jerry said. "We drive him to the dump."

Shoot the guy?

Jerry was talking about me.

The dump? My nerves were pumping again. If these three had their way, it sounded like my final resting place would be among the debris at the foot of Leslie Street. Nothing like advance knowledge of your grave's location to get the adrenalin flowing.

Instinct took over. I made a move at Grimaldi's desk, more of a lunge than an orderly dive. It was sudden enough to avoid arm-grabbing from Nicky and Jerry, and Grimaldi remained separated from me by the desk. My target was the envelope with Wansborough's cheque. It rested beside the pile of computer printouts. I snatched the envelope, held it high over my head, and danced to the side of the desk.

"Get that thing away from him," Grimaldi barked at Jerry and Nicky.

Grimaldi meant the envelope, or more specifically the cheque with all the numbers on it, and the two heavies went for it instead of for me. The difference was small but crucial. It gave me room to create my simple-minded diversion. I threw the envelope in the air. It fluttered over Grimaldi's desk, and both Jerry and Nicky reached their arms after it. Grimaldi was busy with the top drawer. He pulled a gun out of it. In the couple of seconds that the three guys were occupied with the envelope, the drawer, and the gun, I broke across the office and out the door.

No gunshots followed my flight, but Nicky was about four steps behind me. His boots hit the floor with thumps that sent echoes bouncing off the walls. If I kept going straight down the hall, his seven-league strides would catch me before I made the front door. I turned right down the steps to the basement. The door to the backyard was my objective. Game over if it was locked. It wasn't. I turned the handle and the door swung outwards. Nicky was coming down the short flight of stairs two at a time. I stepped through the door and paused. Nicky hit the landing at the bottom of the stairs and flung himself toward me. My timing was gorgeous. As Nicky flew in my direction, I slammed the door on his head. Smacking Nicky with doors was getting to be a habit.

It was fifteen yards to the first row of trucks. They were parked sideways to me, facing into the yard. I ran across the open space, and behind me I could hear Grimaldi urging on the troops. His voice didn't vibrate with good cheer. I rounded the first truck, and before I disappeared from the sight of my pursuers, I took a swift look backwards. Grimaldi was in the lead. He had the gun in his hand. Jerry hurried along beside him, and Nicky trailed by a few yards. Nicky was holding his forehead with both hands.

I ran down the line of trucks, and when I'd passed six of them, just as Grimaldi and company made an appearance around the first truck, I ducked left. That put me in between two of the monsters. I jumped up on the steps that led into the cab of the seventh truck in the row. I tried the door. If it were a Humphrey Bogart movie, the door would be unlocked and the keys in the ignition. It wasn't a Bogart movie. The door failed to open and I didn't bother checking for keys in the ignition.

Grimaldi's voice sounded somewhere back along the line of trucks. I couldn't make out what he was saying. Jerry's voice answered back. Also unintelligible. I pulled myself up onto the hood of the truck and crawled over the windows to the roof of the cab. The manoeuvre put me ten feet above the ground, and when I flattened myself on the roof, I was invisible from down below. It made a temporary refuge.

I waited two or three minutes. No noises drifted up from Grimaldi or the other two. I raised my head a foot from the roof and surveyed the territory. Grimaldi came into view first. He was standing beside the office building, gun in hand, and looking toward the row of trucks that began the next aisle over from my row. Where were Nicky and Jerry? Grimaldi must have split his trio into separate search parties.

He was playing the backup man, the guy with the gun who'd ensure I didn't get out the front way.

I shifted around on the truck roof, trying to locate Jerry and Nicky. My truck stood in the middle of its row, seven vehicles from the office building and another seven to the garage with the bays for servicing the trucks. The garage seemed a logical place to seek my next temporary refuge. Might find a weapon in there. A crowbar, a wrench, something metal and heavy. How the hell did a crowbar get its name? Any connection with the ugly black birds?

"He ain't along here."

The voice, Nicky's, came from immediately below me. I dropped my head so sharply that it hit the metal of the roof and made a small noise. Boing. It was as loud as a thunderclap to me. I sucked in my breath and waited. Nothing happened. No shouts of discovery. No Nicky scrambling up the truck. The noise hadn't been as loud as a thunderclap to him. Not even as loud as a boing.

I stayed unmoving, and after half a minute I lifted my head again. Nicky was standing beside Grimaldi at the office building. Grimaldi was waving his arm, the one that wasn't holding the gun, apparently delivering fresh instructions to Nicky. Jerry wasn't to be seen, but reason told me that if Nicky had been searching my row of trucks, Jerry must be on another section of the grounds. Reason went on to advise me that this was probably a good time to make my switch to the garage.

I slid from the roof of the truck and trotted to the outside of the row of trucks, putting them in between me and the spot Grimaldi had staked out as his field headquarters. I ran down the row past seven trucks, watching in every direction for Jerry and not spotting him.

At the side of the garage, one truck stood separate from the rest. It wasn't in any of the tidy rows with its brother trucks. And there was something else different about it. Its windows were open. So was the driver's door. Only one answer. It must be the truck that Jerry and Nicky intended to employ in transporting my remains to the dump after Grimaldi finished with his execution job. Must be. If the windows and door were open, the keys might be in the ignition. I hoisted myself up the step into the truck's cab and looked across the dash-board. No keys.

Maybe in the garage. I dropped back to the ground and hustled around to the rear of the garage and through the open entrance into one of the bays. The bay door had been lifted high overhead. I looked around for a board where keys to the trucks might be kept. I didn't see a board or any keys.

All I saw was Jerry.

He had his back turned. He was in the garage and he was looking for me. He held a hammer in his hand. He was trying to be stealthy. Two could play at all of those games. Another hammer, many hammers in fact, lay on a workbench that was within reaching distance of my right hand. I picked one up, a ferocious-looking instrument, and tiptoed after Jerry. He was about six paces in front of me, back still turned, and I covered the space in four fast tiptoes. Jerry didn't hear me. There was something to be said for Rockports with cushiony soles. I hit Jerry in the centre of his head with the flat side of the hammer's business end. He fell forward on his beard. I waited, and Jerry didn't move. No blood appeared from the centre of his head. Clean knockout.

I leaned over Jerry and detached the ring of many keys from his belt. One of the keys had to start the truck beside the garage. But which? There were at least a dozen on the ring. The vision in my head, as soon as I located the right key, was of making the great escape. Start the truck, drive down the rows of trucks past Nicky and Grimaldi, crash through the gates, and soar to freedom. Well, rumble to freedom.

The only way to put my vision on the path to reality was to test the keys in the truck's ignition. I started back the way I'd come, through the open bay door and around the rear of the garage. Before I reached the truck, I stopped, returned to the garage, and picked up the ham-mer I'd used to deck Jerry. I hefted it in my hand. It made me feel semi-secure.

Back outside, I climbed into the cab of the truck and began testing the keys. It was aggravating work, slowed by the shakes in my hands and the necessity to keep a watch for Nicky and Grimaldi. I got through five keys without finding the one that fit the ignition when Nicky came into sight. He was about twenty yards away and walking down a row of trucks in the centre of the yard. As he walked, he was checking under each truck, no doubt on the lookout for my running legs. My legs weren't running. They were in the cab of the truck and they were beginning to tremble.

The eighth key slid into the ignition. Eureka. Soon be on my way. That was the upside of the situation. The downside was that as soon as I started the engine, I'd attract Nicky's notice. And Grimaldi's. No choice. I turned the key in the ignition. The truck's motor started on two sound levels. First it burped. Then it roared. At the burp, Nicky straightened up. At the roar, he came barrelling toward the truck.

"I found him," he shouted as he ran. Liar. It was me who found me for him.

At Nicky's shout, Grimaldi steamed into view at the top of the row of trucks to my left. He had the gun at his side and he was running hard. But Grimaldi was still eighty or ninety yards away. Nicky was closer. Nicky was coming around the front of the truck to the driver's side.

Inside the cab, the space was a confusion of gears and levers and chains. The levers and chains worked the bin on the back of the truck. I wasn't concerned with them. It was the gears that were giving me trouble. I couldn't find a forward shift, something that would get the truck in motion. I was stuck in neutral. I pressed the clutch with my foot and pushed and pulled on the gearshift. The sound of grinding metal emitted from somewhere below me in the truck's bowels. Nothing moved forward.

Nicky's head popped up outside the open window on my side of the truck. He was on the step and he had one hand around the handle of the door. The other hand reached at my head. No chance to pull the old door trick, not as long as Nicky controlled the outside handle. My hammer routine was called for.

I abandoned the hopeless wrestle with the gears and picked the hammer off the seat with my right hand. Nicky had me by the neck and he was squeezing hard. That hampered the hammer-wielding and the cozy confines of the cab didn't leave much room for swinging it. I pushed it instead. Straight into Nicky's nose. A direct hit. His forehead was already bloody from the bang I'd delivered with the back door. The bleeding nose gave him a companion piece in crimson.

Nicky was tenacious. Through the blood and pain he held on to my neck. His hand was weakening, but he didn't need to maintain the hold for long. Help was now fifty yards away. Grimaldi and his gun were covering the ground at a rapid pace. I whapped at Nicky with the hammer. It caught him on the left cheek. He kept his grip. I felt a choke deep in my throat where Nicky's fingers pressed at me. I gave him another whap on his right cheek. He let out a scream. But he wouldn't quit. Another whap, smack on the bleeding nose. That got results. Nicky let go of my throat. His hand went limp and fell away. Nicky's eyes blinked, his head wobbled, but he didn't fall to the ground. I used the hammer to tap him once lightly in the chest. He dropped from sight. A real gamer, that Nicky.

Grimaldi's first shot zipped through the windshield a foot to the right of where I was sitting. He was thirty yards away, crouching and gripping the gun with both hands straight out in front of him. I ducked in my seat and went back to the clutch and gearshift. Another shot from Grimaldi produced another hole in the windshield. This one was two feet farther to the right. The crouch and all the *Hill Street Blues* shooting style weren't doing much for Grimaldi's aim.

During the non-stop action, the tussle with Nicky and the shots from Grimaldi and the sprinkling of tiny pieces of windshield glass on the seat beside me, the truck's engine hadn't stalled. Small mercies. It kept on roaring. And when I heaved at the gearshift in ultimate desperation, I got something to work. The truck lurched ahead. I'd found a gear, not the right gear but something that put the truck in forward motion. It wasn't making for a smooth journey. The truck lurched. Then it leaped. It felt as if the damned thing were leaving the ground and taking miniature hops. I wouldn't be going anywhere fast.

Grimaldi was holding his fire, probably waiting for a clear shot. He might have to wait awhile. The truck's heaving and bucking made me a difficult target. Grimaldi was off to the right. I caught a glimpse of him, still crouched, still holding the gun at arm's length, backing away, looking for a shooting angle. The truck, carrying on like a kangaroo, cut down his chances.

My hippity-hoppity progress carried me down the row of trucks, past Grimaldi, and almost to the office building. The gate was beginning to shape up as a realistic objective. I examined the rearview mirror for a sighting of Grimaldi. He was nowhere in range. While I was examining, the truck stopped hopping and skipping. It stopped altogether. The engine had stalled.

Without the roar of the motor, the yard was suddenly still. I could hear Grimaldi's footsteps on the pavement. He came into view in the rearview mirror. He was about fifty yards back of the truck and he was dashing toward it. He had his gun at the ready. His strategy seemed clear. He'd come up from the rear, directly behind the truck, under cover and out of sight, and circle around until he had an unimpeded pop at me with the gun.

I needed a strategy of my own. Never mind taking another crack at starting the truck. Too unreliable. I couldn't leave the cab and take off on foot. Grimaldi would pick me off. In the matter of weapons, my hammer didn't measure up to Grimaldi's pistol. The possibilities of escape had become less than infinite.

I looked around the interior of the cab. The lever that operated the bin on the back of the truck stuck out of the floor. It had three indicated positions: Release, Lock, and Hold. It was in Lock. The chains that held the bin in place were overhead and had two positions: Secure and Release. It was in Secure.

Back to the rearview mirror. Grimaldi had drawn to within twenty yards. He was holding on course toward the back of the truck. I put my right hand on the lever and my left hand on the chains. I waited and watched Grimaldi. Fifteen yards away. Ten yards. Then he disappeared. He was too close to the truck for the mirror to catch him. I counted one, two, and pulled simultaneously on the lever and the chains until both hit the same position.

Release.

The silence of the yard was broken. So, I gathered from the tumult at the rear, were many other things. The noises came swiftly on one another. The sound of chains unravelling was first followed instantly by a thick scrape of metal, then a whoosh of air and the crash of a very heavy object thudding into the pavement. The heavy object had to be the truck's empty bin. No other heavy object back there.

I gave myself sixty seconds of careful listening before I dared to sneak a peak from my perch in the cab. The sixty seconds brought quiet back to the yard. It brought no sound of activity from Grimaldi. I stuck my head a few inches out the window. The bin was gone from the back of the truck. Without it, the truck looked naked. I climbed down from the cab and walked slowly toward the truck's rear. I had two reasons for taking it slow. One was wariness of Grimaldi, the other was the ongoing case of shakes in my legs.

The bin had flipped over. It rested upside down on the pavement. The sudden release of both lever and chain, not the usual way those controls were operated, had sent the bin into a 180-degree mid-air turn. It went up, flopped over, and smacked to earth.

Grimaldi and his gun were not to be seen.

I banged my fist on the side of the bin.

"Hey, Charlie," I shouted, "you in there?"

I didn't think Grimaldi heard my voice. The walls of the bin were too thick. But he heard my pounding. He pounded back. His pounding had an angrier quality than mine.

Grimaldi wouldn't be keeping any appointments in the immediate future. Not even for the funeral of the woman he had killed. Charles was immobilized. I'd caught him. Like a rabbit in a snare. A Grimaldi in a bin.

I walked across the yard and into the Ace office building. My legs had a new steadiness. The envelope from the bank was on Grimaldi's desk and the cheque was inside. I carried it across the street to the Volks in the Majestic's parking lot. Noon-hour customers were arriving. Couple of beers, a hamburger, and the nurse in the shower. Zowie.

I unlocked the trunk on the Volks, tucked the cheque behind the spare tire, and went back to the Ace office.

I made my phone calls from a secretary's desk on the street side of the corridor. The first and briefest call was to the cops. The dispatcher said it might take an hour to get a cruiser to the Ace property if I couldn't be more specific about the crimes I was reporting. I told him murder, fraud, burglary, and a nasty attitude. The dispatcher said he'd put in a rush call for all cruisers in the area.

When I got Ray Griffin, he wanted to quiz me on the phone. I told him to come on out to Ace and he'd earn himself a banner headline. Ray didn't bother telling me they'd done away with banner headlines. He said he was on his way. Tom Catalano said nothing about being on his way. He asked on the phone if the cheque was valid. Yes, I said, and he asked if it was in a safe place. Another yes. He said he'd let Wansborough know and, oh yes, he said to me, nice work.

The person who answered at the CBC radio arts program took two minutes to pull Annie out of the editing room.

"Here's the choice for this evening," I said to Annie. "Sweat over your tapes or come with me and sip Dom Pérignon."

"You forget," Annie said. "I'm the girl who doesn't perspire."

"How's eight o'clock at Scaramouche?"

"You're teasing."

"When it comes to champagne and expensive restaurants," I said, "I don't tinker with the truth."

"You've closed the case or however lawyers phrase it."

"I've got Alice's killer."

"You're a darling."

"Just for closing the case?"

"For that and other compelling reasons."

"I'll need until eight," I said. "I anticipate a few hours of explaining matters to the authorities."

Outside the fence around the Ace property, the first police officers arrived. There were two of them, uniformed and in a yellow cruiser.

"You're all right?" Annie asked. "Nothing violent done to you?"

"Piece of cake."

There was something familiar about the cops and the cruiser out front. The cruiser number was 3148. Oh-oh. The two cops were the smoker and the apple-eater from the encounter early Saturday morning. Annie was saying on the phone that she was ahead of schedule and she'd be done with editing the tapes by dinnertime. I interrupted her.

"Maybe nine o'clock for the champagne," I said. "I see an extra hour of explaining coming my way. Can you wait?"

Annie said she'd consider waiting forever. I said it wouldn't take that long. Not quite. I hung up the phone and went to let the cops in.